An Autumn to Remember

An Autumn to Remember

Remember

A Brooks Bend Romance

Robyn Neeley

TULE
PUBLISHING

Chapter One

THERE WAS ONLY one thing in life that could move Executive Chef Sloan Leary from zero to sixty in three seconds flat—the unfathomable horror of witnessing a slice of pumpkin cheesecake about to leave her five-star restaurant's kitchen completely naked.

"Hold up!" She flew around the steel cooking island she'd spent her entire career and most of her childhood behind, ordering her new server, Lyndsey, to halt in her rubber-soled tracks.

The waitress spun around, her straight, black ponytail whipping across the long white whiskers she'd painted onto her cheeks, a totally appropriate look for Halloween.

The entire staff enjoyed dressing up for their shifts on this day.

Except for Sloan.

She straightened her white jacket over her black pants, not having the slightest interest in being anything but an award-winning chef of Seasons of San Francisco all three hundred and sixty-five days of the year.

Because that is what would move her one step further to

achieving her goal of franchising her restaurant in destination cities all over the world.

Unwavering determination.

"I'm so sorry," Lyndsey apologized. "Did I pick up the wrong order?"

"No, it's the correct one." Sloan's panicked expression softened into a supportive smile as she bent down and retrieved the black cat ears headband that had fallen off the waitress's head.

She handed back the cat ears in exchange for the slice. Right now was one of her favorite teaching moments.

"It's not quite dressed for the party, but we can easily fix that." Sloan picked up a small maroon bottle from the spice rack her grandmother had mounted in the middle of the island fifty years ago. "You see ... every single dish we serve—from our Parmesan-butternut squash soup to the stuffing-crust turkey potpie—cannot leave the kitchen until it receives a generous sprinkle of seasoning." She turned the bottle upside down and gently shook it across the dessert, beaming down. "Now it's ready."

She handed Lyndsey back the robin's-egg blue plate with gold leaf etching along the rim, a pattern she'd driven three hours south down the winding California coastal roads earlier this year through the pouring April rain to purchase from an antique dealer.

It was the perfect plate pattern to show off her fall menu and well worth the drive.

"Thank you, Chef. I won't make that mistake again."

Sloan flipped shut the spice bottle's lid and returned it to the rack. After five years leading the back of the house, she knew no evening was perfect. It never was. "Mistakes are always welcome in my kitchen. It's how we learn." She winked. "Besides, you have eight more lives left."

The grateful waitress scurried out.

Sloan maneuvered to the double swing doors and pressed one open a crack. Nothing pleased her more than watching her customers take a first bite. Her knack for picking the perfect seasoning for each dish was what kept them coming back.

Whether they lived in the neighborhood or visited the Bay Area on occasion, they always returned.

The delight on the young woman's face as she dug her fork into the cheesecake for another bite said it all.

Mission accomplished.

Grinning, Sloan turned back around and joined her staff, who'd already begun breaking down the kitchen. To some, it would seem insurmountable, but helping her team was often a nice bonding moment.

After it was done, she'd start packing up her spices for the much-anticipated Culinary Exchange program, an annual event sponsored by the Executive Chef's Institute and the only reason she'd ever even consider abandoning her kitchen for two weeks.

The program was known for making careers.

All up-and-coming chefs knew that participating could not only sharpen their skills but was an amazing way to network and introduce their signature dishes to even more clientele.

Many of the big celebrity chefs with multiple restaurants all over the world had gotten their start participating in the Culinary Exchange.

And Sloan planned on one day being one of them.

Plus, working in a new five-star restaurant was a ton of fun. Being the executive chef and owner of Seasons of San Francisco, she simply had no time for vacation, let alone to leave the city. The Culinary Exchange scratched an itch to take in a new scene.

So what if it involved slicing an eight-inch blade into a thawed chicken breast at the start of each day and ending her nights more often than not exhausted and covered in sauce stains? It was her ritual, and she loved it.

Each year, she looked forward to traveling to a new place. Now in her fifth year, she'd asked her longtime agent, Erika Palmer, who brokered the exchange, to look for opportunities to match her with a Parisian restaurant.

IT ALIGNED PERFECTLY with her goal to open up a Seasons of Paris as the first restaurant in her expansion plans. She'd spend every single minute soaking up the city, the people, and the fine dining culture.

A spotless kitchen later, Sloan made her way through the front of the house to chat with her last two customers before packing up her spices. Norman and Lucy Banks were seated at their usual table in front of the beautiful picture window. The couple lived a few blocks away and often finished out their week with a stroll along the pier before dining in her restaurant.

It was her nightly ritual to spend a few minutes chatting with her last customers, just like her grandmother had done each evening, until she couldn't walk anymore.

She'd taught Sloan that ending the day showing kindness and gratitude was the only way to end it.

"Thank you so much for coming in tonight." She grinned down at the empty soup bowls and plates. "I hope you enjoyed the pumpkin sage soup."

Lucy rested a bony hand over Sloan's, her fingers shaking ever so slightly. "It was almost as good as your grandmother's."

She'd take that compliment. Her grandmother's signature fall soup had been second to none. "I'll keep working at it. I'll see you both when I get back in two weeks."

Norman slid up his glasses. "Who will be running your restaurant this year?"

"Good question. My agent was supposed to stop in tonight with the big reveal." Sloan reached over and centered the bright-orange and yellow flower arrangement on a nearby table, looking out the window as a Frankenstein passed by with his bride. "Maybe her broomstick is in the shop."

"I hope it's not another chef like last year's." Lucy wrinkled her nose, taking a sip of her after-dinner espresso. "Nice man, but the catfish he served us could have stayed in the ocean."

"You mean bayou, love," Norman quipped, giving his wife a gentle pat on her arm.

Lucy set her cup down and touched her cloth napkin to one corner of her bright-red lips and then the other. "I'll stick to a good old-fashioned Dungeness crab, thank you very much."

Sloan laughed. She'd received dozens of texts last year from her frantic staff, begging her to come home early.

While she'd thoroughly loved last year's exchange that took her to a popular Gulf-to-plate restaurant in New Orleans, her routine customers were less than pleased to find a menu full of catfish.

"Don't worry, Mr. and Mrs. Banks. I've left instructions to keep three Sloan Leary fall specials on the menu each night, just in case." She chuckled, adding, "I promise, only Bay Area fish, and all the Dungeness crab you can eat."

That seemed to appease the couple. She said a final good night and crossed the room to the front door, pushing it open. A cool crisp breeze greeted her as a Little Red Riding Hood raced by in shrieks, followed by a Big Bad Wolf, who stopped in his tracks to howl at the bright full moon before chasing her down the sidewalk.

"How was tonight?" she asked Connor, her sous chef, who on a normal night was her steady second-in-command, but he'd worked so hard on the green-and-purple makeup for his warlock costume that she didn't have the heart to ban him to the kitchen all night. Instead, he'd spent his shift next to a large black cauldron, doling out Sloan's ginger-cinnamon apple cider.

"Some potion for you, Chef." He dipped the ladle into the green mixture, thanks to the generous amount of food coloring they'd added in earlier and offered her a cup.

"Don't mind if I do." She began to take a sip but stopped, inching up a playful eyebrow. "Unless it's cursed?"

That got a wicked chuckle out of Connor. "I cast only one spell, and it was on an old boyfriend who walked by an hour ago. He should be turning into a toad any minute now."

"Oh my. I hope he doesn't get stomped on by this crowd," Sloan joked back and took a sip, the ginger spice filling all of her tiny taste buds to their brims as she peeked into the cauldron. "I can't believe how much you have left."

"Well, the little ones aren't fans. Your scarecrow cinnamon twists, on the other hand . . ." He bunched his fingers and brought them to his lips for a kiss. "Perfection. I ran out hours ago."

"Why am I not surprised that bread coated in cinnamon and butter would be a hit?" She tilted her cup and drained it.

"They don't know what they're missing."

The ghoulish fun continued all around when a woman's voice rose high above the crowd, admonishing a ghost for not watching where it was going.

Erika! Sloan whipped around. *Finally.* "I've been waiting for you all ni—" She stared at her agent, who was dressed in an enormous, bright-yellow cardboard box, her long, black hair pushed off her face in a high ponytail. The neon-blue arms of her sweater stuck out and matched both her lipstick and tights perfectly.

What on earth?

"I'm sorry I'm late." Erika waddled closer to Sloan, nearly being taken out by six football players and a referee jogging by. "Taking public transportation in this getup wasn't my smartest idea."

That wasn't her smartest idea? Sloan cocked her head, reading the word Palate scribbled across the box in bright-blue cursive. As far as creative costumes went, she wasn't sure this was going to win Erika any Halloween contest. "What are you supposed to be, exactly?"

"I'm your surprise." Her agent stretched her arms out with her palms up. "Ta-da!"

Sloan studied the getup for a beat. "A box?"

"Not just any box. Oh, I forgot the props in my pockets." Her arms disappeared, returning with an apple and a sweet potato. "Ta-da," she repeated with even more gusto, holding the produce high in the air.

Sloan stared at her blankly.

"Ta—" She dropped the produce to her sides. "Oh, for Pete's sake. I'm as plain as day."

"Of course you are. You're a . . . a . . ." Sloan thought for a second. Her agent was here for only one reason. "Am I going to be working in a place named Palate for the Culinary Exchange?" Sloan asked, racing through the vast restaurant directory she'd built up in her memory bank over the years but coming up short.

Wait a minute. Her eyes widened. Palate sounded French enough. "Oh my God. Is Palate a new Parisian restaurant?" It had to be. Her arms flew around her agent, not waiting for a response. "I knew you could do it. I'm going to Paris, aren't I?"

Erika hugged her back, the sweet potato pressing into Sloan's spine. "Better. Way better."

Way better? Sloan stepped back. What could possibly be better than finally getting her dream culinary exchange?

"You, Sloan Leary, are going to spend the next fourteen days working on an audition meal for Palate." Erika emphasized that by running the sweet potato under the word.

Sloan blinked. "What?"

"Palate, you know, the meal kit service."

Of course, she knew Palate. Everyone did. It was only the most sought-after meal kit service, with billions of subscribers worldwide.

Her heart began to accelerate as she asked the next question. "Are they looking for a chef?"

Erika's head bobbled up and down, nearly causing her to tip over. She regained her balance. "They're looking for their next up-and-coming celebrity chef to create signature Thanksgiving dinner recipes." She took a bite out of the apple. "Yours truly got you an audition."

Sloan parted her lips. "No way."

"Yes!"

"No," she repeated, still trying to process the news. It couldn't possibly be. Over the years, several chefs had partnered with the popular meal kit service, but they were way more established and internationally known.

She was a far, far cry from being one of them.

"Is there any alcohol in that brew?" Erika asked Connor. "Your hearing is just fine, Sloan, dear. You've got two weeks to plan a traditional Thanksgiving meal. The winner will have their recipes in next year's Holiday Palate line."

Holiday Palate line! Sloan's hands went to her cheeks. "I can't believe it."

"Believe it. Thanksgiving meals by Sloan Leary will be on thousands of dining room tables from here"—she waved her hand in the air, pointing east—"to Maine. All you have to do is wow the judges panel, and I know you will."

This was the moment Sloan had worked so hard for—her chance to finally step into the elite celebrity chef circle, which would elevate her further to realizing her goal of franchising, beginning with Paris.

"Wow. Palate." Sloan couldn't help but take a second to let it sink in.

Her agent had always looked out for new opportunities to elevate her culinary career ever since Sloan and her grandmother had signed with Erika to publish a cookbook, *A Dish for Every Season*, ten years ago.

Erika had been there, especially after Grandma Gabby passed away. It was she who had approached Sloan about the Culinary Exchange as a good opportunity to raise her profile.

Yes, Erika was a fabulous agent and friend. Still, there was one clarifying question that needed to be asked: "You really think I'm ready for this? You have other clients who are more established."

Erika's expression softened. "But I only have one Sloan Leary."

That validation was all she needed. She clapped her hands. "I guess I should get started right away. My grandmother's maple-ginger apple pie recipe would be so perfect for this." She paused, adding, "I'm assuming this means I'm sitting out the Culinary Exchange this year."

"Oh, you're still participating." Erika finished the apple and dropped the core in a trash receptacle next to the cauldron. "I've found the perfect place for you to cook up a storm. You're going to love it."

Wait, what? Sloan bit down on her lip. How was she possibly going to work on her audition recipes while running an unfamiliar restaurant? To knock it out of the park, she really needed to stay here and cook in *her* kitchen with her utensils, not some stranger's, never mind access to all of her spices. "I'm not sure I can do both—" she started.

"You can, and it's already arranged. Where you're going has a steady stream of customers but will also give you enough downtime so you can focus on creating your audition recipes. Plus, it's in New England—the epicenter for all things fall—to really inspire you and get your creative turkey juices flowing." Erika shook her arms to accentuate that point. "How marvelous is that?"

New England. Now was not the time to go clear across the country. "I don't know . . ." Sloan's voice trailed. Leaving her familiar kitchen to work on something so life changing seemed like a bad idea.

Terrible, really.

"I know it seems like a lot, but I really do believe I've found the best place for you to be," Erika continued her pitch. "Think miles and miles of bright-orange, yellow, and red foliage as far as the eye can see; warm, apple cider donuts on every farm stand; and pumpkin spice everywhere."

"Pumpkin spice everywhere," Sloan repeated, inching an eyebrow up.

"Everywhere."

"Well . . ." She'd always wanted to go to Boston, and cooking there in the fall would, no doubt, be a wonderful experience. With all of its fall foliage charm, it probably would inspire her. "Okay. Fine. I'll go." She could get a jumpstart by sorting out her Thanksgiving recipes on the long plane ride over.

"You're going to love it, trust me. I've booked your flight for six a.m. tomorrow."

"Oh wow . . . that early?" Being a chef who worked well into the night, to say Sloan wasn't a morning person was an understatement.

That question got a supportive pat on her arm. "No time to waste. We've got to get you in the kitchen. It's a quaint bistro in the heart of everything." Erika looked down at her Apple Watch. "I've got to run, but I'll e-mail your ticket and all the details later tonight."

"Wait." She reached for Erika's arm. "Who will be working in my restaurant?" Given her team would be working with someone new, she should at least know who.

"It's a lovely woman named Dee Dee Edwards, with more than forty years of restaurant experience owning a small bistro. The Executive Chef's Institute raved about her and her chocolate-pecan pie. Apparently, it won some award. I talked to her this morning, and she sounds like an absolute delight. Your regulars are going to love her."

Small bistro. Would Dee Dee be able to keep up with an upscale operation? She dismissed the question. Erika was clearly excited about this, and her agent would never hand over Seasons of San Francisco to just anyone—even if it was only for two weeks.

Plus, Connor would be here, ready to step up.

She'd check in on this Dee Dee in a day or two, see how she was settling in, and answer any questions she might have. Maybe they could set up a few video sessions. "So, Palate is really happening?" she asked, still not believing it was true.

"I didn't dress up in this getup for nothing. You got this, girl. I'll talk to you in a couple of days. Palate is going to send you a shipment with some of the ingredients they'd like you to use in your recipes." She reached for Sloan's arm, hooking hers around it. "Now do me a favor and help this meal kit to the curb."

Sloan laughed and guided her agent to her Uber, then said a quick good night to Connor, before stepping back into her restaurant, reeling over the amazing news.

She had a bounce in her step as she crossed the dining room and pushed through the swinging doors. Her gaze rested on her favorite framed photo of her grandmother seasoning a Christmas pudding their first year cooking together after Sloan began working full-time professionally.

Her heart squeezed. Her grandmother would have been over the moon-excited about this opportunity. "Paris, here we come," she said to the photo.

It wasn't the way she'd planned, but if she won the Palate audition, she wouldn't need the culinary exchange to get her there.

Her grandmother's dream for a Seasons of Paris could be within grasp.

That thought spurred her into action as she began transporting spice bottles into the portable rack. "Get ready, my loves, we're going on a big East Coast adventure," she said to the amchur powder and juniper berries seasonings before placing them into the rack with all the others.

A few minutes later, she scanned her kitchen one last time, making sure she hadn't forgotten anything, while trying to ignore the needling feeling that setting up shop clear across the country to work on an opportunity of a lifetime might not be the best idea.

"You love the Culinary Exchange," she gave herself a pep talk before flipping off the lights. Plus, two weeks in Boston surrounded by beautiful fall foliage. How bad could it be?

Chapter Two

S LOAN LUGGED HER two suitcases off the Amtrak and let out a deep sigh into the darkness, her wispy, brown bangs lifting off her forehead. She gazed around at the wet orange leaves scattered across the secluded platform.

This was *so* not Boston.

And given the fact that her agent had e-mailed her a ticket to JFK late last night with zero explanation—other than a cryptic 'trust the process'—should have tipped her off that her culinary exchange was far from Bean Town.

"Trust the process . . . yeah, right," she muttered, staring at the BROOKS BEND destination sign for a beat before yanking up the zipper to her brown leather jacket. Her frustration built as she made her way down the long platform, her suitcases rolling over the dead leaves.

She entered the one-story brick train station and glanced around. Her agent's client roster was about to be reduced by one as soon as she got ahold of her. Sloan had spent the better part of the flight demanding Erika e-mail her an explanation as to why she was flying into Manhattan.

She was on the tarmac before she received a brief text

from Erika with instructions for Sloan to make her way to Grand Central Station. She was to then hop a train north to Brooks Bend, Connecticut, where she'd be staying at a place called The Bend.

After twelve hours in a plane, Uber, and train, she was utterly exhausted, famished beyond words and, thanks to the frosty evening temperature and her lack of a warm wool coat, freezing her tush off.

If she had known she'd be spending her entire day stepping in and off different modes of transportation rather than simply going from an airport to a nice hotel via a warm Uber, she'd have dressed differently.

Strike that. If she had *known* she'd be spending two weeks in some Podunk small town in the middle of nowhere, she never would have headed to the airport this morning in the first place, let alone boarded the plane.

Okay, to be fair, "nowhere" might be a bit of a stretch since she was only on the train for about an hour—but still. She doubted she'd be spending her evening looking at the bright lights of a city landscape, enjoying a Boston cream pie.

Stepping farther inside the station, she opened her Uber app, frowning down at the "No Cars Available" message.

Just terrific.

She glanced around, her gaze jumping the empty bench seats all the way to the ticket window, where an old man sat behind a glass counter engrossed in a book.

Maybe he could help. She stepped up to the counter, her

gaze landing on the book's cover.

The title *Pie or Die* accompanied a picture of an enormous pumpkin pie in the middle of a Thanksgiving spread, a butcher knife dripping in red lodged in its smooth, orange center.

"Excuse me, sir." She tapped on the glass screen that he sat behind. Nothing. *Wow. Must be a real page-turner.* "I don't mean to interrupt, but does this town have taxi service?"

Before he could answer, the front door opened and a woman that looked to be Sloan's age stepped inside, bundled up in a black parka and jostling a large, orange pumpkin in her arms. "You must be Sloan Leary." She nodded to the man behind the window. "Hey, Earl. You were supposed to call me when Sloan's train left Grand Central. Have you been reading that book this entire time?"

"Just two more chapters, but I think I know who did it."

"Honestly." The woman rolled her eyes, stepping closer to Sloan. "I'm sorry for Earl's rudeness. I hope you haven't been waiting long. I'm Kimmie Evans, the town's taxi driver."

"Sloan Leary," she said, but the stranger apparently already knew that.

"We're so excited to have you here. Earl, can you please put a bookmark in it and help us get Sloan's luggage into my trunk?" She narrowed her gaze when the man didn't make any effort to move. "Or we can make ourselves comfortable here. I finished the book this morning and would be more than happy to start talking to you all about it. I never could have predicted that the murderer was th—"

"Okay. Okay." Earl shut the book and made his way from behind the counter.

"Thought so," Kimmie said with smug lips.

"My agent has me staying at The Bend. I'm assuming that's a hotel?" Sloan asked as Earl grabbed each of her suitcases. "Oh, please be careful with the smaller one. It's full of glass bottles." The last thing she needed was her spices mixing.

"You're going to love The Bend. It's very popular with out-of-towners." Kimmie followed behind Earl and held the door open with her backside for Sloan to walk through. "World famous."

"You don't say." Sloan stepped outside, shoving her hands into her jacket pockets. Being that she was the only passenger who'd gotten off the train, she doubted anything in this place was world famous.

"Well, maybe not the entire world." Kimmie glanced down at the pumpkin in her arms. "Oh heavens. Where are my manners?" She extended it toward Sloan. "This here is for you. Dee Dee gave it to me this morning before she boarded her train for the airport. She asked that I give it to you the minute I saw you."

"Wow. Uh . . ." Sloan took the pumpkin, her arms dropping from its weight. "Thank you," she said, taking the odd gift, as she didn't want to be rude. This nice woman was, after all, getting her to her final destination, where she could soak in a hot bath, eat a warm meal with perhaps a glass of wine to wash it down, and pass out underneath the covers.

"She told me to tell you that it will bring you good luck when you most need it, so don't slice into it right away."

Sloan followed Kimmie outside to her silver Toyota. "How far is it into town?" she asked. *Man, this pumpkin is heavy.*

"Super quick. You can sit up front. There's more legroom." Kimmie swung open the passenger's side door and tossed some grocery bags to the back seat so Sloan could get in. "I'm going to take The Vine all the way through the woods."

"To grandmother's house we go," Sloan whispered under her breath, sliding into the car seat. She placed the pumpkin on the floor between her legs.

"Dee Dee was so excited for her flight to San Francisco this morning. I told her that if she cooked for any celebrities, she'd better take a picture." Kimmie started up the car, cranking the heat. She adjusted her messy, ash-blond ponytail, giving it a yank.

Sloan smiled politely and fastened her seat belt. Rarely did anyone of celebrity status come into her restaurant if you didn't count the occasional San Francisco 49er or local politician. She glanced down at the *Pie or Die* paperback resting on the console between the driver's seat and the passenger seat. "Popular book."

That got a chuckle as Kimmie backed out. "More like required reading. The author, Mia Graves, is from Brooks Bend and is in town. The mayor made sure we all received copies. Apparently, it's a"—she took her hands off the steering wheel and made air quotes—"*New York Times* best seller. We're all supposed to have it read by tomorrow."

Sloan raised an eyebrow. "The entire town?"

Kimmie nodded. "Well, at least those over sixteen, on account of the murder element."

"Ah, of course." Sloan used to be a reader and longed for the days when she could curl up in a coffee shop on a crisp autumn day and get lost in a good fiction story.

Although, she did enjoy her annual tradition that she began five years ago of starting each fall by flipping through one of her grandmother's old notebooks filled with recipes while enjoying a pumpkin spice latte on Pier 39. She'd select one recipe to then be her signature fall special throughout the season.

Somehow, that ritual always made it feel as if her grandmother was still in the restaurant's kitchen with her night after night.

This year's chosen recipe for an autumn harvest brisket was in her stash of 5x7 cards she'd packed last night. She planned on experimenting with it for a potential side dish for her Holiday Palate audition.

"We've got book club tomorrow night, and it just happens to be at The Bend," Kimmie continued, pulling Sloan from her thoughts. "Hey, if you'd like to read it and join us, you could have my copy. We're doing a murder reenactment. Should be a fun time."

"Oh." The only person she'd like to murder at the moment was her agent. "I'm probably going to be working late tomorrow getting settled and all, but thank you for the invitation. It sounds like fun."

A couple of twists and turns down darkness finally led them to a beautifully lit wooden bridge.

"Oh my goodness." Sloan leaned forward to get a better look at the white lights twisted along each side.

"I know, right?" Kimmie sighed and slowed down to let a vehicle in the opposite direction cross first. "I've lived here all my life, and I never get tired of driving over this bridge."

"It's beautiful." Sloan took in the twinkling lights as they made their way across. "I feel like I'm in Stars Hallow," she remarked, referring to the popular fictional town.

"We get that a lot." Kimmie made a few turns into town and stopped at the red light.

Sloan gazed down Main Street, taking in its many brick buildings, the trees along the sidewalks all decorated in the same white lights as the bridge.

"You're going to enjoy your stay at The Bend. Real nice place."

"As long as they have room service." She patted her

stomach. "Then I'll be all set."

"Actually, the kitchen is currently undergoing a remodel job. The only thing open on a Sunday at this hour is the Pizza & Pop Shop."

At this hour. Sloan glanced over at the dashboard clock. It was 6:45 p.m.

"It's open for another fifteen minutes. It'll be the best pizza you've ever tasted." Kimmie clamped her lips. "You don't make pizza for a living, do you?"

Sloan laughed a little at that. "No, it's not my specialty. You can drop me off at the pizza place." She'd feel better once she got some sustenance, and a cheesy, saucy slice would do the trick.

"The Bend is all the way down at the end of the street." Kimmie hopped out of the car and grabbed Sloan's suitcases from the trunk, placing them on the curb. "Three-story white building with black trim. It'll be all lit up. You can't miss it."

"Thank you so much for the ride." She reached into her purse, pulling out her wallet. "How much do I owe you?"

"Dee Dee already covered it this morning. You're all set."

"That was very kind of her." Sloan set her wallet back in her purse. She wished she'd thought of returning that kindness when Dee Dee arrived in San Francisco. She'd ask Erika to send her a nice welcome to the Golden Gate City gift basket with a copy of *A Dish for Every Season*. She kept a box of copies signed by both her and her grandmother in the office closet for special occasions. Dee Dee might enjoy having one as a memento of her time in the restaurant.

Kimmie went to get into the car, but spun around, snapping her fingers. "Oh, I almost forgot. Dee Dee wanted me to tell you that she left a set of keys with her nephew, Alex. He'll meet you at 5:00 a.m. at the inn and bring you over."

5:00 a.m.? What time did this bistro open? Perhaps this Alex nephew needed to meet her before he went to work. She pulled up the suitcase handles and turned to go into the pizzeria. Once she ate, she was definitely headed straight to bed.

"Sloan."

She glanced over her shoulder to see Kimmie had rolled down the passenger's side window to get her attention. "Don't forget your lucky pumpkin."

"Right. Lucky pumpkin." She opened the door and retrieved it from the floor, hoisting it up with all her might. "Wouldn't want to forget this."

"Remember. Don't slice into it. It won't bring you the luck you need if you do it too soon."

"Got it. No slicing." She rested it on top of her suitcase. Couldn't Dee Dee have picked a miniature one to give her?

"Enjoy your night, Sloan. I'll see you in the morning."

"See you . . ." Sloan rolled her suitcases toward the entrance. *Why would the taxi driver see me in the morning?* She opened the glass door and maneuvered in her suitcases, the aroma of tomato sauce and fresh dough filling her nostrils as she made her way up to the counter. "I'll take a cheese slice," she said to the man behind it.

The nice man named Colin, according to his nametag shaped like a pizza pie, handed it to her within minutes. "Enjoy."

"I'm sure I will." She took an enormous bite, unable to wait any longer, a delicious blend of seasoning giving her taste buds a bonus delight. "What kind of spice do you use?" she asked, since the man was not waiting on anyone at the moment.

"It's a secret." He grinned, reaching for a dishrag and wiping down the counter. "The only two that know are me and my pop."

"A secret, huh?" She took a bite, accepting the challenge. "Oregano, basil, and thyme."

He smiled. "Close."

She raised up a more than curious eyebrow. "It's not those three?"

"Nope." He grinned, shaking his head.

"Hmmm . . . there's definitely an interesting, sweet note. I'll get it right next time," she said, liking a good seasoning challenge. She made her way outside with the help of Colin, who carried her pumpkin and propped it on her suitcase for her. She stood alone on the curb, taking a few minutes to finish her pizza before continuing on. "Definitely basil," she said into the dark night.

She went for another taste, when out of nowhere, huge

brown paws landed squarely on her chest while a furry mouth snatched her pizza.

She let out a scream, falling to the ground. Was she being attacked by a brown bear?

"Oliver. No!" A man in a red baseball cap turned backward and a red-and-black flannel jacket jogged across the street, calling off her assaulter. He extended his hand. "I'm sorry to scare you. My Labradoodle got out. He's harmless."

Labradoodle. Okay, not exactly a dangerous brown bear. She got up on her own, refusing his help. "I wasn't scared. Just surprised."

He bent down and latched a leash on the collar, giving the dog's head a scratch behind its fluffy chocolate ears, its tail going a mile a minute while it finished off the pizza crust. "That's a good boy."

Her eyes narrowed at his baby dog talk. The pizza snatcher was anything but a 'good boy.' "Well, I sure hope your dog enjoyed my dinner."

The man looked up and quirked his lips into a half grin, causing her pulse to quicken. She immediately dismissed it as aftershocks from the fact she'd been almost trampled over by a fifty-pound Lab with poodle curls.

"I can get you another slice," he offered, standing up.

Just then, the pizzeria's lights turned off.

"Tomorrow." He coiled the leash around his wrist.

"Uh-huh." It appeared she was going to go to bed hungry, but that wasn't the worst of it as a wet tongue gave her hand a giant lick and then another. "Ew!" She snatched it away. "Does your dog like human fingers too?"

"He only likes the chicken variety," the man said with a chuckle that she didn't find the slightest bit amusing. He pulled gently on the leash, maneuvering his dog to the side. "What he really loves is pizza from the Pizza & Pop Shop."

"I can see that," she said, wiping the dog's saliva off her hand with a paper napkin and then thumbing through her purse for her sanitizer. She retrieved the tiny bottle and squirted two pumps, rubbing her hands together, and then squirted a few more drops because you could never be too careful.

Who knew what that dog had gotten into before salivating all over her?

"C'mon, fella, we'll get you some dinner." He turned to Sloan. "Are you visiting Brooks Bend?"

Normally, she wouldn't share that kind of information with a total stranger, but her suitcases inevitably gave her away. "I thought I was going to Boston," she deadpanned.

"Um . . . you're about three hours south of that goal."

Oh, the cute guy has a funny bone. She ignored his quip. "I'm staying at The Bend."

"You'll find it across the street all the way down." He pressed the crosswalk button, which was kind of pointless since there were no moving vehicles in sight. "You wouldn't happen to be Sloan Leary by chance?"

Sloan's lips parted. How did he know who she was?

"Um . . . why, yes."

"I'm Alex. Alex Edwards. Dee Dee's nephew."

"Oh, hi," she said, taken aback but, nevertheless, extending her hand. "It's nice to meet you."

"Nice to meet you too." He crooked a lopsided grin that kicked her pulse up a notch.

At that moment, his dog wanted in on the introductions with a nudge to her knee. Maybe she overreacted earlier. She bent down to pet his wavy ears, trying to be all cool in front of the cute nephew. "It's nice to meet you too."

The Labradoodle gave her face an enormous lick and then got in another before she could block it with her hands. She was going to have to bathe in sanitizer tonight. "Wow, your dog sure is friendly."

Alex chuckled, pointing to the side of his mouth. "He won't leave any pizza sauce left behind."

Her hand flew to her lips, feeling some of the coating on the corner of her mouth. She closed her eyes.

Just terrific. Nothing like having a conversation with a cute stranger with pizza sauce all over her face.

Not the first impression she wanted to make to anyone in this town.

She slowly stood and reached for her suitcases because it was time to end this night. "I should get going," she said abruptly, not looking at Alex.

"Oliver and I could walk you to the inn."

"Thank you, but that won't be necessary." Head down,

she secured her pumpkin for the short trip to her final destination and maneuvered her suitcases off the curb.

"Your next slice is on Oliver," she heard Alex call out.

"I won't be here long enough for that, but thanks," she replied, not bothering to look behind her shoulder.

She continued down the street, finally gazing up at the three-story white building with black trim, a single candle-light glowing in every window.

She stopped at the wooden steps decorated with white and blue pumpkins.

"Inn, sweet inn," she grumbled and picked up the orange pumpkin, setting it on the bottom step before dragging up her suitcases.

It was going to be a long two weeks.

Chapter Three

"MORNING, HANDSOME."

Alex Edwards stepped inside The Bend, his home away from home for the last few months.

"Mornin'." He ushered Oliver inside and greeted Hayden Merry, the inn's general manager and an old friend. A friendship that went way back to their early days of playing hide-and-seek in the enormous three-story inn, while his mother made beds and mopped floors.

Last spring, he'd been hired by the inn's owner and Hayden's father, Bill Merry, for a huge kitchen remodel and an addition of a new library on the first floor.

He wasn't an official contractor and his renovation and remodeling experience had been limited to what he did for mainly his aunt, but as the town's unofficial handyman, doing "all the things" for the last three years, Bill gave him a shot.

His hand shook, signaling his furry companion was demanding to break loose. "Hold on a second, buddy." He grinned as the Labradoodle went dashing toward Hayden, who was now flashing a bone she'd taken out of her sweater's pocket.

"You spoil him," he said with a smile. "Where's my treat?"

"Your maple hazelnut coffee is brewing on the coffee bar, even as we speak." She adjusted her headband keeping back her long blond hair.

"A woman after my taste buds." He coiled up the leash and set it down on the front desk, stretching his back until it cracked. "I don't know how people get up at this dark hour, let alone work."

"It's called a paycheck." She laughed and gave the bone over, giving Oliver a pat on the head.

Alex let out a big yawn. Normally, he didn't arrive until well after nine, but he'd promised his aunt that he'd escort the woman who was taking over her cooking for the next two weeks to the restaurant and help her settle in.

He didn't quite get the concept of turning over your business to a total stranger. Nevertheless, his aunt could barely contain her excitement last night when she'd shown him pictures on the internet of the fancy San Francisco restaurant she'd be working in.

"Sloan should be down any minute." Hayden lowered her voice, making her way over to the coffee bar. She reached for a yellow coffee cup and a bottle of maple syrup. "Kimmie said she had a rather long trip. I felt so bad giving her a four a.m. wake-up call."

Alex couldn't help but smile, glancing over at Oliver,

who'd made himself at home in the living room, sprawled out on all fours while going to town on his bone. "I wouldn't worry about it." He took the coffee cup Hayden handed him, his lips parting for a nice, warm jolt of caffeine. "She's probably used to getting up early, being a chef and all."

"I hope so." Hayden made herself a cup of coffee. "You ready for your new job?"

He nodded. Along with her meat loaf special, Aunt Dee Dee had handed him a list of repairs she'd hoped he'd take on while she was away.

A paint job here, a light fixture there. Nothing he couldn't handle while he was finishing up the inn's new library. She'd even suspended dinner service for the next two weeks so he could work on sprucing up the place at night.

He didn't mind. He loved his aunt and appreciated not only the work, but the vote of confidence. She'd been there for him when he first came back to Brooks Bend after years stationed overseas, giving him a free place to stay until he got back up on both feet.

Literally.

Since he had to open the restaurant for Sloan and show her where everything was, he figured he could get a head start taking a look at what he had to work with before the breakfast rush began. He'd make a list of materials he'd need and snap some pictures.

Not that he needed any photos. He'd grown up in the diner, eating most of his meals at the counter while his mom was working two jobs to make ends meet.

"Hey, do you think we'll see you for tonight's book club?" Hayden asked as she made her way back around the front desk.

"I've got some work to do in the library. That is, if I'm not at Dee Dee's."

Spending the evening with a jackhammer sounded way better than attending the mayor's well-orchestrated event that had all the town buzzing about the stupid book.

"You know I heard from my hairdresser, Jackie, whose sister, Devyn, is best friends with Mia's cousin, Stephanie, that Mia's single."

"Good to see our small-town grapevine is intact." He moved toward the coffee bar for a little more cream, reaching for the ceramic cow creamer.

"I'm just sayin'."

He knew exactly what Hayden was "just sayin'." He'd dated Mia all through high school and while she was at college before she dumped him her senior year. "I think I'll pass. Besides, I didn't read the book."

"Well, if you change your mind, the party starts at seven." She glanced toward the stairs, breaking out in a wide smile. "Sloan, good morning."

Alex turned to see the attractive chef descending the staircase in a crisp white jacket and black pants, her long brown hair pulled back in a ponytail as she carried down the small suitcase she'd had with her last night.

He sipped his coffee, not moving from the coffee bar. Her outfit seemed a little over the top for slinging eggs and hash. Maybe that's what they wore in San Francisco.

"Hi." Sloan descended the last step and set down her suitcase.

"Welcome." Hayden extended her hand. "I'm Hayden Merry, the inn's general manager. We're so excited to have you here. I trust my assistant manager, Izzy, provided you with a smooth check-in last night."

"She did, thank you." Sloan shook Hayden's hand. "It's nice to meet you. You have a lovely inn."

Alex stood off to the side, dropping his hand to pet his inquisitive Labradoodle to keep the pup from greeting Sloan. "Glad to see you found your way last night," he said when her gaze reached where he was standing.

She smirked, nodding down to his dog. "If the pizza snatcher is here for my breakfast, you'll have to tell him the kitchen's closed."

He returned her smirk. He knew that. He and his crew had finished their work last week, and he was proud of what they'd done. The new-and-improved kitchen with state-of-the-art equipment was now waiting for inspection.

"Sloan, this is Alex Edwards. Dee Dee's nephew," Hayden launched into an introduction. "He's going to open Dee Dee's for you and show you where everything is."

"We met last night. It's nice to see you again, Alex." Sloan reached for her suitcase handle. "I appreciate you meeting me this morning."

"Happy to." He set down his coffee cup and grabbed Oliver's leash from where he'd left it. "Let's go, buddy." He made his way to the front door, opening it for Sloan.

"Wow, it's cold." She let go of her suitcase and ran her hands up and down her arms. "Is it even twenty degrees?"

"Actually"—he pulled out his phone from his jacket pocket—"thirty-eight. Do you want to go back in and get your coat?"

"No. No. I'll be fine. You're probably anxious to get to work. I appreciate you making a detour to help me settle in."

He made his way down the steps to the lighted sidewalk since it was still dark outside and would be for a bit longer. "I don't usually start until nine a.m., sometimes ten."

"You don't?" She carried her suitcase down the steps, meeting him on the sidewalk. "Then why are we going there so ear—"

"Sloan, wait." Hayden flew out the front door, coming down the steps. "I think you might have left your pumpkin outside last night. Maybe you'd like to take it with you for your first day?" She brought the orange pumpkin to Sloan.

"Thank you." Sloan looked a little busted. "I thought it would be better to set it outside last night in the crisp autumn air with the others."

Alex fought back a smile. Leave it to his aunt to select the biggest pumpkin in the patch to declare it was Sloan's lucky pumpkin. "I can take that if you'd like."

"It's fine." She set it down on the top of her suitcase and pulled up the handle, glancing over at him. "I'm ready."

"Okay then." He led them across the street. "So, my aunt gave you a lucky pumpkin," he asked, never really good at small talk with strangers.

"Seems so."

He blew out a cold breath. Guess the chef wasn't either. Definitely not like the women in this town, or at least the ones he knew. "Did they tell you not to slice into i—"

"I got the memo," she cut him off, then stopped in her tracks. "But do I need to carry it around *everywhere* I go?"

He grinned at that. She had a good sense of humor, or at least a dry one. "I think it'll make an excellent restaurant decoration."

"Thank God, because this thing weighs a ton."

"Have you been to New England before?" he asked, not bothering to ask if she'd been to Brooks Bend because he suspected he knew that answer.

"No. First time." She picked up her pace. "Is it normal for it to be so cold this time of year?"

"It can be. This week we're expecting a warm-up."

"Oh, good. So, where is this bistro exactly?" she asked as they made their way down the street.

"Bistro?" he repeated.

"Your aunt's restaurant. Dee Dee's Bistro. The place where I'm working."

He stopped in front of the signature sky-blue brick

building. "We're here, but I wouldn't exactly call it a bistro," he said, pointing to the white cursive lettering above the entrance.

"Dee Dee's *Diner*." She stared up at the sign, and her jaw dropped.

It was going to be a long day.

ERIKA IS SO getting scratched off my Christmas list this year. Sloan took a deep breath as she followed Alex in. Why would her agent arrange for her to cook in a *diner*?

This was not a typical exchange.

Alex flipped on the lights. "Let me get the heat cranking. Should be nice and toasty in about thirty minutes."

Thirty minutes?! She took a deep breath and closed her eyes. Maybe this was simply a bad dream.

She squeezed her eyes tight. A very bad one.

"Hey, you okay?"

Her eyelids opened to see Alex staring at her from behind the counter, looking all sorts of amused. "I'm fine," she said, wheeling her suitcase across the black-and-white-checkered marble floor away from the Labradoodle, whose ears instantly perked up as she approached the counter. "I probably just need some coffee."

"On it." Alex turned around and flipped on a coffee maker, a loud noise spurting out. He gave it a good whack on its side. "It's been doing that for years. Usually takes a few minutes to really get percolating."

"I'll wait." She glanced around the dining room at the red vinyl booth seating along both walls and matching vinyl stools. Gold and yellow leaf decorations were strewn everywhere, along with small orange pumpkins and cornucopias set on each booth and table.

"Is fall your aunt's favorite season?" She pointed to the maple leaf string lights around the large cutout in the wall showing the kitchen.

He laughed at that and switched them on before setting an empty ceramic orange cup in front of her. "Every season is my aunt's favorite. She prides herself on her decorations. You should see this place at Christmas."

She smiled politely, picking up a nearby menu and flipping it open. That wouldn't be happening. "Wow, this is quite a breakfast selection."

"Best scrambled eggs and home fries in New England."

"*All* of New England. You don't say." She pinched the bridge of her nose, trying to reset her bad attitude that she was sure was coming out loud and clear.

It wasn't that she couldn't make breakfast food. It just wasn't her specialty. At home, she rarely cooked it since she rolled out of bed way past nine most days.

She glanced over her shoulder, staring out the front window, where dawn was barely beginning to break.

"One cup of Brooks Bend's finest." Alex poured the hot

coffee into her mug. "How do you take it?"

"With a lot of cardamon."

A line formed across his forehead. "I'm not sure my aunt has that."

"Don't worry. I brought some with me." It took her a few seconds to set the lucky pumpkin on the counter, where she planned on having it take up permanent residence, and open up her suitcase, carefully pulling out her portable rack. She retrieved the tiny bottle, popped the lid, and sprinkled it in. "Voila."

"I'll have to try that sometime." He pointed at the spice rack. "You've got quite the collection in there."

"I never start a shift without at least thirty of them," she said.

He reached for a couple of condiments, placing them in front of her. "You might find that we're more 'ketchup and Tabasco sauce on eggs and home fries' kind of people."

"We'll see about that." She hopped off her stool and picked up her spice rack. The simple fact of the matter was she was going to have to play with the cards dealt to her. If it was serving breakfast for two weeks, so be it. Her eggs Florentine with garam masala powder and tarragon seasoning was a real hit during a brunch she hosted a few years ago for her grandmother's book club and would be her special for today.

Oliver came over to her, sniffing her suitcase. "I've got nothing in there for you." She glanced over at Alex. "Are dogs even allowed in here?"

"This one is," he said, and that seemed to be the end of that as he moved from behind the counter. "Come here, boy. I'm sure Aunt Dee Dee has some snacks in the kitchen." He made his way to the double doors. "Care to join us?"

"For some dog treats?" She set her cardamon back in its spot. "I'll stick to my coffee, thanks."

He chuckled, and for some reason, the sound of his laughter caused her pulse to quicken. She brought the coffee cup to her lips.

Yeah, Alex was cute with his blondish-brown hair and rocking beard stubble that barely hid the cleft in his chin, but so what? He was just being friendly.

Besides, she'd always been more of a cat person.

He pressed open one of the doors with his back. "How about I give you an exclusive tour of the kitchen?"

"That would be great." She straightened her chef's coat, and followed him in. "Oh wow." She glanced around the tiny kitchen with two stoves, a walk-in refrigerator, and an industrial prep table a quarter the size of what she was used to chopping on.

"You'll set the food here and tap this when the order is ready." He rang a small silver bell on the counter line. "I'm sure it's a far cry from Seasons of San Francisco."

She parted her lips. *He knows my restaurant.* "My kitchen is a little bigger, but this is . . . this is . . ." She searched for the right words as to not offend the owner's nephew. "It's cozy."

He walked into a small pantry and pulled out a box of dog biscuits, showing it to Oliver. The dog's curly brown tail going a mile a minute. "I've been trying for the last couple of years to convince my aunt to buy the space next door." He pressed a hand along the wall. "There are so many things I could do if I could knock this down. Really open the kitchen for her."

"Are you an architect?" she asked, bending down to see the assortment of pots and mixing bowls stored underneath the prep table, and then popping back up to inspect the frying pans hanging above the stove.

"Nah." He smiled, lifting his hand off the wall and shoving it into his jacket pocket. "I'm more of a contractor. I come in after the plans are designed. I'm actually doing some work at The Bend right now."

"That must be fun. I've never been good at renovating anything." She opened the walk-in refrigerator, happy to see each shelf fully stocked.

"My aunt arranged for another food delivery on Friday."

Her gaze moved along the acorn squash, sweet potatoes, and pretty much everything else she'd need. "Thank you so much for opening the diner for me. I'm sure you're eager to get on with your day." She stepped out of the refrigerator, pointing to the stove. "Unless you want breakfast."

"No, I'm good." He pulled a set of keys out from his coat pocket. "These are for you. Justine, who is one of Dee

Dee's waitresses, should be here any minute."

"Great. Thanks again." She stepped into the refrigerator, retrieving a carton of eggs and a container labeled fresh spinach as Alex left the kitchen. Setting them on the prep table, she maneuvered to the bell, pressing it three times because she did have one last question.

Alex spun around; his lips turned up. "That's not quite how that works."

She laughed, coming out of the kitchen, and was immediately greeted by Oliver, who apparently wasn't going to stop doting on her until she petted him. She relented and bent down, patting his furry head. "What about my sous chef? When will they arrive?"

"Your sous chef?"

Okay, this place with a bell to announce a plate was ready for pickup probably didn't have an official sous chef. "Prep cook?" she asked, looking up.

"Um . . ." He pulled his face, his eyebrows squinching.

"Dishwasher?" She stood and made her way behind the counter. Maybe her voice sounded a little desperate, and it wasn't that she couldn't wash dishes, but his expression couldn't be implying that she'd be working the back of the house entirely by herself.

Could it?

"You're the only one on Mondays for breakfast on account of it being a little lighter in here than the rest of the week." He bent down and secured the leash to Oliver's collar. "Tom will be with you for lunch. The diner's closed on Sundays."

"And dinner?" She couldn't possibly run that shift alone.

"You're off the hook. My aunt suspended dinner service while you're here."

"Really? No dinner." That actually could work out well. She'd close the kitchen by three p.m. and have the rest of the afternoon and evening to work on her Holiday Palate audition meals.

"Have a great day." Alex flipped the closed sign and opened the door, turning around. "Remember, Chef. Ketchup is your friend."

"Noted." She slid the red bottle far down the counter, making room for all of her spices. Grinning, she pulled out her garam masala powder and tarragon bottles.

The good people of Brooks Bend were about to get seasoned.

Chapter Four

ALEX TOOK HIS hand off the Pizza & Pop Shop's glass door, observing the enormous line leading up to the counter.

"Looks like no pizza for us today, buddy," he said down to Oliver. For a Monday, the joint was jam-packed, and he was never one to wait in a long line.

At least not this afternoon, when he wanted to spend some time pricing out light fixtures a few towns over for his aunt's diner. He'd decided, after leaving earlier, it would be best to let Sloan settle in for a day or two and then he'd tackle his aunt's list.

In hindsight, he probably shouldn't have left her alone before Justine arrived for her shift, but judging from their interaction last night and earlier, he suspected Sloan Leary was a confident woman who, when faced with the unknown, did perfectly fine on her own.

"Alex."

He froze in place. Speaking of confident women, he knew that voice anywhere.

Mia.

He turned for their inevitable reunion, ten years in the making. "Hi," he said to his ex, who was standing in front of him in a black wool coat and purple scarf, her fiery-red hair the same as he remembered, just a few inches shorter and straighter. "It's good to see you."

"You too. It's been so long." She threw her arms around him.

Oh, we're doing this. He patted her back for his part in this really awkward hug. "You look great," he offered when they moved apart.

"So do you."

He stood silent for a beat and then another. He'd wondered over the years what this reunion would be like. Now that it was finally here, he wasn't quite sure what he was feeling or how to act. "Congratulations on your book."

"Thank you. Is this your dog?" She smiled, and he instantly went back to a time where they'd stood in front of her locker after a homecoming pep rally. A seventeen-year-old Mia in her cheerleading uniform, smiling up at him.

He nodded. "Oliver Edwards, this is Mia James . . ." He paused, correcting himself. "I mean, Graves." He'd heard her pen name was what she was going by these days.

She bent down to pet him, but in an uncharacteristic move, Oliver turned away and sat with his back to them.

Alex bit back the laugh bubbling up. *Good boy. Stay away.*

Mia didn't seem to notice the pup's snub, standing back

up and tugging on her purple gloves that matched her scarf. "I'm meeting some friends right now to do some early Christmas shopping, but did you hear about the book club event tonight at The Bend?"

"I did." He'd received his book and orders in the mail from the mayor's office. "I don't think the mayor gave many of us much of an option but to attend."

She laughed. "I did include your name on my invite list."

He laughed back, and it was nice for them to be smiling at one another after all these years. "I'll be there for a few. I'm actually doing some work on the inn."

"That's great." She tightened her scarf. "It was really good to bump into you, Alex. I'll see you tonight."

"See you." He watched as Mia crossed the street and entered the Belle and Beau Boutique. As far as awkward reunions went, that wasn't a root canal type of excruciating. Maybe catching up with her wouldn't be so bad.

Although their going down memory lane that ended with her dumping him over the phone from her UCLA dorm room wasn't a road he was anxious to take a second time.

"C'mon, Oliver. Let's go get a hoagie." He scratched his dog's head and headed down the street to The Sandwich Spot, a few buildings away.

Normally, he'd have lunch at the diner on the house, as his aunt always insisted when he pulled out his wallet, but it seemed kind of weird to ask Sloan to make him something, even if he did pay for it.

He stopped in front of the sandwich shop, also wildly popular today, with a line outside the door for some reason. The owner, Matt Simmons, was by the entrance, pulling out two folding chairs and setting them around a small table.

A bit odd for alfresco dining this time of year.

"Hey, man," Alex greeted him. He'd always liked Matt since their days of playing football together in high school. "Are you having a special?"

"Yeah, it's called Any Alternative to Dee Dee's." Matt chuckled, patting Oliver. "You want this table?"

"Nah, I'm good." He'd rather eat without his fingers turning purple. Curious about what Matt meant exactly by "Any Alternative to Dee Dee's," he headed down the sidewalk, only to see a couple of truckers exiting the diner, followed by Sloan flying out.

"It's called seasoning, people!" she yelled, holding two plates up high. "Deal with it."

Maybe the chef wasn't fine on her own. He pulled gently on the leash for a waggy tailed Oliver to hang back. Now wasn't the time for his dog to dote on the chef. "Hey there," he greeted her.

She whipped around, her nostrils full-on flaring.

"Everything okay, Chef?" he asked, but clearly it wasn't.

"No one will even give my chicken saffron rice pilaf a try. Do you know how expensive saffron is?"

"Can't say I've ever priced it out." He offered a smile

that she clearly wasn't interested in accepting.

She nodded to the untouched chicken. "All they want are greasy burgers and fatty french fries. Can you believe that?"

"Yeah, why would anyone come to a diner and want that?"

His attempt at humor got a serious, pointed stare. It was time to diffuse the situation. He opened the front door, motioning for her to go in. "Why don't we step inside?"

"Honestly. Do East Coasters not like tasty food?" She let out a sigh, but followed him in, heading for the kitchen. "I just don't get it."

He glanced around the empty dining room that, on a normal Monday at lunchtime, would have been full.

"Oh, good. You're here." Justine greeted him with a hug before patting Oliver. She nodded to a booth with four abandoned plates. On them was barely touched food. "This has been happening all day." She picked up a plate. "They take one bite and head straight to the Pizza & Pop Shop."

"Wow." He cocked his head. "Does it taste that bad?"

"No one wants whatever she's sprinkling. I mean, she's nice and all, but Tom and I have scraped more food off plates today than I do in an entire week. You know how people talk. We won't make any profit this week or next if she keeps this up. Please go reason with her."

"On it." The last thing they needed was his aunt's business to lose customers while she was away. He walked over to the counter where Sloan was now muttering to herself while examining a burger at eye level.

So, she did know how to make one. Good. That was the first step. He slid onto the stool.

"There's absolutely nothing wrong with this burger." She set down the plate. "The man didn't even try it."

"You didn't take my advice, did you?" He waggled an eyebrow as to hint that question was more playful than accusatory.

"Why would I drench my roasted wild mushroom cumin burger in ketchup?" She pushed the plate toward him. "Here, take a bite."

"Oh, I'm not all that hungry," he said, despite his stomach letting out an enormous growl.

"Please. The guy didn't even touch it. I need someone—anyone—to tell me it's good."

He smiled, thoroughly defeated by the plea in her warm brown eyes. "Okay." He picked up the bun and took a cautious bite. The chef might be cute and all, but he wasn't about to ingest a lot of something foreign to his taste buds that might make him hurl.

The seasoning had a sweet and nutty kick that actually . . . man, was quite good. "Hmmm."

"You hate it."

"No. No. It's different, but I like it." He took a bigger bite to show that he truly meant it. "Here's the thing. You're obviously good at what you do." He set down the burger. "When customers come here, they're expecting simple diner food. Not mushroom burgers with cinnamon."

"Cumin," she corrected him, handing over a paper napkin. "What should I do?"

He wiped his mouth. "Maybe try sticking to the menu?"

She bit down on her lip, appearing to think about that, and darned if that look didn't make him melt a little.

He reached for the burger, taking another bite. How attractive Sloan was even in distress was really not the point. "Could you make a simple cheddar cheeseburger with, say, lettuce, tomato, and grilled red onions?" It was his favorite classic burger that his aunt had made for him on several occasions.

"Yeah, I could. I guess."

"Perfect. I'll be your first lunch customer tomorrow."

She snapped her fingers. "And I could pickle some of my ginger seasoning tonight and prepare a ginger relish."

"Nope. Nope." He shook his head, putting his hand up. "Stop right there."

She cracked a smile—finally. "You know, the whole point of this culinary exchange is for me to bring my signature style and give Dee Dee's customers an opportunity to try something they've never had before."

"But to do that, we need to keep them *in* the diner."

She looked out at the empty dining room and frowned. "I really screwed up, didn't I?"

"Nah, they'll come back, but how about you ease into introducing your spices? Maybe you make a dessert or side dish with one of your seasonings." He paused, adding, "But keep a plain cheesecake on the menu too."

His suggestion got both a groan and a big ol' eye roll. "There's nothing worse than a naked cheesecake."

Before he could question what that actually meant, the door flew open, followed by a delivery man rolling in a dolly with three white insulated boxes. "I have a delivery for Sloan Leary," he said to them.

"That's me." She clapped her hands together and moved quickly around the counter. "I was hoping you'd come today."

Alex watched as Sloan signed for the delivery, asking the man if he could set the white boxes on the booth closest to the door.

"Did you order more food?" he asked, hopping off the stool. His aunt's refrigerator had been stocked and given that Sloan didn't do a lot of cooking today, there might not be much room for more.

"No." She shook her head, looking all kinds of excited for whatever had arrived. "It's for this amazing audition that my agent set up for me. If I win, I'll be contracted to make prepared Thanksgiving meals for next year's holiday."

That sounded important, judging by her emotional flip from agitation mere minutes ago to jubilee. "Must be a big deal."

She glanced up, her gaze locking with his. "It could lead to everything I've ever dreamed of."

He gulped. "Everything you ever dreamed of, huh? Well, let's get these opened." He went into the kitchen and grabbed a knife, rejoining her in seconds. He held it up. "Shall I?"

"Please." She scooted over and Oliver jumped up by her side. "Yes, you can join me," she said, patting his back.

Alex sliced into the first box. Popping open the foam lid, he started to do the same to the second, while Sloan rummaged through its contents.

"What in the world?" She held up what looked like individual frozen meat packets.

"Is that chicken?" he asked. It sure looked like a cutlet.

She flipped over both, reading the labels. "Chicken and turkey *gizzards*," she said, making a face. "What's in there?"

"Some grain." He reached inside and pulled out a bag. "And rice."

"Rice?" she repeated, leaning over and inspecting the box for herself. Her sweet, fruity scent went straight to his head.

"Looks like that's it inside this one," he said. "Want me to open the last?"

"No, that's okay." She reached into her pants pocket and pulled out her phone. "If you'll excuse me, I need to text my agent because I'm clearly not cooking turkey gizzards on a bed of rice for Thanksgiving."

"Sure." He got up and whistled for Oliver to join him. His dog was completely fixated on the gizzards in Sloan's hand. He guided the pup gently out of the booth. "Oh, by the way. I forgot to mention that I'll be doing some minor renovations in here while my aunt's gone. I'll do them in the evening to stay out of your way."

"Okay, no problem," she said, mid-text. "I'll see you later."

Once on the street, he glanced over his shoulder to see the pretty chef in meltdown mode as she opened the remaining box.

He put his hand on the door to go back and see if there was anything he could do, but then he lifted it.

Sloan's time here was only a pit stop on her way to getting everything she ever dreamed. She'd sort out whatever the issue was that currently had her in a tailspin. It was best if he didn't get involved.

He glanced down at his dog, who was now stationed on hind legs in front of the glass door, staring in. "Okay, fine. I'll give you that—she's cute—but don't get excited, buddy. She won't be here for long."

"ERIKA, PLEASE TELL me you have a good explanation as to why I received these from Palate?" Sloan waved the turkey and chicken gizzards in front of her phone. Her agent had responded to her frantic text earlier that she was on the case and to give her an hour to get some answers from the company.

Erika leaned back in her chair, and Sloan could easily tell from the artwork in the background that her agent was sitting at one of the Seasons of San Francisco's two-top tables. She and her grandmother had commissioned a talented local artist for all the vibrant pink and orange pictures decorating the restaurant's pale-blue walls.

"Okay. I know this seems confusing," Erika started, picking up a glass and taking a sip of water. "I spoke to my contact for the Palate audition and got some clarity on your audition."

"There was a mix-up on the ingredients, right?" Sloan asked, all but sure.

Erika held a finger in the air. "Well, what they sent you is actually correct."

Sloan cocked her head. Her agent couldn't be serious. "I can't possibly be making anything with the digestive organ of a turkey as my base," she said, not masking her irritation.

Not this time. From her unexpected trek thousands of miles away to being assigned to work in a small-town diner, she was finished with Erika throwing her one curveball after another.

Absolutely done.

She took a deep breath and asked the only question she needed an immediate answer to: "Do I have an audition or not?"

"You do. So, here's what happened." Her agent smiled up at someone who Sloan suspected was Dee Dee. "Oh, hey.

I'm talking to Sloan right now. I'll bring her in when I'm done. Your chocolate-pecan pie was delicious. I understand how you got that award." She turned back to Sloan. "You are going to love Dee Dee, and you really do need to try her pie when you get back. I'll ask her to leave you a big slice in the freezer."

Sloan's blood was bubbling up to a boil. She didn't care about some dessert that probably won first place in the Brooks Bend dairy festival. "Can we please get back to the topic at hand?"

"Okay. Here's the situation. A really big celebrity chef became available at the last minute, and Palate decided to sign her for the Holiday Palate line."

Sloan's heart sank to her stomach, taking her upper body with it as she slumped into the vinyl booth. "So, I lost the audition?"

"No. No. You still have an amazing opportunity with those ingredients in front of you. You, Sloan Leary, have a chance to be the exclusive chef for another new line that they just announced."

"Another new line?" She picked up a gizzard. "No *human* is going to eat this."

"Bingo!"

"Bingo, what?"

"No human will be eating them."

Sloan tipped her head. "I don't understand."

"You'll be auditioning to be the exclusive chef to their

Puppy Palate line." Erika clapped her hands. "Isn't that marvelous?"

"They want me to make dog food?" Had her agent lost her mind?

"They want you to make fun holiday meals for pampered pooches."

"Pampered pooches," she deadpanned, pressing her thumb into the mushy gizzard.

"Yes, and they are so excited to see what you come up with. My contact said you are a lead contender."

"Well, you can tell your contact I'm not interested." She sat up, pushing her shoulders back. This was not the step she'd planned to get closer to realizing her dream.

A total nightmare was what this was. "Audition is off."

"Sloan . . ." Erika started, giving her that infamous look she often served up with some of her sage "I've been in this industry and know a thing or two" advice. "I realize this is a bit of a detour."

"Detour." Sloan scoffed at that understatement. "You're asking me to make dog food."

"No. I want you to create scrumptious meals that pampered pooches will no doubt run to their bowls and lick clean."

This couldn't be happening. This wasn't happening. "I'll be the laughingstock of the culinary world. My reputation—"

"Will be just fine," Erika finished Sloan's sentence. "Listen, I know it's not what we were hoping, but this *is* a big deal. I've been doing some research and the culinary pet industry is enormous. People pay top dollar to feed the bellies of their fur babies with wholesome, natural ingredients."

Culinary pet industry. Sloan shook her head, staring at her phone screen. How did the last forty-eight hours go so seriously off the rails?

Erika continued, "You would be one of a very small handful of chefs lending their name to this market. If you win the audition, I'll do everything in my power to make sure we walk away with a major deal, and nothing less."

"I don't know." Sloan was very well aware of how many zeros could be included in a major deal. Enough to expand Seasons of San Francisco, but could she even pull off such a pivot in her cooking? "I've never even owned a dog. I haven't a clue what they eat."

"Why don't you take a day to think about it? I'm going to e-mail you some sample recipes to help you brainstorm. There are thousands of kibble combinations."

She raised an eyebrow. Somehow, she doubted there were thousands of things you could do with a mushy part of a chicken.

She glanced over at the box of rice. But, like it or not, she also knew that her agent had always had her best interests at heart and would never steer her to a deal she didn't wholeheartedly believe in. "I guess I could try."

"That's my top chef! I'm going to run and give this table

up to a customer. I'd put Dee Dee on so you can meet her, but this place filled up fast while we were talking. She's probably flying around your kitchen at the moment."

"Okay." Sloan glanced around the empty diner, feeling awful that she'd spent the good part of the day scaring Dee Dee's customers away. "Please tell Dee Dee that I hope she has a wonderful time, and I'm looking forward to chatting with her soon."

"I will." Erika paused, then added, "Sloan, dear, Puppy Palate *is* a good thing. Trust me on this."

"Uh-huh." Sloan said a final goodbye and pulled herself up, picking up a turkey gizzard and flipping it over. Could she make anything out of this that dogs would eat?

She tossed it back into the box, closed the lid, and frowned.

Did she even want to?

Chapter Five

I'M AUDITIONING TO *make meals for dogs.* As she made her way down Main Street, Sloan continued to wrestle with the bombshell her agent dropped, smiling politely to an old couple that passed her.

Didn't matter if it was dressed up in a pretty Puppy Palate holiday-inspired package, it was still dog food.

She rolled her suitcase behind her, picking up her pace. It'd been a long day and what she needed more than anything was to peel off her uniform and put on her cozy yoga pants and favorite comfy long-sleeved Henley.

She paused at The Bend, taking in the scene. *What do we have here?* The beautiful inn was all lit up with the drapes pulled back, revealing a nice-sized crowd who'd gathered in both the foyer and the living room.

The last thing she wanted to do was crash the event or have to engage in painstaking small talk with total strangers. She made her way up the wooden steps and did her best to slip through the crowd with her suitcase, while jolly laughter and conversation filled the first floor.

She stopped in front of a giant poster of a beautiful red-headed woman who looked around her age, wearing a dark-blue apron and holding up a *Pie or Die* paperback in one hand and a butcher knife in the other.

Oh, right. The town's book club event. She glanced around. Kimmie hadn't been kidding when she said all of Brooks Bend was invited. While maybe not the *entire* town, the place was jam-packed.

"Sloan!" Hayden greeted her, all dressed up in a long, burgundy velvet dress and matching headband. She put a hand on her hip. "Where's your lucky pumpkin?"

"Oh." Sloan placed a palm on her neck. Why all the obsession with this pumpkin? Maybe she should have brought it back. "Um, Alex told me I could leave it at the diner."

Yes, that's right. Blame it on the cute nephew.

"It's okay." Hayden gave her shoulder a pat. "I'm just teasing. Can I get you some hot apple cider?" She leaned in. "It's an adult one."

A spiked warm drink actually sounded really good right about now. "Yes, thank you."

"Come right this way, then. You can leave your suitcase off to the side there by the counter. No one will touch it."

"Oh, I'm good. Thank you." She didn't like to leave her spices unattended; some were rare and would take many weeks to replace. She rolled the suitcase into the living room, following Hayden. The furniture had been pushed to the walls to make room for a long, skirted table displaying a nutty cheese ring with crackers, colorful fruit and vegetable platters, and mini pumpkin pies with a little toothpick-sized knife plunged into the center of each.

Cute, and a nice promotional touch.

A bar had been set up to the far left of the room next to a beautiful redbrick fireplace with a couple of logs crackling inside. Sloan inched closer to the fire, extending her hands to let the heat warm her fingers while she waited for her drink.

"Here you go. Pure autumn in a cup." Hayden came up beside her, handing her the beverage.

"Thank you." Sloan took a sip. The general manager was right. It *was* pure autumn deliciousness. "Your fireplace is exquisite," she said, admiring the red brick behind it.

"Thank you. My grandfather built it with his bare hands when he first bought the inn." Hayden picked up a long black poker propped up against the wall and gave the logs a good poke. "I've been thinking about replacing it with an electric one. But there are so many precious memories dancing around in those flames, I've never had the heart."

Sloan smiled, taking a sip of her cider. Though it had only been her and her grandmother for most of her life, she understood the power of holding on to special memories any way that you could. "Well, it's lovely." She paused, adding, "And I've always admired people who can build something with their hands. Your grandfather was clearly talented."

Hayden nodded. "You know who else is talented?" Hayden pointed behind her, and Sloan's gaze followed it to see the handsome contractor in conversation with two other guys over by the guest check-in counter. Oliver laid on the floor next to him. "Alex is great at building things."

"He'd mentioned this morning he was doing some renovations here." Was the general manager playing matchmaker? It sure felt like it.

"And he's single." Hayden winked.

Yep, she is. Sloan brought her cup to her lips. Sure, Alex, with his floppy, dirty-blond hair and lopsided grin, was cute and all, and yes, he'd been really nice to her today, sweet even, but there was no reason to get her flirt on. She'd be on the first flight out of here in thirteen days.

Eager to change the subject from Alex's single status, she turned back to the fireplace, taking in the various empty picture frames along the mantel. "Are you working on adding in new pictures?" she asked, curious as to why there were no actual pictures in them, just the black-and-white stock photo paper that came with the frames.

"Oh, no. They're perfect as is." Hayden picked up one photo, pointing to the young woman posing with a man and two small kids on a beach. "This is my younger sister, Rachel."

"Your sister?" Sloan glanced down at the picture.

"Yeah, she's a stock art model." She placed the photo back on the mantel, laughing. "That was the first photo frame she sent my parents nine years ago. She'd been living in New York City and was so proud to land the gig."

"That's cool." Sloan stared at the photo next to it of her

AN AUTUMN TO REMEMBER

posing with the same handsome man as in the first. For this one, they were bundled up in winter coats and wool hats, ice skates slung around their shoulders. "Does she always work with the same model?" she asked, noticing the man was in the next three photos.

"She did for a few years." Hayden set the fire poker back along the wall. "That's her ex-boyfriend, Josh. They met during their first assignment together and then became a package deal. They'd send us a framed picture every year for Christmas, and we'd all have a good laugh."

"I'm sorry it didn't work out between them."

"Yeah, we were too." Hayden picked up the last frame on the mantel. "Rachel still sends us frames, though." She paused, adding, "Josh has a new stock photo family, but we don't buy those frames."

Sloan couldn't help but let a chuckle slip. She put her fingers to her lips. "Understandable."

While Hayden excused herself to tend to a guest checking in, Sloan stepped off to the side, taking in everything going on around her. Kimmie and Earl were at the back of a line that had formed to have their books signed by the celebrity author, who was now seated behind a round table next to the stairs, chatting it up with her readers while signing their books.

Everyone seemed to be having a really nice time. She cocked her head, gazing over at the guest check-in counter.

That is, all but one.

Alex was still there, but now at the far end, all alone, leaning against the counter and sipping on a longneck while watching the signing.

She grabbed two of the mini pumpkin pies, resting them in her palm, and then wheeled her suitcase with her free hand over to Alex. Oliver greeted her immediately, rising on all fours when he saw her.

She caught Hayden's eye, who gave her a mischievous smirk before pretending to busy herself behind the counter with some papers.

What a little matchmaker.

"Pie or die?" she asked Alex, holding out her hand.

"Die," he said bluntly, but nevertheless, took the mini pie she offered and placed it on the counter.

She bit into her pie—mmm, really good. Although, a sprinkle of her pumpkin pie spice that she created each year by combining some of her sweet and savory fall seasonings would make it even better. "Don't want the author's signature?" she asked in between bites, tipping her head toward the line.

"Didn't read her book." He took a long pull of his beer and scowled.

Okay then. Sloan moved over beside him, swiping her bottom lip for any pumpkin remnant. There was probably a story there, judging by his silence, but she wasn't one to pry.

"Sloan Leary. I'm so glad you could join us. Hey, Alex. Nice to see you." A short, thin man with wire-rimmed glasses, sporting an orange-and-green argyle sweater vest with a crisp white shirt underneath, greeted them. A tall brunette in a tight-knit black sweater dress and white pearls, her lips a perfect ruby red, was with him.

Sloan smiled politely at the attractive couple as the man extended his hand.

"Evan Hertzberg, mayor of Brooks Bend. This is my wife, Jillian. Jillian owns the flower shop a few spaces down from Dee Dee's Diner."

"It's so nice to meet you both." Sloan shook Evan's hand and then Jillian's. "You have a lovely town," she said. *Despite it being full of people with no taste buds.*

"I'm looking forward to stopping into the diner and sampling your cooking," Jillian said.

Sloan pressed her lips together. At least someone was.

Although, because this was a small town and since Jillian's flower shop was near the diner, the florist probably already knew how much of a disaster today had been. "I've decided that I'm going to stick with Dee Dee's fall menu and offer only one or two of my own seasonal side dishes and desserts."

Jillian touched her pearls. "Probably a wise move."

Ouch! Yep, the florist had gotten the 411. Sloan prayed people would come in tomorrow and give her a chance.

"I hope to see you both at tomorrow night's Wishbone Wishes event," the mayor said.

Her ears perked up. Wishbone Wishes event. That

ROBYN NEELEY

sounded fun. God knows she could use a wish coming true.

"Wouldn't miss it," Alex said dryly.

Whatever the event was, Dee Dee's nephew sounded as enthused as one would be spending the whole day in line at the DMV. "I'd love to attend," she offered, although the way the couple was now looking around the room, they were clearly done talking with her.

Alex leaned in when the couple was out of earshot. "Don't let Jillian get to you. She's snide like that with everyone."

"It's fine, and I probably deserved it." Sloan pushed off the counter. "I promise that starting tomorrow, every single egg, pancake, burger, and BLT will be straight off your aunt's menu. My spices will stay nestled in their bottles, awaiting their journey back to San Francisco."

That visual seemed finally to spark a laugh out of him, which was better than the sourpuss face he'd been sporting. "So, did you get ahold of your agent?"

"Yes, I did." Now it was her turn to go silent.

"Didn't go well, I take it?"

"More like, took an unexpected turn. That audition I was telling you about is for . . ." She didn't even have it in her to finish the sentence. What chef who oversaw a Michelin-starred restaurant would seriously consider auditioning to make puppy kibble?

"Wasn't everything you ever dreamed?"

"Not even close." She dropped her hand to pet Oliver.

"They want me to make dog food. Can you imagine that?" she asked Oliver, ruffling a fluffy ear. "Food for you."

"Dog food?" he repeated. "You're kidding."

"I wish I was. I mean, it'd definitely be a major pivot in my career, but if I were to get the contract, I could earn enough to branch out. Open up a new restaurant in Paris."

"Paris?" he asked, sounding taken aback. "Is that your dream?"

"Yeah," she said softly, lifting her hand off the dog. She rarely talked about her expansion plan with anyone besides Erika, but for some strange reason had no problem blurting it out to this man she'd only met twenty-four hours ago. "I'd love to expand one day. This could get me to that goal much faster than I had planned."

"So, then you're going to go through with the audition?"

Her gaze met his and something in his bright-blue eyes was causing her legs to wobble. She straightened one and then the other. It was silly to think Alex really cared what some random woman he met by chance wanted to do with her life, but for some reason, it felt . . .

Well, it felt nice that he seemed interested. "I'm going to sleep on it."

Just then, Oliver pressed his black nose into her white jacket. "I don't have anything for you, but if you stop in tomorrow, I can cook you up some yummy turkey gizzards." She glanced over. "Does your dog go everywhere with you?"

"Do your spices go everywhere with you?" he asked,

nodding down to her suitcase.

Touché. She wanted to say something funny back, but judging by his deep frown as he watched Mia now chatting with the two guys he was hanging out with earlier, he had other things on his mind.

Just then, one of the guys put his arm around the author.

"I've got some work to do in the new library." Alex whistled, clapping his thigh a couple of times. "Let's go, buddy."

Sloan watched Alex dodge the crowd, avoiding the signing table altogether as he disappeared down the hall. She turned around to Hayden, who wasn't far behind the counter, and no doubt heard their conversation. "What's with him?" she asked.

"Oliver's his emotional support animal."

Sloan's lips parted. *Emotional support animal.* "I didn't know," she said, feeling awful for asking the question the way she had. Of course, the dog went everywhere with him.

"It's okay. Alex doesn't talk about what led to his getting Oliver. He was honorably discharged from the Army. When he finally came home, Oliver was with him."

Sloan touched her chest. "I feel so awful. I should go apologize."

"I'm sure he'll be fine. You didn't know, and honestly, that's not the reason for his bad mood tonight." She nodded to the guest of honor. "Mia's his ex."

"Ah." Sloan picked up his untouched pumpkin pie. "I get his choice now."

Hayden leaned in, resting her elbows on the counter. "They were *the* class couple in high school. He was the cute football player every girl had a crush on, and she was the bubbly cheerleader. We all thought they would be the first in our class to get married, but she dumped him her senior year in college."

Sloan glanced over at the author, who exuberated sophistication in her style and manner. "College breakups are hard," she said, thinking about her own with a nice business major, David, she'd met her sophomore year. When she wasn't studying or in the Seasons of San Francisco kitchen with her grandmother, she was with David. It had broken her heart when he decided to end things, just before he moved to Chicago to start his MBA.

Hayden continued, "Alex would never admit this, but he was staying around Brooks Bend, hoping Mia would get a job in New York City when she graduated college. When she took a job in Los Angeles and broke up with him, he enlisted and le—"

A loud noise coming from another room cut her off. Hayden shook her head. "Oh dear. He's gotten out the sledgehammer, and we're just about to start the murder reenactment. I can't have any of the guests wandering over there. I'm going to go talk to him."

Sloan set down the pie, straightening her chef's jacket over her hips. A fictitious murder mystery reenactment and an upset ex swinging a potential weapon didn't feel like a good combination.

But she did know what would make one. "Let me do it."

She bent down and unzipped her suitcase, pulling out a tiny bottle toward the front of her rack.

"What are you doing?" Hayden asked.

She smiled while opening the lid and sprinkling some of her spice across the pumpkin pie, swirling it in with the little knife. "Giving Alex a taste of some of Sloan Leary end-of-day kindness."

And, hopefully, he won't kill me.

ALEX BROUGHT THE sledgehammer back and put all his muscle into the swing, slicing into the wall. He'd thought peeling off his flannel, rolling up his sleeves, and doing something physical that would fire up his adrenaline would improve his mood.

Turned out, it didn't.

It wasn't that he cared that Mia was here and had easily caught the eye of every single guy.

Okay, he cared a little.

But their ship had sailed years ago when he arrived at Fort Benning for basic training, determined to forget her. He'd joined the Army to finally make something of himself.

He glanced down at the sledgehammer. Now, he was a glorified handyman at best. He pulled back the ax.

"Hey there."

He swung around to see Sloan jump back, her hands up above her shoulders. "I *knew* it was the contractor, in the library, with a jackhammer all along."

He laughed because that was funny. "Sledgehammer," he corrected, setting it down along his workbench he'd set up a couple of days ago while prepping the room for the wall demolishment. He nodded at the mini pumpkin pie she was holding. "I thought I made my choice clear."

"Well . . . you did, but I thought I'd give you another chance because this one is special."

"It is, is it?" He found her refreshingly amusing, and let's face it, this night could use some humor.

"This pie right here is swirled with none other than the best pumpkin spice made by yours truly." She laughed, handing it over. "I used the tiny knife to swirl it in. I'm calling it 'sweet revenge.'"

His lips curved up as he accepted the mini pie and took a bite. "Not bad."

"Not bad?" She shot him a horrific expression that was super cute. "I'll have you know that that spice has been enjoyed by tens of thousands of my customers."

"Tens of thousands, huh?" He smirked, taking another big bite. He didn't doubt it. It was pretty tasty.

"Yep." She stepped onto the protective plastic sheet that he'd dropped down to not get dust and other remnants from smashing a wall in all over. "So, this is going to be a library when you're done?"

"Yes. The inn's owner is pretty jazzed about providing a quiet space where guests can come in here and relax."

"That sounds lovely." She gazed up at the arch windows with the stained wood paneling. "This room is already gorgeous."

"It's going to be better once I knock this wall out. There's going to be a floor-to-ceiling bookshelf with a spiral staircase to retrieve books on top. Both were specially made this summer and are arriving early next week for installation. Then I'm going to give the hardwood floors a cherry stain."

She closed her eyes, which gave him a few seconds to take in the tiny freckles that dusted her nose. "It sounds magical." Her eyelids flew open, and he immediately looked away.

"May I?" She came up beside him and picked up the sledgehammer, and darn it if she didn't look adorable, taking a few wobbly steps backward from its heaviness.

He reached over and gently took it back. The last thing he wanted was for her to throw her back out. "Maybe you should stick to culinary utensils."

"You're probably right. So . . ." She hopped up on the workbench. "You left the party suddenly."

He finished off the pie, licking a spiced finger. "The author and I had an ending a long time ago that was far from happy, but I'm thrilled for her success. No ill will there."

Sloan's raised eyebrow suggested she didn't buy it.

"Okay, I was a little sour tonight."

"A little?"

"Her success, I am happy for," he reiterated because that certainly was true. "She deserves it. It's hard seeing other guys we grew up with all over her." He raked a hand through his hair. *What's the matter with you, man?* Here he was alone with a pretty woman having a nice conversation. The last thing he should be talking about was his ex.

"I bet it's a little awkward for her too." Sloan seemed to want to continue talking about Mia. "I get not buying her book, but maybe you could take a break from your demolition and congratulate her. My grandma Gabby used to say that ending your day showing kindness to others was the best way to end it."

He grinned. "Is that what you're doing here?"

"Maybe." She shrugged a shoulder. "It might make you feel better."

"Probably." But he didn't have to do it right now.

"I'm really sorry, Alex, for what I said earlier."

Her apology took him by surprise. "What did you say?"

"About Oliver always being with you. Hayden told me . . ." She paused for a second. "Well, she didn't really say much. She said you were in the Army and that he's your emotional support animal."

"I was. He is, and it's fine."

He kept his gaze on Oliver to avoid the pity he was all but sure had taken over Sloan's expression. He'd seen the same look on friends and family members over the years. "He's my bud, aren't you, pal?" He scratched Oliver behind his ears. "Plus, he's a good dinner date. You can borrow him if you need a taste tester."

That got a laugh from her. "I might need to take you up on that."

"I'm sorry I asked you if you always bring your spices everywhere you go." He glanced around. "Although, I guess you don't."

"I'm trying something new." She laughed and pulled herself off the bench. "I should probably head to bed. I'll see you both tomorrow for your cheeseburger and gizzards."

"You've got yourself two paying customers." He smiled, disappointed that she was calling it a night, but he understood. It'd been a long day. "Remember, Chef, ketchup is your friend," he teased as she crossed the room.

"Yeah, yeah, yeah." She shook her head but didn't seem put off by his advice. "You wait and see, Alex Edwards. I'm going to make a gourmet seasoning connoisseur out of you yet." She waved goodbye and disappeared out of the room.

Alex picked up the mini pie wrapper, swiping a crumb with his finger.

He certainly hoped so.

Chapter Six

ALEX MADE HIS way down Main Street, Oliver trotting behind him, squeaking his favorite rubber pizza slice toy that Aunt Dee Dee had gotten him for Christmas last year.

He'd spent the last hour hauling in materials for the inn's library, working up an appetite for a stack of buttermilk pancakes.

Yep, his urgent need to stop in the diner had all to do with his famished stomach craving some Vermont maple syrup, and nothing to do with the pretty brunette doing the cooking.

He tugged up the zipper on his brown leather coat. He'd decided to ditch his heavy flannel when he walked out his front door this morning.

Nope. Nothing at all.

After Sloan left last night, he'd taken her advice and pulled up his big boy pants, rejoining the party to congratulate Mia. The chef had been right. It'd been nice to engage his ex in more than the small talk they'd done earlier outside the Pizza & Pop Shop. They had a nice conversation over hot ciders as the guests began to leave. Sitting by the fire, she showed off to him pictures of her home in L.A. and the summer vacation she took to Spain.

He'd even offered to buy her book, but they'd long since run out of the extra copies her publicist had brought for the event for those who might want a second copy in addition to the complimentary ones the mayor's office mailed out. Mia said she was staying with her folks through Thanksgiving and promised to stop by the diner and leave a signed one for him and one for his aunt.

Even if she didn't, it was highly probable they'd run into each other again, Brooks Bend being the size of his hand and all, but he now knew it would be just fine if they did.

Adulting 101 at its best.

He stepped into the diner, glancing around at the empty booths and tables.

Shoot.

Guess he'd underestimated Aunt Dee Dee's customers, who clearly were extending their boycott another day.

Sure, it was late for the breakfast crowd, being almost eleven a.m. and all, but usually there were at least a couple of retirees milling about, enjoying a second or third cup of his aunt's strong coffee.

He crossed the room to the counter where Justine and Tom were huddled together up on barstools, working on a crossword puzzle.

"Hey, guys." He unleashed Oliver, who went right over

to them. "Are you both relaxing after the morning rush?"

That question got a big ole cackle out of Justine, giving him that answer. He took a deep breath. This wasn't good. "Where's Sloan?" He was almost afraid to ask.

"Oh, she's in the kitchen, preparing for the lunch stampede," Justine quipped, putting a hand on his jacket. "But if you're hungry for a grab-and-go breakfast, you've come to the right place."

"Alex!' Sloan called out from the service window.

"Hey." He raised a hand. She looked in a good mood, her hair pulled back, but unlike yesterday's slick ponytail, loose strands were flying in every direction and a noticeable white powder streaked across her left cheek.

"Come on back. I want you to taste something." Sloan waved for him to join her in the kitchen.

"Oh, lucky you," Justine joked under her breath.

Alex threw the waitress a pointed look to cool it with her jabs and pushed through the double doors. His eyes widened at the sight of the long prep counter filled with tall stacks of muffins, breads, and croissants. "Wow, you've been busy."

"I know, right?" She reached for a cup of coffee, brought it to her lips, and tilted it way back. "I woke up at three a.m. with all this boundless energy, so I decided to get a head start to the day." She handed him one of her many baked goods. "Here, you *have* to try my apple-sweet potato muffin."

"Thank you."

"I didn't even put any cinnamon in it," she said with a

smirk.

"Well done." He took a bite. "It's really good." Although, it probably *would* have been better with cinnamon, but he decided to keep that review to himself.

She slipped on two oven mitts and opened up the range door. In seconds, she showed off buttery, light-brown bread bowls. "I thought I'd make a few dozen of these to hold your aunt's New England clam chowder. I found the soup recipe in a folder she left for me in her office." She pointed to a large stainless steel soup pot on the stove. "Tom was a doll and got it started."

"I didn't realize my aunt left you her recipes," he said, finishing off the muffin and tossing the foil in a nearby trash dispenser. "I would have given them to you yesterday."

She brushed off his apology with her hand. "No worries. I am a woman of my word, determined to stick to Dee Dee's menu." She removed the bowls with a spatula, transporting each to a cooling rack. "I just hope we get a few customers for lunch." She nodded in Justine and Tom's direction, lowering her voice. "Did they tell you that no one came in for breakfast?"

He reached for another muffin since there appeared to be no shortage. "They mentioned it."

"I hate that I'm the reason your aunt isn't making any money this week."

He didn't like that his aunt's bottom line had taken a nose-dive either but didn't want to alarm Sloan. He reached for a paper towel near the sink and wetted it, handing it to her. "You've got a little flour on your cheek."

"Oh." She took the towel and wiped it across the wrong one. "Is it gone?"

"Other side." He took the paper towel and gently swiped her cheek. He could blame it on feeling sorry for the pretty chef, but the slightest touch of her skin setting an electric jolt straight through the towel. "There."

"Thank you," she said softly.

Embarrassed, he turned to look out the serving window while Sloan disappeared into the walk-in refrigerator, mumbling that she needed more eggs.

His gaze moved across the empty dining room. What could he do to help bring customers back in besides waiting for people to tire of pizza and hoagies?

"Is there anything else I should bake?" she asked, coming up right beside him. The scent of her sweet perfume tickled his nostrils.

"I think you've got it covered." He glanced over at the dozens of muffins and breads. If she baked any more, they'd have to start giving them away.

Actually . . .

An idea started to form. What they needed to do was get Sloan and her food in front of customers. It was a zany idea, but it could work. He reached for her hand. "Let's get out of here."

"What?" she asked, despite letting him lead her out of

the kitchen, which he took as a good sign. "Where are we going?"

"It's time to get your food in the bellies of the good people of Connecticut." Yeah, that's exactly what needed to be done, and he had three ideas on how to do so. He called out to the first reinforcement: "Hey, Justine, Tom, can you both work on that puzzle by the door and give out some of Sloan's muffins and breads when people walk by? Let them know Dee Dee's New England clam chowder is today's special with homemade bread bowls."

"On it," Tom said, and he and Justine both pushed off the counter stools and headed into the kitchen.

Alex leashed up Oliver and pushed open the front door, holding it for Sloan, who'd gone back into the kitchen to grab her purse.

"So, I'm just going to leave for the day?" she asked, sliding the strap over her shoulder.

"Yep. Tom can handle the kitchen and make more chowder if they run out."

She arched up an eyebrow, pausing in the doorway. "I don't think your aunt would approve of you forcing me out on my second day."

He laughed while leading her down the sidewalk, stopping only when they reached the end of the street to cross it. On the contrary, he had no doubt that his aunt would approve of what he had planned.

If—and that was a big if—he could pull it off. He'd have

to make a call, but first they needed to make a quick stop.

"Where exactly are we going, may I ask?"

He grinned down at the pretty chef, catching the amusement in her eyes. *Good.* Her sense of humor was going to be needed for the next few hours. It was time to execute idea number two.

"We're going to get you a coat."

"A COAT," SHE repeated. Why had Alex, all of a sudden, developed such a concern for her outer wardrobe that he needed to take her to get one right this second? What he should be worried about was his aunt's restaurant.

A business that was tanking this week, and it was all her fault.

"Thank you, Alex, but that's not necessary." She spun around. "I'm going back."

He reached for her hand and pressed the crosswalk sign. "Chef, with all due respect, there aren't any customers for you to go back to."

Wow. Her stomach tightened from that hard blow. She lifted her chin, determined to show her trademark confidence. "A good chef is always prepared. Besides, I already have a coat."

"Then why aren't you wearing it?"

"Because it's . . ." She wrapped her arms around her as

they crossed the street. "Not that I owe you an explanation, but it's a short leather jacket that I have a hard time getting on over my uniform. I didn't exactly pack to trek down a small-town main street every morning before dawn."

"Oh, right . . . the planning on being in Boston thing. Newsflash, it's cold up there too."

She pressed her lips, shaking her head. "Just when I thought you were a cool guy."

He showed off his lopsided grin. "I still am."

"Uh-huh." She gave him a sideways glance.

"I promise you this won't be painful." He stopped in front of a clothing boutique and opened the glass door. "After you, Chef."

She paused for a second. Annoyed at Alex or not, it would be nice to not freeze her tush off walking to and from the diner. "Okay, but if I see one I like, I'm buying it."

"Of course."

"Alex!" A petite woman with short black hair came over and greeted them, giving him a huge hug and then dropping down to give Oliver some love.

"It's good to see you, Gwen. How've you been?"

"Doing great." She popped back up. "Living the dream."

Sloan stood politely by the door while the two caught up for a minute taking in the super cute boutique that displayed men's and women's clothing along the walls and several round racks throughout the shop.

If she weren't preoccupied with returning to the diner,

this would be the kind of place that she loved getting lost in for hours back home. Supporting small business had always been her favorite thing to do, especially around this time of year as they moved into the holidays.

"Gwen, I'd like to introduce you to Sloan Leary," Alex began making introductions. "Sloan's running Aunt Dee Dee's diner while my aunt's working in Sloan's San Francisco restaurant as part of a . . ." He turned to her. "What's it called again?"

"Culinary exchange. Hi," she greeted the boutique owner, extending her hand.

"It's so nice to meet you, Sloan." Gwen motioned around the boutique. "Welcome to the Belle & Beau."

Aw, what a cute name. "You have a lovely shop."

"So, what brings you in? Are you looking for something special?" the boutique owner asked, giving Alex a wink. "Perhaps some nice jewelry."

"She needs a warm coat." Alex picked up a black knit cap with a fuzzy burgundy ball attached to it and tossed it to Sloan. "And maybe a hat and mittens." He reached for a pair of burgundy mittens and handed them over to her too.

"You have come to the right place." Gwen headed for a rack near the wall, a woman now on a mission. "I spent all of last week in the Garment District, picking up winter threads. I've got some great coats that you're simply going to love, Sloan. Come on over."

"Go on, Chef." Alex gave her an encouraging nod.

Sloan smiled wryly, glancing down at the hat and mittens. All of this was silly. They really shouldn't be wasting time here. No. What she needed to be doing was firing up the burners for all the cheeseburgers she planned on flipping.

She studied Alex, who gave her a dopey grin while nodding again for Sloan to join Gwen. "Okay. Fine. You know, I liked you better when you were brooding with your sledgehammer."

He laughed at that. "I'm going to take Oliver outside for a bio break and make a phone call. I'll be right back."

"What do you think of this one?" Gwen pulled out a waist-length navy-blue wool peacoat from the rack.

"It's nice." Sloan touched the fabric. Simple and probably would do the job.

"You know what?" Gwen snapped her fingers. "I've got this gorgeous burgundy number in the back that I haven't tagged yet. I think it would look fabulous on you with your brown hair and skin tone. Hold right here. I'll be right back."

Sloan stepped in front of a full-length mirror and let her ponytail down, slipping on the wool cap that Alex had tossed her. Suddenly, her phone buzzed inside her purse. "Hey," she greeted Erika, who was doing the video call while standing in a long line at the coffee shop across the street from Seasons of San Francisco.

Sloan's heart squeezed. She missed her routine of stopping in there for her large latte before heading into her restaurant.

She missed her home.

"Hello, dear," Erika said. "Why are you wearing a hat? Where are you? Shouldn't you be in Dee Dee's kitchen? It's got to be almost noon there, right? You didn't quit, did you?"

Sloan waited for the bombardment of questions to stop before answering. "I'm taking a break in between the breakfast and lunch shift and buying a coat. It's quite cold here in Connecticut, especially when I have to walk to work down Main Street at four a.m."

"The hat is cute on you. You should get it." If Erika picked up on Sloan's frustrated tone, she was ignoring it. "I wanted to check in to see if you received my e-mail."

Sloan pulled a pine-green cashmere sweater off the rack and admired it while she continued to talk.

She had received the e-mail. Ten pages of dog food recipes had been waiting in her inbox when she checked it before climbing into bed last night. "I really appreciated that you included pictures," she deadpanned.

"I wanted you to see the vast number of combinations. The possibilities are endless."

"Uh-huh." Mash it, whip it or sauté it, it was still dog food.

"And I have more news."

"Let me guess. Dee Dee absolutely hates working in my restaurant and wants to end the exchange early?" Sloan asked. One could hope.

"No. On the contrary. She's having a ball. Your customers are loving her specials."

"That's really terrific." With her free hand, she scratched the guilt that now crept up her neck. At least someone was having success with this exchange.

If things didn't improve, she was going to have to write Dee Dee a personal check to make up for the financial loss.

Erika continued, "So, Puppy Palate e-mailed this morning. They have scheduled your audition for next Tuesday. You'll be going up to their headquarters office in Boston. They have a fully operating kitchen studio, where you'll prepare the meals and present them to a panel of judges."

Sloan bit her lip, glancing away. She could say that she'd been baking up a storm all morning only for Dee Dee's customers, but truth be told, she'd also spent the whole morning doing everything *but* making a decision.

Now, time was up.

"Sloan, you are going to go through with the audition, right?"

She took a deep breath, closed her eyes, and envisioned the Seasons of Paris red marquee above her cute and trendy restaurant on Rue St. Dominique, her grandmother's favorite street.

She lifted her eyelids. Heaven help her for what she was about to say. "Yes, I'm going to do it. I'll get started on coming up with my audition meals right away."

"Yes! She's going to do it," Erika shouted in the coffee shop, fist-pumping the air before spinning around and hugging the guy standing in line behind her.

Sloan waited for her agent to finish her celebration and return to the screen, seeing the back end of the man's dark blue suit.

Erika's face finally reappeared. "I think I might have a coffee date," she said in a low voice.

Sloan laughed. Only her agent would get a date out of Sloan's agreement to make pooch casserole. "I'm going to try my best, but I can't promise you I'll be any good at it."

"Are you kidding?" Erika shook her head. "I have no doubt that you are going to knock it out of the park—the dog park."

Sloan glanced behind her out the window. Alex was still on the phone, Oliver by his side. "I think I know where I can borrow a four-legged taste tester."

"Good. I've got to run. I'm at the counter. I'll check in with you in a day or two."

"Fine, go have your coffee date." Sloan ended the call and slid the phone back in her purse, watching Alex continue his conversation. Whoever he was talking to must be important.

"He's cute, isn't he?"

She spun around to see Gwen had returned with the burgundy coat.

"Um …" Sloan's cheeks warmed as she took the coat and

pushed her arms through the sleeves. It was probably not appropriate to rate Alex's attractiveness with the boutique owner. "He helped me get settled yesterday in his aunt's diner. He's really nice."

So nice that when he wiped the flour off her cheek earlier, his touch had set off fireworks inside her.

"That's our Alex. He's got a heart of gold, along with his purple one."

Purple one. Sloan fiddled with the top button on the wool coat. If she understood that high military honor correctly, it meant he'd received it for his being wounded while serving.

Her chest tightened. Had he been hurt? "He hasn't really shared much of what happened. I mean, I know that he served."

"My fiancé is stationed overseas right now and was the same way when we first started dating. Alex will open up to you when he's ready."

"Oh. We're not—we barely know each other." Feeling flushed, Sloan loosened the belt, and stepped in front of a nearby full-length mirror. It was the perfect fall coat. "I think I'll take it." She pulled the knit cap off her head and handed over the mittens. "And these too."

"I knew it would be a beautiful color on you," Gwen said, moving behind the counter. She cut off the tags for both the mittens and knit hat and gave them back to Sloan to wear out of the shop as Alex returned.

"I thought you two might have left me," Sloan kidded, putting on the hat and sliding her hands into the mittens.

"Doesn't she look ready for winter, Alex?" Gwen beamed over at Sloan.

"She does." Alex flashed a grin. "I like that hat. Who picked it out?"

"Ha, ha." Sloan tugged at her mittens. "You may have missed your calling as a personal shopper."

"Maybe." His voice softened. "You look really great. Very warm."

Sloan touched the side of her hat, feeling a bit shy. It wasn't that men hadn't commented favorably on how she looked on occasion, but something about the compliment from this man made her all warm inside.

Or maybe it was the coat. It was probably the wool.

"So, Gwen." Alex came over to the check-out counter and leaned in with one elbow on the glass. "I'm hoping you can do us a favor."

"Whatcha need?" Gwen processed the credit card that Sloan had given her, then handed over a receipt.

"Tomorrow we're going to run a two-for-one special price for breakfast over at Dee Dee's, and I'm going to hang up my toolbelt for my aunt's spatula for the day and help in the kitchen."

"You are?" Sloan asked, taken aback. Why would he do that?

"Yes." He smiled over at her. "It's going to be fun."

"Well, that sounds fantastic," Gwen said. "I'll make sure to tell everyone I know. I'm in charge of our local businesses' social media accounts so I can start getting the word out immediately."

"Thank you." He pushed off the glass. "I knew I could count on you. Make sure to let them know I'm bringing out my APOP special for this occasion."

"APOP! Oh. My. God." She clapped her hands together. "I haven't had one since high school. I'll be your first customer."

"Get your spandex out, girl, and come by during lunch."

Whatever this APOP was, it had definitely gotten Gwen excited.

"I've got an idea." Gwen snapped her fingers. "You know, the nursing home up on the hill likes to bring their residents down for a meal out every once in a while. My great-aunt Mary Lou is one of them." She turned to Sloan. "Would it be okay if I called the manager to tell them about the two-for-one price for breakfast? There's about fifty of them."

Fifty customers! Sloan would normally not blink an eye at that number, but given she didn't even have five this morning, fifty sounded pretty amazing. "That would be wonderful."

"My pleasure. The old ladies will crush all over Alex."

Sloan shared that laugh. "If they'd like to come, perhaps we can honor the rate an hour earlier just for them?"

Alex nodded. "Love that idea. Special starts at seven a.m. for the nursing home and eight a.m. for everyone else. Thanks again, Gwen."

"I'll call them right now. It was so nice to meet you, Sloan." She smiled over at Alex. "Make sure Sloan has a good time in Brooks Bend."

Alex chuckled, and darned if that sound wasn't really cute. "I'll do my best."

They said their goodbyes, but Sloan halted outside on the curb. Alex was brilliant. "This wasn't about getting me a coat, was it?" she asked, as they crossed the street.

"Oh, it was." He flashed her a mischievous smile. "But we also need to get customers back in the diner, and Gwen's our best bet. She's well connected, as you witnessed, and quick to offer her assistance."

"And you want to cook with me?" she asked, her smile fading. "You don't think people will come back until I'm gone, do you?"

"Chef," his voice softened. "Tom just started with my aunt last month and hasn't created a reputation. People know me."

"Do you even know how to cook?"

He touched his chest. "That hurts."

Okay, maybe she shouldn't have blurted it out like she did, but it was a legitimate question. "Well, do you?"

He shot her over a playful, cocky smile. "I'll have you know I worked every summer in my aunt's kitchen after I turned fifteen and for four years after high school."

"Oh." *I guess he does know his way around the kitchen.*

"My APOP special is legendary and will bring people in once Gwen gets the word out. Trust me."

"So what's in it?"

"It's not something you just tell someone." He zipped up his jacket. "It's got to be experienced."

She didn't bother holding back her eye roll. But despite it being a blow to her ego that she needed someone else with her in the kitchen to get Dee Dee's customers back, what Alex was offering could work.

People in this town did seem to like him; plus, he was the owner's nephew. It might go a long way to their coming back if potential customers knew Dee Dee's bloodline was working the back of the house with her.

An image of her and Alex, side by side, him holding up a soup spoon to her lips to sample soup, popped into her head. She pushed that thought away. "You know I'm going to cook circles around you."

"Game on." He stopped at a black Jeep that must be his.

"Well, thank you again." She turned to go back inside. "I guess I'll see you tomorrow."

"Whoa, Chef, where do you think you're going?"

She pointed to the door. "Back inside." She peeked through the glass. The diner was still empty. "Not that I'm needed," she mumbled.

"Good, because we're not done yet." He opened the passenger-side door and made his way to the driver's side, opening the back seat for the pup. "There's somewhere else you need to be." He glanced down at his watch. "And we're a little late."

Somewhere she needed to be? What was Alex up to? She hesitated, shoving her hands in her new coat's pockets.

She'd trusted him with their first excursion, and it paid off. Plus, she kind of liked hanging out with him. "Where are we going?" she asked, resting her hand on the Jeep's roof.

"Somewhere where we can find you some kindness." He grinned, starting the car. "Hop in."

Chapter Seven

"IT'S THE MOST beautiful thing I've ever seen." Sloan stared out the windshield at the bright-yellow and red leaves decorating the trees on each side of the road.

"It's pretty awesome, isn't it?" Alex tapped along on the steering wheel to the country music song playing as he made his way through The Vine's twisty road full of fall foliage.

He knew his passenger would enjoy the view.

Driving through the back road's fiery burst of colors was especially popular this time of year. It was one of the things that made this small town the best place to live, in his opinion.

"How long will it last before the leaves fall?" she asked with a sigh.

"Usually happens in early November, so any day now."

She smiled over at him. "Then I guess I came at the right time."

His heart ticked up a notch. *Yeah, she did.* He didn't quite know what was going on, but he was enjoying their moments together.

It was probably stupid to feel whatever he was feeling,

since she was only here for a limited time. He maneuvered his steering wheel, taking the curvy road.

But she wasn't leaving tomorrow.

"This hill will be full of leaf peepers this weekend. I'm kind of surprised there aren't some up here now."

"Leaf peepers? Like people who come here just to look at the leaves." She bunched her eyebrows. "That's a thing?"

He nodded, gently hitting the brake as they descended the hill. "It sure is."

"Hmmm." She pulled out her phone and held it up to take a few photos. "Simply gorgeous."

He grinned to himself, taking in Sloan's excitement as she continued to *ooh* and *aah* over the trees.

She turned to face him. "Oh, before I forget, do you think you could bring Oliver by the diner tomorrow evening? I need his assistance."

"You want to borrow my dog?" There had to be only one reason for it. "You decided to go through with the audition, didn't you?"

"Yes, my agent called while we were at the boutique, and I told her I'd do it. So it's finally official. Sloan Leary is making dog food."

"And you're good with that? You seemed hesitant last night. What changed your mind?"

She sat silent for a few seconds. "The pros outweighed the cons, and I'm nothing if not a realist. If I get it, it could lead to other good things."

He tilted his head in her direction. "Like Paris."

She nodded. "Like Paris. Do you think I'm crazy?"

"No. Not at all." He shook his head, finding it comical she'd ask that question to someone she only met three days ago. "Going for your dream is admirable, no matter what route you take, and Oliver would be more than happy to sample whatever you make out of the gizzards." He glanced up in his rearview mirror at the pup going to town with his pizza slice toy in the back seat. "Won't you, bud?"

Oliver gave a bark on cue.

"Thank you, Oliver." She settled in her seat. "I haven't the foggiest idea how I'm going to come up with a unique Thanksgiving meal that dogs find scrumptious."

"You will, and I'm sure it will be great." He hadn't known her long, but he'd seen enough this morning at the diner to know Sloan would put her all into it.

"Oliver, question for you." She glanced over her shoulder. "What would you like most to eat for Thanksgiving besides pizza?"

Alex chuckled, thinking back to the other night when his dog had stolen her dinner. "I'm pretty sure he'd like a nice stuffed turkey with gravy. Maybe a little cranberry sauce on the side."

"That could work; although, cranberry sauce can be high in sugar." She pulled out her phone and said into it, "Is cranberry sauce safe for dogs?" She scrolled the screen. "Nope. Doesn't look good for you, Oliver."

"You're kidding?" His dog had slurped up all the Thanksgiving sides placed in his bowl last year, including cranberry sauce on a small bed of stuffing, thanks to his aunt's delicious spread. She and her new husband, Fred, had invited him over to celebrate with Fred's daughter, Charlie, and her fiancé, Spencer.

He'd thought he'd feel like a fifth wheel among the love-birds, but he really liked Fred. Plus, Charlie and Spencer were cool. The couple was spending some time in Italy for Spencer's job, so they weren't around much this fall.

Sloan continued, "While it says cranberry sauce is okay in tiny amounts, its high sugar content could cause gastrointestinal upset."

She extended her hand to pet Oliver. "No tummy ache for you on my watch."

"He appreciates that." Alex winked. "And so does my carpet."

"Ew." She scrunched her nose at that visual, continuing to look at whatever website she'd pulled up on her phone. "Creating these recipes might be harder than I thought. I'm going to have to do some research before I get started. I don't want to cook with any spices that could be toxic for dogs."

"So you're going to do the spice thing?" he asked.

"Of course." She nodded, her tone indicating that skipping that step wasn't an option. "That's what I'm known for. It'll set me apart from the competition." She leaned back on the headrest. "This has been a wonderful distraction. Thank you for your kindness. I'm going to take some more pictures on our way back."

Oh. Alex pressed his lips together. She thought this was the kindness he'd referred to earlier. "So, there is something else that I'm hoping you'll be receptive to doing before heading back, and we're almost there." He continued to travel down the bottom of The Vine, taking the left turn that would take them straight into the neighboring town and to what he'd arranged while Sloan was trying on coats at the boutique.

It took him only a couple of minutes to arrive at a light. Taking a right, he turned into a parking lot that he'd driven into many times over the years.

"LIAM'S LUNCHBOX." She read the sign to the popular diner. A line formed across her forehead. "You want to have lunch together?"

He took a deep breath because it was time to confess. "Not quite."

"YOU'RE GOING TO work the lunch shift," Alex said, pulling into the only spot left in the back row.

"Yeah, right." She laughed, but when he didn't return her laughter, her lips turned down. "You're joking."

He shook his head. "The owner's a family friend. He'd be happy to have you join his crew today. He's waiting for you."

Sloan sat silent, staring at the diner, trying to process this absurd conversation. "So let me get this straight. You're dropping me off to work in there."

"Yes."

"In some strange restaurant in an unfamiliar town. Where I know no one." Had Dee Dee's nephew lost his mind? "Why would I do that?"

"It's not a totally foreign concept. You did it yesterday."

"For a culinary exchange that was arranged by my agent. This . . . this . . ." She folded her hands in her lap. "This is not happening. I'd like to go back to Dee Dee's, please."

"Sloan, I know this is crazy, but I think it could help you. Liam Fisher and my aunt go way back, and he taught her everything she knows. He's got this special technique you'll really enjoy."

She shook her head. This was absolutely insane. "I don't have to learn how to flip burgers and make sandwiches." She counted to five before speaking, hoping to find her Zen. "I know I screwed up yesterday. I admit it, but I told you I plan on sticking to Dee Dee's menu."

"I believe you, and it's not that. I just thought it might be nice for you to cook for a restaurant full of diner enthusiasts."

"Diner enthusiasts," she repeated, trying to process what Alex was saying—or what he wasn't. "So, you think I can't cook for anyone who doesn't pay sixty dollars for one of my plates?"

"That's how much one of your entrees costs?"

Her muscles tightened. "Not the point."

"I didn't mean to offend you. What I thought would be nice is for you to enjoy a day cooking in a New England diner." He threaded his fingers, cracking his knuckles. "Maybe inspire you for our face-off tomorrow."

"Oh, it's a face-off now, is it?" she joked, despite herself. "I don't need this Liam's help to whip your butt around a kitchen."

His gaze met hers for a beat and then stayed for another. He finally turned on the Jeep and put it in reverse. "You're right. This was a bad idea. I'll take you back."

She sat silently. It *was* a bad idea. At the very least, he should have clued her in on what he had planned way before their arrival at the diner.

Her head dropped to her new mittens. Still, she couldn't deny everything Alex had done today was to help her turn things around at Dee Dee's. From giving out the baked goods she'd made to people walking by to coming up with tomorrow's two-for-one special and enlisting Gwen's help to spread the word had both been his ideas.

And he was even going to take a day off from his work to cook with her because he believed that would help bring his aunt's customers back.

Not when Dee Dee eventually returned in two weeks, but now.

She glanced out the windshield at the bright-red LIAM'S LUNCHBOX sign. If Alex truly believed this Liam could help, too, she owed it to him to see it through. She let out a deep sigh and reached for his arm, hardly believing what was about to come out of her mouth. "Stop. I'll do it."

"Really?" he asked.

"Yes," she said. "But only one shift. That's it."

"That's all you'll need." He shoved the console in reverse and pulled back into the spot.

"You're going to love him."

"Uh-huh." She opened up the passenger door and stepped down. What would Liam show her in three hours that she didn't already know?

In seconds, Alex and Oliver were by her side as they made their way through the busy parking lot. "Tell me about how your aunt started working for Liam," she said, pulling her new hat down over her ears to block out some of the cold.

"So, when Aunt Dee Dee started at the diner in her twenties, she wasn't much of a cook."

Sloan shoved her hands in her coat pockets. *Oh, we're going way back.*

He continued, "She was working in an office job in New York City and hated it. One day she walked by a sign in the diner for a short-order cook and the rest was history. Liam was the lead cook at the time. He not only taught her everything he knew, but showed her how unique cooking in an American diner was from just about any other eating establishment. It's about the people and making real connections."

She stopped in her tracks. That wasn't unique to diners. "I know all about relationship building. I do that in my restaurant. I make sure I leave the kitchen and say good night to my last customers before closing down each and every night."

"So you leave your kitchen only once during your shift?"

She realized that effort to speak to two to four customers out of the hundreds that might come through her restaurant on any given day might sound pathetic. She pressed back her shoulders and raised her chin.

"I'm very busy leading my kitchen. I can assure you my front of the house team is second to none in making sure our guests feel welcome, and when I can, I do make an effort to spend time in the dining room." She paused, mumbling, "I love my customers."

"You don't have to convince me. I really think you're going to like Liam. All of Dee Dee's employees spend a day with him when they first start. Seeing him in action is quite something."

"So, this is like orientation?" She narrowed her lashes.

"Yes." He opened up the glass door and held it open. "You're about to get 'lunched.'"

"Terrific," she said flatly. What did that even mean? Alex could go ahead and put away that cute lopsided smile he was now flashing her. She was still mad at him, despite her heart speeding up.

She laid one hand over the offending organ and took a deep breath to calm down. Nope that didn't help. Still mad.

"You'll love cooking here. This is the best diner in Connecticut." He twisted Oliver's leash around his wrist so the dog didn't run off. "Don't tell my aunt I said that."

"I wouldn't dream of it." She served him up a serious side-eye because that was the only thing on her menu.

"This is going to be a lot of fun. Trust me."

She wanted to. She really did, but this was just . . . it was just . . . well, it was weird. She'd been cooking professionally all her adult life. She didn't need some strange man to show her the ropes.

As they made their way in, she gazed around the crowded dining room. Conversation mixed with loud music filled the air. At least, it'll be nice to cook for actual customers.

"Alex!" A thin, old man with gray hair in a deep-red chef's coat and black apron greeted him with a hug before turning to Sloan. "You must be Sloan from San Francisco."

"I am. Seasons of San Francisco is my restaurant. It's so nice to meet you, Liam." She gave the man a warm smile as he shook her hand.

"So, Sloan." Liam slid his wire-rimmed glasses along his nose. "You know how to make a BLT, extra crispy, light on mayo, with the thinnest of marinated tomatoes?"

She nodded. *In my sleep.* "Mixing a little olive oil with

balsamic vinegar is one of my favorite ways to marinate." She also liked to sprinkle some smoked paprika along the cooked bacon, but decided to leave that fun fact out since she was on a seasoning hiatus.

"And those are rubber-soled?" Liam asked, pointing to her shoes.

She lifted one, showing off the bottom. "I've also got on my chef's uniform. I'm ready to go."

"Good. Good. What dessert are you known for in your restaurant?"

"Oh, that's easy. My spiced caramel-pumpkin cheese-cake. It flies out of the kitchen from October through November."

"I'll have to try it the next time I'm in San Francisco."

"It's delicious. I would love to serve it to you."

"Deal." He clapped his hands. "All right, let's get start-ed." He paused, turning to Alex, "Sorry, Alex, you're going to have to leave. No four-legged friends allowed, even yours."

"That hurts, Liam," Alex joked.

Liam laughed and gave Oliver a friendly ruffle up of his ears. Slipping a hand in his apron pocket, he pulled out a small bone and gave it to the dog. "You almost finished up with the inn's job?" he asked Alex, seemingly not in a hurry to kick out Alex or his dog.

"Yes, sir. We finished the kitchen last week, and it's now waiting on the inspection happening tomorrow afternoon. I started to knock down a wall last night for the new library."

He crooked his lips over to Sloan. "But was interrupted."

Heat began to pulsate through her neck. She loosened the top buttons on her coat. *Whatever.* No one forced him to talk to her. He could have politely told her he needed to get back to work and to scram.

But he didn't.

"You must be doing a number on your leg," Liam said. "How's it holding up?"

"It's doing okay. Some days are better than other. My heating pad is getting a lot of use this fall," he admitted, with a chuckle.

Sloan mentally began putting two and two together. Had Alex's leg been hurt in the Army? Was that why he received a Purple Heart?

Liam motioned for a waitress holding a large cup with a bright red straw behind the counter to join them. "Hi, Alex. One Strong Bones Smoothie on the house." The waitress, whose nametag read TINA, handed it to him.

Alex accepted the drink.

"That smoothie is loaded with calcium, so drink up and get lost." Liam turned to Sloan. "You can head up to the counter. Once you're done with your lunch, ring the bell three times, and I'll meet you in the dining room."

And with that, Liam made his way back to the kitchen.

Sloan narrowed her gaze. "Am I working or eating?"

Alex removed the straw from his lips. "You're working. Trust the process." He paused, adding, "And maybe move your sense of humor up to the front burner. You're going to want it nearby."

She shook her head. Her sense of humor was still in San Francisco.

He turned to leave, but hesitated. "Oh, Sloan, I hope it's okay, but I've asked Kimmie to pick you up after your shift. I've got to finish knocking down the inn's wall and clean up the area for the floors to be stained tomorrow."

"Sure." She couldn't help batting her eyelashes. "And I hope you don't get disturbed by the successful owner of a Michelin-starred restaurant offering you a choice to eat a seasoned pie or die."

He laughed. "I wouldn't mind."

His gaze met hers, and that wobbling in her legs she felt last night came back for a second round, this time stronger. She pointed to the kitchen. "I should probably get started."

"Yeah. I'll see you later." He lifted the leash. "Let's go, bud."

She walked past the counter to the double doors. It was nice and all of Liam to offer her lunch, but what she really wanted to do was get to work.

An invigorating rush went through her as she pushed through the doors and took in the familiar sight of a fully operating kitchen with line cooks flipping, mixing, sautéing, and plating.

It may not be her kitchen, but the energy felt like home.

Liam was steps away, putting the final garnish on a burger. "Sloan, you didn't eat your lunch."

"Oh, I'm good, but thank you." She peeled off her coat. "Where do you want me?"

"On a barstool, eating your cheeseburger." Liam looked up. "Unless you don't eat meat."

"I do. I love cheeseburgers."

"Good. Good." He reached for a tasting spoon and moved over to the stove. "And how do you feel about pancakes? Got any specials planned at Dee Dee's?"

What a weird segue. She stepped closer, closing the distance between them. "My grandmother's sweet potato pancakes with fresh whipped cream and maple syrup are delicious. That's what I'm planning on serving tomorrow. We're running a two-for-one special."

He nodded toward the right. "I've got a bag of sweet potatoes and five bottles of maple syrup from Jenkins Farm in the pantry that you can take with you. Now go eat."

He turned to face the stove, dipped a spoon in a big soup pot, and pulled a face. "This needs some more onions, Mick."

He turned back to Sloan. "Ring the bell three times when you've finished your lunch."

"Let me take your coat for you." Tina came up to her and took it. "Your cheeseburger is ready for you at the far end of the counter."

"Remember, Sloan," Liam called out, picking up a butcher knife and thrusting it into a slab of beef. "Don't forget to ring the bell."

Yeah, Yeah, Yeah. What was she? A lab animal? "Three times. Got it."

He clearly wasn't interested in her cooking in his kitchen and was probably being nice to Alex's request because of his friendship with Dee Dee.

She pushed through the double doors. When she returned to Brooks Bend, there was going to be a fourth ring—this time around Alex's neck—for wasting her time and Liam's.

SLOAN FINISHED HER steamed cheeseburger, which was hands down the best one she'd ever tasted and washed it down with her equally delicious pumpkin cheesecake shake.

"You liked your lunch?" Tina asked from the other side of the counter, picking up Sloan's empty plate.

"Very much so. Thank you." She glanced around the dining room, sipping her milkshake. Over the last thirty minutes, the diner had gotten even busier, with a long line now formed outside.

"I think it's time for me to get to work." She hopped off the stool. She'd give it one more try with the owner. If he kicked her out of his kitchen again, she'd call Hayden at the inn and ask for Kimmie's number to see if she could pick her up earlier.

Liking that plan, she started to head into the kitchen, but an exaggerated throat clearing stopped her.

She turned to see Tina pointing to the bell on the pickup window.

"Oh, right." She made her way behind the counter. Heaven forbid if she didn't ring it. She tapped the bell three times.

The diner erupted in applause.

"What on earth?" She spun around to see every single man, woman, and child on their feet, cheering for her. *All this from ringing a bell?*

Liam came out from the kitchen, holding a red lunchbox. "Congratulations, Sloan, on having your first official meal with us." Liam handed her the lunchbox. "You have been 'lunched.'"

"Aw." So that's what Alex meant.

Liam grinned, pointing to her shake. "I know it probably isn't as good as your cheesecake back home, but did you like it?"

Her heart squeezed a little as she connected the dots. He'd made the shake just for her. How sweet. "Very much. Thank you."

"Good, because you'll receive one on the house on your anniversary and every year after. There's a coupon inside your lunchbox."

"Wow," she said, holding up the pail. "If I have a reason to come back to this area next year, you will definitely be my first stop."

"I hope it is." He turned to his customers. "Everyone, listen up," Liam raised his voice high. "Sloan is the celebrity chef at Dee Dee's Diner in Brooks Bend through next week."

Sloan placed a hand on her neck. "Oh, I don't know if you can call me a celebrity."

Liam seemed to disagree. "Stop in for her grandmother's legendary sweet potato pancakes with fresh whipped cream and Jenkins maple syrup anytime between tomorrow and . . ." He turned to her to complete that sentence.

"Next Saturday." She paused, then added, "And tomorrow, we'll have a two breakfast plates for the price of one special, where I'm facing off with Dee Dee's nephew for charity. Come on by."

Wow. She didn't know where the improvised charity bit came from, but it sounded like a good idea in the moment. She made a mental note to talk to Alex as soon as she saw him.

As the customers took their seats, Sloan greeted two women who came up to her to introduce themselves as residents of Brooks Bend. They were looking forward to stopping in tomorrow with their knitting club. "Feel free to bring your yarn and stay as long as you'd like," she replied.

"Looks like you're going to have some customers tomorrow," Liam said.

"It does look that way." She grinned over at the old man, who was pretty brilliant. "Thank you for the plug to your customers." She held up her lunchbox. "And thank you for this."

"You're welcome. Dee Dee and Alex mean a lot to me. Anyone in their circle does too."

"Oh," she started, taken aback. "I don't know if I'm in their circle. I've never even met Dee Dee, and I barely know Alex."

He winked. "You're in. Now let's get you in the kitchen so that this crowd can taste your special BLT."

"So I do get to cook?"

"It's not every day a chef from a Michelin-starred restaurant wants to oil up the pans in my kitchen. It would be my honor to have you in there." He turned for a second to greet a customer who'd sat down on a stool.

Sloan straightened her chef coat. What a truly wonderful man.

Not only had he done an incredibly generous thing introducing all of his customers to her, but she'd witnessed some true displays of his thoughtfulness in his work—from the dog bone in his apron for Oliver to a special smoothie for Alex after asking him about his leg.

And then he'd gone ahead and made her a shake based on the most popular dessert on her menu.

She could learn a thing or two from him. It might only be another hour or so, but she was all in.

"You ready, Sloan?" Liam asked.

"I'm ready." She followed him into his kitchen. "Hey,

Chef, you wouldn't happen to have some smoked paprika, by any chance?"

"I read online about your specialty." He reached into his pocket, pulling out a bottle. "Not smoked paprika, but this is my special burger seasoning that has the same kind of woodsy kick."

She grinned, taking the seasoning, and twisting off the cap.

It was going to be a great shift.

Chapter Eight

SLOAN TIGHTENED HER bathrobe and slipped on her slippers. When she'd returned to the inn, her first matter of business had been to soak her tired bones in a long, hot bath.

True to his word, Liam had her cooking up a storm in the kitchen. He also had her follow each waitress out into the dining room to introduce herself to the customers and share that she was a guest chef at Dee Dee's until next Saturday.

She picked up the brown bag of sweet potatoes and syrup off her bed and set it on her nightstand next to her new red lunchbox. It'd been a great day for so many reasons.

And she owed it all to Alex.

If only there was something she could do to repay him for everything he'd done for her today.

Maybe a bottle of wine or a gift certificate somewhere?

No. She reached for the lotion provided in the little pale-lavender basket and sat down on her bed, slathering it on.

She needed to do something big for him that showed her enormous appreciation.

A knock pulled her out of her thoughts. "Coming." She

crossed the room and swung the door open.

"Hey, Hayden," she greeted. The inn's general manager looked more casual than normal in a long green sweater, along with a heavy beige coat and tall brown boots.

"Hey, Sloan. I'm headed to the Wishbone Wishes event and wanted to see if you'd like to join me. It's across the street in the town square."

Ah, the Wishbone Wishes event. She'd forgotten about it. Maybe she'd bump into Alex there and could fill him in on her time at Liam's Lunchbox and thank him for arranging it. "Sure, it sounds like fun. I'll put some clothes on and meet you in the lobby."

It took her less than five minutes to change into her favorite black crewneck sweater, dark jeans, and black boots. She opted for her leather coat instead of her new wool one, sliding it on, because in an ironic twist, the temperature had actually risen throughout the day to a much more pleasant fifty degrees.

She grabbed the hat Alex had picked out for her, smiling as she stowed it in her purse, just in case her ears got cold, as they often did.

And not because she wanted to take something with her that he'd told her she looked adorable wearing.

Nope, that wasn't the reason at all.

Hayden finished chatting with an inn guest. "Hey, Sloan. I left my purse in the kitchen. I'll only be a minute." She turned back. "Unless . . . do you want to see it? Alex did a fabulous job."

"Sure." Sloan followed her down the hallway into the kitchen, her excitement growing as she took in the various stations in their pristine shiny glory. "It's stunning."

"Isn't it? We really needed it. The old one was a relic. Smaller than Dee Dee's."

Sloan lifted an eyebrow. "That small, eh?"

"Yep."

Sloan ran her hand along the center island with its ovens, ranges, and fryers. "The island layout has always been my favorite."

"Why's that?" Hayden grabbed her purse off the prep station and threw the strap over her head to rest on her shoulder.

"My grandmother used to say the cooking area is where the kitchen's heart beats and should be in the middle." She laughed. "And the more practical reason I say is, it's easier to communicate with the prep cooks and front-of-house staff coming into the kitchen from this location." She glanced around at the cream walls with the pale-lavender trim that she'd seen on other walls of the inn but seemed a little out of place for a kitchen. "Is pale lavender a significant color? I've seen it around the inn."

"It was my grandmother's favorite color." Hayden's voice softened. "When my grandfather developed Alzheimer's, we'd bring him to the inn. For some reason, just seeing the color brought him back to us, even for a few minutes. It was the only thing that did."

Sloan's throat thickened and she touched her heart.

"Alex did a really nice job honoring her memory and my grandfather's."

"It's perfect." Sloan took in the digital order display system and the framed picture next to it. "Is this your entire family?"

"It is." Hayden pointed at the people in the picture. "The little girl is me and that girl over there posing is Rachel. She was a model for the camera even back then. That's my mom and dad and grandparents." She smiled. "It was taken the day my dad took over as inn owner. We'd thought we'd lost that picture years ago, but Alex found it buried in our pantry. He even repainted the frame."

"That's so sweet."

"Oh, do you want to see something really sweet that he did?" She clapped her hands. "My mom doesn't know this yet, but Alex also found these old wooden carvings of our names that my grandpa had made for us one year when we were little." She bent down next to the service table next to the entrance and waved for Sloan to join her. "Each station is named after one of us. See."

Sloan crouched down to see an intricate carving with Hayden's name seemingly built into the station. "This is awesome." She stood. "When will you be opening up the kitchen?"

"Not until next month. The first time we cook in here,

we want to make sure it's for a really special occasion, so my dad's going to surprise my mom and cook a Christmas dinner. I've already started planning it and Rachel is going to come home."

Sloan's heart squeezed. She'd already planned the dinner she was going to prepare for her first night when she opened up Seasons of Paris. She'd set a table by a window for two. "A special meal prepared to enjoy with the ones you love is the only way to christen a kitchen, as far as I'm concerned. I'm sure they're going to love it." She paused, adding, "Alex is truly talented. I see why your family hired him."

"He's so skilled," she agreed. "I'm hoping that this job propels him to start his own business."

"He should." Sloan nodded. "There's a demand for commercial kitchen remodels all the time with new culinary inventions and techniques. My grandmother and I did a big one a couple of years before she passed away." She gazed around at Alex's fine work, her gaze resting on the wooden nameplates. "His special touches would certainly set him apart."

"There's only one problem."

"What's that?" she asked.

"Our guy didn't bring his confidence back from Iraq." She sighed. "And I'm not sure if he'll ever find it." She motioned for the door. "We should get going. Don't want to miss the event."

"Right." Sloan took one last look. She knew a lot of people in the culinary industry on the East Coast, mainly from an executive chef's social media group for alumni of the Culinary Exchange. Maybe there was something she could do to give Alex a boost: make an introduction, get him connected.

That's it! That social media group often had chefs post when they were looking to hire freelancers. "I just remembered I have to send a quick text. Can I meet you in the foyer?"

"Sure. If you could flip off the lights when you're done, that would be great."

"Will do." Sloan moved around the room, taking a few pictures of not only the kitchen remodel, but of all of Alex's special touches. When she was done, she typed out her post and tapped to post it.

Grinning, she turned off the lights. With any luck, she was on her way to giving Alex her thank-you.

A big one.

SLOAN REJOINED HAYDEN in the lobby. Nothing might come of her posting, but if she could help Alex in getting his next job, and maybe his confidence back, she had to try.

They made their way out of the inn and down the street toward the park. "How was your day?" Hayden asked as they waited at the crosswalk.

"Busy, but really great, thank you."

"I heard about tomorrow's egg slam competition between Alex and you."

"So now we're calling it an 'egg slam.'" She laughed, not surprised at all. "I'm a little worried about this 'APOP special' he keeps boasting about."

"You should be. It's amazing. For prom, he skipped the after-party to make the entire class breakfast. We all piled into Dee Dee's at three a.m." She closed her eyes, no doubt basking in that memory. "I can taste the eggs, sausage, honey baked beans, and macaroni salad now."

"Together?" Sloan asked, pulling a face. "That's what's in it?"

"Oh, yeah. Sometimes he throws in cheeseburger and a few other things, always with a generous amount of ketchup."

Hayden's eyes flew open. Sloan tried to erase her look of utter disgust, but it was too late.

"You just wait, Sloan. It's amazing."

"I believe you." There was *no* way she'd be trying it.

They arrived at the park, and Sloan took in all the small, orange vendor tents set up with fall-inspired food, crafts, and games. "Wow. This looks fun." She glanced in a tent where you could throw apples into mini propped-up barrels to win cornucopia displays as prizes. "Very fall festive."

"We are nothing without our festivals. You should see us at Christmas for the Elfcapades. This place really kicks up its holiday game."

"Elfcapades?"

"It's our twelve days of Christmas kindness, where we all come together for twelve different holiday activities while giving back to the community. Cookie and cocoa crawls, ice-skating games, a trivia contest, all kinds of Christmassy-type things. You'll be long gone by the start of it."

"Yeah. Long gone . . ." She shoved her hands in her pockets. A cookie-and-cocoa crawl sounded fun. A tiny part of her was sad she'd miss it.

She brushed off that feeling. Having one good day here didn't change the fact that where she truly belonged was in San Francisco in her restaurant, making plans for her expansion.

Tomorrow she'd get to work on making that dream come true. After the lunch shift, she would work the entire evening on her Puppy Palate meals.

"Let's go get an apple cider." Hayden leaned in. "I have such a crush on the guy who ferments it. He also makes donuts."

"Donuts, huh?" Sloan tilted her head to get a good look at the attractive man behind the rectangular cider table. Wearing black-and-white-checkered flannel, he was uncorking a bottle. "He's cute."

"Is there anyone special in your life back home?" Hayden asked.

Sloan blinked at that question. "Um, not really. I date

here and there, but I've been pretty focused on my restaurant. That doesn't leave a lot of hours in the day to meet anyone. I mean, I've gone out with different chefs casually from time to time . . . thinking about getting on one of those dating apps."

She gave herself a mental slap to stop rambling. *You only need one excuse for your pathetic love life, not twenty.*

"Well, maybe you'll find someone in Brooks Bend and you'll stay longer."

"Maybe." She had a better chance of skipping merrily down Main Street after midnight in her uniform while eating Alex's APOP special in a takeout tray.

She chuckled to herself at that silly image. *Never going to happen.*

While Hayden chatted with two women in line, Sloan watched as a group of teenage cheerleaders jogged by, clapping and kicking, followed by a line of football players, who were hooting and hollering. "Is this a pep rally?" she asked, feeling quite old.

"It's part of the activities," Hayden said. "The Brooks Bend High School football team plays our rivals each year during their homecoming weekend, which is this weekend. The Wednesday before, we gather here in the square where the class seniors all write down their wishes for what they'd like their lives to be like in ten years, and then they attach them to wishbones." She paused, adding, "Not real ones. We use wood."

"That's so cool."

"And it gets really funny. We read the wishes that were written ten years ago that were put in a capsule. It's my year for our class wishes to be read."

"I wish my senior class would have done something creative like that." Although reading out wishes for her large graduating class of more than three hundred at the Bay Area school she'd attended would have taken hours. She guessed there were far fewer seniors in Brooks Bend. "It sounds like fun."

"And somewhat embarrassing. I wished to be a Rockette married to Ryan Reynolds." Hayden laughed. "Guess I'll have to settle for general manager of an inn and single."

"A successful general manager of a charming, cozy inn with"—Sloan raised a finger—"a potential new leading man. You should totally ask him out." Sloan nodded to the cute apple cider guy.

"I might," Hayden said shyly, which seemed so uncharacteristic for her. From what Sloan had seen, both Hayden and Kimmie were outgoing women.

Sloan spun around, taking in all the festive merriment. This town really did know how to come out for a good time. Her gaze zoomed across the park over to some of the scattered benches, her breath catching at the sight of Alex sitting alone with Oliver.

She turned back as they reached the front of the line and purchased two apple ciders, winking at Hayden. "I'm going to leave you here to learn how cider is fermented, if that's okay. I need to talk to Alex."

Sloan grinned as she walked away, hearing Hayden asking the cute cider guy that very question. *Go, Hayden.*

She made her way through the crowd, reaching a preoccupied Alex with his head down, scrolling through his phone.

"Is this seat taken?"

He looked up. "Hey, you survived today. I was wondering how it went."

"I should have texted you a picture." Although that would have been difficult since she didn't have his number, but Liam probably did. She sat down, inhaling his spicy scent. "For you." She handed him the cider.

"Thank you. What's this for?"

"For everything." She pulled out her mittens from her pockets and waved them at him. "For making me buy these to arranging for me to spend the day with Liam. Today was really great, and Liam was so cool."

"Did he make you ring the bell?"

"Three times, and I got 'lunched.'" She laughed. "Although, first, he kicked me out of the kitchen when I told him I didn't want to eat."

Alex laughed back. "Sounds like him. Did he have you introduce yourself to everyone that you cooked for?"

"Every single one."

He tapped the tip of his bottle to hers. "Cheers. I'm glad

you had a good time."

"I really did. I love how he wears his thoughtfulness, literally, with his apron full of goodies."

"It's something, for sure. He's been doing that for as long as I've known him." He leaned back.

"He even had a spice bottle in it." She gave his shoulder a nudge with her elbow. "At least someone from Brooks Bend appreciates me."

He took a long pull of his cider. "He's not from Brooks Bend."

"Okay, fine." She rolled her eyes. "Connecticut, then."

Alex grinned, letting her have this moment. "He's one of a kind. Don't make them like that anymore."

That wasn't exactly true, because she was sitting next to a man just as thoughtful, who had single-handedly orchestrated all of today's wonderful events.

She took a sip of her cider. "Man. This is amazing."

"Never had cider before?"

She nodded. "Once. My grandmother served apple cider champagne for a private fall dinner in which the client bought out the entire restaurant for his wife's fiftieth birthday. I wasn't old enough to drink, but my grandma let me have a sip." She closed her eyes and smiled, remembering it like it was just yesterday.

"Your grandmother sounds like one cool lady."

"She was. I miss her every single day." Sloan took another sip, not quite ready to let go of that memory. "How did

AN AUTUMN TO REMEMBER

your work on the library go?" she finally asked, settling into the bench as two little kids ran by, both wearing hats of turkey feathers.

"Good. The wall's knocked down. Floors are prepped. The bookcases and stairs are being installed once the floor is refinished."

"If you need to skip out on tomorrow, I completely understand." The town would crucify her, but she'd deal with it.

He shook his head. "We're good. I don't need to be there while the floor is being done. I might have to leave you with the dishes to check them out."

She smiled. "I think I can handle that, but there is something else happening that I should fill you in on."

"What's that?"

"While I was working with Liam, he announced to the dining room that I was the celebrity chef at Dee Dee's until next Saturday and encouraged his customers to stop in for breakfast."

"We're so going to rock it tomorrow." He made a fist and reached over for her to tap it, and the most amazing energy flowed through her.

"I'm glad you feel that way," she said, her hand still tingling as she opened up her fingers, giving each a wiggle. "I kind of got carried away in the moment and said that her nephew would be joining me for a face-off for charity."

"For charity," he repeated.

125

"I'm sorry. It just flew out of my mouth. I obviously don't want Dee Dee to lose any profit. I can make a donation."

He leaned back, dropping his free hand to pet Oliver. "I think it's a great idea, and I'm sure my aunt will too."

Just then, Mayor Hertzberg's voice boomed into the microphone that wishbone wishes reading would begin in five minutes. She touched her ear, all but certain her eardrum had been blown out. "He likes being mayor, doesn't he?"

Alex chuckled. "You have no idea."

Sloan was watching the flurry of activity around them when a teenage girl approached their bench. "Would you like to make a wish?"

"Oh, I'm not . . ." How young did she think she was? "I thought this was for the senior class."

"We also sell wishes to other attendees. It goes to fund our senior class trip to Toronto in April."

"Toronto. That sounds like fun." Sloan reached for her purse, glancing over at Alex. "Would you like to make a wish, Mr. Edwards?"

"I'm good," was all he said and pressed the cider bottle to his lips.

Okay, then. "I'll take one." She paid for her wish and took the free pen the student offered. "Thank you."

She glanced down at her wooden wishbone and the small piece of paper attached to it to write in her wish. What should she wish for?

"Did you know, years ago, wishbones were considered sacred collarbones of chickens?"

She turned to him. "Really? Not turkeys?"

"Well, eventually, we adopted the tradition from England and then it became part of the Thanksgiving tradition. The Romans believed chickens had divine powers and wanted in on the action. The term 'catching a lucky break' refers to pulling the long end of the wishbone."

"I never knew that. Thanks for the history lesson."

"You're welcome."

"Did you ever catch a lucky break?"

He leaned back on the bench. "Still waiting."

She clicked her pen and scribbled her wish: *I wish Alex would catch his lucky break.* And with any bites from her earlier post, he just might. She'd make sure to go online and check the group later.

"What did you wish for?" He nudged her shoulder. "To win the audition?"

"I'm not telling you." She folded the paper and slipped it in her purse. That would have been a good one, but this was much better. "If I did, it might not come true." She leaped off the bench. "And I'm counting on it definitely coming true. Let's go try to win a cornucopia."

"Nah, I think I'm going to head home. It's going to be a long day tomorrow."

"Oh, c'mon. You can't leave me." She reached for Oliver's leash. "I won't have anyone to hang out with, and half these people think I poisoned them."

He laughed, standing. "Did anyone ever tell you you're a bit dramatic?"

She shook her head, feigning surprise. "No one."

"Alex," a voice called out.

Sloan turned to see Mia, bundled up in a long purple coat, walking toward them. So, the ex was sticking around.

"Hey, Mia." He paused, turning to Sloan. "Did you two meet last night?"

Sloan shook her head and extended her hand. "It's nice to meet you and congratulations on your book. I'm staying at the inn and saw everyone having a good time at your event."

"Thank you. It's nice to meet you too."

"Sloan's cooking in Aunt Dee Dee's Diner for a couple of weeks while my aunt works in her restaurant in San Francisco."

"Really?" Mia cocked her head. "Which one?"

"Seasons of San Francisco," Sloan said.

"Hmmm, Seasons of San Francisco," Mia repeated, raising her eyes, thinking on it. "I don't believe I've been there, but I will make a point of stopping in the next time I'm in the Bay Area."

"You're welcome anytime," Sloan extended a genuine offer.

Just then, a woman Sloan didn't recognize grabbed Mia's arm. "Mia, come join us."

"I'll see you later," Mia said to Alex, her gaze resting on his for an extra second before turning to Sloan. "It was nice meeting you."

"You too." Sloan took a sip of her cider. "She's nice."

"Yeah." He looked away.

"You know what? I take that back. She's awful. Such a snob with no personality whatsoever."

He laughed. "She's not any of that."

"So why the grumpy face? You didn't take my advice to go talk to her last night, did you?"

"I did, and we had a nice conversation." He shoved his hands in his flannel pockets.

"It's silly, really, and I'm happy for her. It's just I'm not a fan of going down memory lane."

Oliver gave her a nudge with his nose. "Are we ignoring you?" She bent down and rubbed behind his ears. "You really do have the cutest dog. Despite being a pizza snatcher."

"Yeah." He reached down and petted his pup. "When you're the only survivor of a military vehicle bombing, you get moved to the top of the list to get one if you want. I found that out the hard way."

Her lips parted. "Alex . . ." She straightened. "I'm so sorry."

"It's okay." He continued to pet Oliver. "This guy's gotten me through some rough nights. It's better now."

She thought back to their earlier encounter with Liam today. "It was your leg that was wounded, wasn't it?"

He nodded. "Shrapnel wound. Shattered it into pieces. I spent a good year in Walter Reed before finally coming home. Even with a leg full of plates, screws and rods, I'm one of the lucky ones. I know that." He stood and nodded in the direction of the stage. "Looks like they're getting ready to start."

Sloan followed. Alex had been through a lot these last few years. She didn't know anyone who'd served overseas, but she imagined he was still working through moving forward with his life after such a horrific event.

She hadn't expected this deep conversation in the middle of an outdoor pep rally, but she appreciated his opening up to her.

They made their way to the crowd where the mayor was doing a warm-up of really corny jokes.

"Why should you never confess a secret to your sweetie while strolling through a maze?" He motioned for the crowd to ask why.

"Why, Mayor Hertzberg?" Alex deadpanned, and Sloan nearly spit out her cider.

"Because the corn has ears! Thank you. Thank you very much." Mayor Hertzberg motioned for a cheerleader holding a box to join him. "All right, it's time for the moment you've all been waiting for, the reading of the wishbone wishes from ten years ago."

The mayor began to read all the wishes and the crowd, that apparently included many of the senior class from ten years ago, seemed to take it all in good fun.

When the mayor read Hayden's, she made her way through the crowd, hopped on stage and did a high kick. "Ryan, I'll be waiting for you at The Bend after this."

The crowd laughed, and Mayor Hertzberg took back the microphone. "Thank you, Hayden. Others, don't feel like you need to make any commentary."

It was clear the people in this town loved being from Brooks Bend and participating in its traditions. Even those who'd left, like Mia, found their way back.

Mayor Hertzberg reached in for the next wishbone. "And here we have a wish from former star quarterback, Alex Edwards."

"That the Patriots would go to the Super Bowl. That wish came true multiple times," someone shouted from the back. "Thanks, Alex."

"I'm going to get out of here. I'll see you in the morning." Alex tapped her shoulder and turned to leave.

The mayor unfolded the paper attached to the wishbone. "In ten years, I hope Mia and I are just as happy together as we are tonight."

The crowd went silent. Alex looked all sorts of uncomfortable, raking a hand through his hair. Right about now, he was probably hoping memory lane had been demolished.

No wonder he'd wanted to leave earlier. He knew what was going to be revealed and his inevitable embarrassment from it. Sloan squared her shoulders. This wasn't the way the event was going to end for him. Not if she could help it.

"I have a wish. I have a wish!" She raised her hand and pushed her way through the crowd to the stage. She could always blame what happened next on the cider, but she couldn't let Alex leave feeling this way. Not after the way he'd come through for her today. She climbed onto the stage, handed the mayor her bottle, and took the microphone.

"I'm ready to make my wish."

"Sloan, that's not quite how this works." Mayor Hertzberg attempted to take the microphone back, but she was too quick for him.

"Good evening, everyone. For those of you who haven't been to Dee Dee's, I'm Sloan Leary, and I'm delighted to be working in Dee Dee's kitchen while she works in mine. I hear her chocolate pecan pie is making quite an impression among San Franciscans."

"Go back home," a man's voice yelled out from the back.

Wow. Tough crowd.

She ignored the heckler. "My wish is for all of you to join Alex and me at Dee Dee's Diner tomorrow for breakfast for a two-for-the-price-of-one special. Some of you may have heard today that we're squaring off in the kitchen. Well, it's true. Your Brooks Bend golden boy and I will settle who is the better cook, and I promise, *no* seasoning."

That last announcement got more applause than she would have liked.

She continued, "And that's not all. We're running a special contest the rest of the week that kicks off with tomorrow's face-off. With a purchase of a meal anytime between tomorrow and Saturday, you will be entered to win a future four-course meal prepared by either Alex or me. That's right. Two winners. A portion of the proceeds will go to Walter Reed National Military Medical Center. We'll see all of you starting tomorrow."

"Thank you, Sloan." The mayor snatched the microphone back and she stepped off stage.

Alex looked amused, or maybe confused. It was hard to say.

"So, that was your wish?" he asked.

She shrugged. "Some of it was improvised."

"And now I have to cook a four-course meal."

She bit her lip. She hadn't had time to think that through. "I'll help you come up with the menu."

Mia interrupted his response. "Hey, Alex. My ride needed to take off early. Do you think you could give me a lift home?"

"Uh, sure." He turned to Sloan. "I'll see you in the morning."

Guess he was no longer concerned about getting up early. "Game on," she said, flashing her brightest smile. It faded as he crossed the park with Mia, Oliver by his side.

Was Alex's wish ten years later on the path to becoming true?

She pulled out her mittens, slipping them on. For some strange reason, that thought came with an ache to her heart.

Chapter Nine

"I CANNOT BELIEVE people eat that." Sloan stared down at the baked beans, hash browns, and macaroni salad Alex had piled high onto a plate. "And why are we listening to this song *again*?"

For the entire breakfast shift, she'd had to suffer through one Air Supply ballad after another. A band she'd barely heard of, but she knew them now.

"My aunt loves their music. She plays this old CD all the time. It's time to rock this, Chef." He waved a spatula in the air, doing a spin while he lip-synced the chorus to "I'm All Out of Love" into it.

She liked a good love song as much as the next woman, but this silly display coming from a man who wore flannel shirts and baseball caps backward was a mismatch if she ever saw one.

He kept singing, flipping an egg onto his heap.

"That's disgusting."

He stopped singing, aiming his spatula at her. "Please take that judgmental nose scrunch to your side of the kitchen."

Sloan laughed at his kidding around. They had made a decision an hour ago after bumping into each other several times that they needed to draw a line. Alex had found some black duct tape in his aunt's office and done just that.

"Sloan, I need four more orders of your sweet potato pancakes special," Justine called out. "One with fruit and one with sausage. The one with sausage would like syrup on the side."

"Got it. *Four* of my pancake specials coming up." Her smile was pinned by playful smugness. "Did you hear that, Alex? *Four* pancake specials."

"Yeah, yeah, yeah. Gloat all you want." He cracked a couple of eggs onto the grill. "Once we start lunch service, my APOPs are going to leave your cheeseburgers in the dust."

"They're your aunt's cheeseburgers, and you were practically begging me to make them the other day."

Sloan hummed to herself as she poured the sweet potato pancake batter onto the hot grill from the batch she'd whipped up earlier. It'd been a busy morning. When she arrived, Alex had greeted her, already dressed in a blue chef's coat and black apron he'd found in the supply closet. He'd made her coffee and then began flying around the kitchen in an exceptionally good mood.

She shot him a sideways glance. Had this pep in his step been because of Mia?

She shoved that question to the side. How he'd ended his

night was not her concern.

She waited for a few seconds as the pancake's bubbles began to take over the batter. Her reaction to seeing Alex leaving with Mia had surprised her. While walking back to the inn, she'd had a long talk with herself to straighten some things out.

She was *not* developing feelings for Alex because that was absurd.

Last night's disappointment in seeing him leave with his ex was merely residual feelings from being grateful to him for everything he'd done for her. She'd been living that high all evening and merely didn't want it to end. That was all.

At least that's what she told herself as she flopped into bed.

And most of this morning while she was getting ready.

And maybe right now.

She flipped the pancake and, in no time, had a stack ready for pickup, hitting the bell. "I'm going to head into the dining room for a bit."

"No making suggestions on what to order," Alex warned with a wink. "I'm onto you, Chef."

"I can't help it if they fall for my charm." Sloan made her way out into the kitchen, where Kimmie and Earl had arrived, rolling in a giant whiteboard. "Thank you both so much for this." Her plan was a simple one. Anyone who bought a meal today went onto the whiteboard under Alex's name if he'd made the meal and hers if it came from her hands. They would take ten percent of the daily sales for the donation, pending Dee Dee's approval.

They planned on Facetiming Dee Dee later today when it was a decent hour on the West Coast.

Sloan was going to match whatever was brought in today, but she was keeping that to herself for now.

She made her way through the crowded dining room. True to her word, Gwen had contacted the senior citizens home, and the majority of its residents were now enjoying their breakfast.

"Do you like your pancakes?" she stopped in front of a booth and asked a group of four older women all in warm fall sweaters and slacks.

The unanimous nods made her heart swell. *Finally.* She'd done something right in this town.

"Dear." One of the women pulled a paper napkin out of the dispenser. "I hate to trouble you, but do you think I could get an autograph?"

She wants my autograph. It'd happened on occasion that a foodie who enjoyed collecting signatures from chefs might ask for her autograph, but given the residents of Brooks Bend had been ready to send her and her seasonings packing, this moment was not only sweet but huge.

"I'd be happy to." Sloan asked Justine for a pen as she walked by. The waitress pulled an extra one out of her hair bun and handed it over.

"Thank you," she said, turning to her customer. "Who

should I make it out to?"

"Actually, I was hoping I could get his." The old woman stretched her arm out and pointed toward the kitchen.

She turned, seeing Alex drop a plate down on the counter and ring the bell. He gave her a satisfied wave. "You want Alex's autograph?"

The woman nodded. "It's for my grandson. He's hoping to make the varsity football team next year. My late husband and I took him to the state championship when he was five years old. That guy there single-handedly handed us our first and only state title."

"He did, did he?" She glanced over her shoulder. So Alex was a hometown hero.

"He's so handsome," another woman in the booth remarked. "Are you two dating?"

"No," Sloan blurted out, turning back. Her cheeks began to heat up by that outburst. "We're just friends." She waved the napkin. "I'm going to ask him to sign this and bring it out to you personally. Don't go anywhere."

Sloan made her way back into the kitchen. Her jaw dropped at the unimaginable sight in front of her. Alex was eating a pancake she'd aborted because the shape wasn't perfectly round. "*What* are you doing?"

"What?" His fork froze mid-bite. "This wasn't for anyone, was it?"

"No, but . . ." She put her hands on her hips. "Today, you are the enemy. I don't feed enemies."

He laughed and continued to eat. "Fall food is my favorite, and this is really amazing." He cut a piece off with his fork. "I get why they're so popular."

She grinned at the compliment. "Okay, I guess you can finish it." She set down the napkin and pen on the prep table. "A cute costumer has requested your presence and an autograph, Mr. State Champ."

He shoved the rest of the pancake in his mouth, taking the napkin and peeking out the service window. "Is she over seventy?"

"I think so."

"Yes." He fist-pumped the air. "Golden girls love me." Picking up the pen, he scribbled his name. "Can't disappoint my fans."

"No, can't do that." She shook her head in amusement and got started on the orders that kept coming and coming. The rest of the morning flew as they moved from the breakfast service to lunch.

Her competition was in his full APOP element as one order after the other came in.

And as he predicted, he easily smoked her.

As the lunch crowd began to disperse, Sloan made her way through the dining room to check out the whiteboard, now completely full with names.

"Did I win?"

She turned to see Alex beside her. "I'm counting now." It was close, but even with Alex's APOP plate outperforming anything she made off the menu, she won the face-off by two. She did a little jig. "Looks like the good people of Brooks Bend have spoken."

He leaned down and whispered in her ear, "I wouldn't take your victory lap just yet."

Goose bumps ran up her arms from his warm breath on her earlobe. "Well, we've broken down service, so I'm pretty sure I won."

"Yeah, maybe you did. I'm going to go grab my things and head to the inn. Great job facing off."

She hummed to herself while moving around the dining room and saying a thank-you to her customers because she could take that victory lap. Making her way behind the counter for a coffee refill, she greeted Hayden, who was at the counter, enjoying her APOP.

"Uh-huh." She lowered her gaze to Hayden's plate.

"What? I told you I was coming in here." She licked her fork before diving back in. "And it's *sooo* delicious. Alex, this is even better than I remember."

Alex had joined them, having changed out of the chef coat and apron back into a red-and-brown flannel shirt.

"Glad you're enjoying it. It was fun to bring back my legendary meal." He touched Sloan's arm. "I am really sorry I can't help with the dishes. I need to head to the inn. I got a text that the floor is finished, and I have to sign off before the men can leave."

"The floor looks amazing," Hayden said. "I took a sneak

peek before I came here. They did a great job."

"Awesome. I'm excited to see it. I'll see you there."

Hayden nodded. "I'll be back after I eat. The kitchen inspection guy called that he'd be arriving by four p.m."

"Oh, great. I'll stick around until he leaves in case he has any questions." Alex whistled for Oliver to get up from his spot on the floor.

Sloan gave Oliver a pet goodbye. The fact that Alex had willingly given up his day to help her when it was jam-packed with his work meant . . .

Well, it meant everything.

Alex tapped her shoulder. "I'll swing back around six with your taste tester, depending on how long the kitchen inspection takes."

"That sounds great." Maybe she could make a simple dinner to thank him. He'd said fall foods were his favorite. "Do you like butternut squash soup? I was thinking of making some for tomorrow's special." She waggled her eyebrows. "You could give it your stamp of approval."

"That sounds good. We'll see you then. Bye, Hayden."

"Bye, Alex." Hayden took a sip of her soda, looking straight at Sloan. "Are you excited about your date?"

"What date?" Sloan asked. She reached for the coffeepot and poured herself a little more.

"Your 'Do you like butternut squash soup?' dinner date."

Sloan took a sip of her coffee. "That is not a date. I made a bunch of bread bowls yesterday that will go stale if I don't use them."

"Uh-huh."

"It's true!"

"I'm just sayin', I see the way he looks at you. I saw it at the book signing, I saw it at the Wishbone Wishes event, and I saw it now."

"There's nothing to see. Besides, I leave next Sunday. Dating anyone in Brooks Bend wouldn't be a good idea when I'm going home soon."

"Okay. But if he shows up in a sweater and not a flannel, he thinks it's a date."

Sloan laughed. "I'll keep that in mind." Though enjoying a relaxing meal with Alex would be fun, tonight was about one thing and one thing only. She needed to get started on her Puppy Palate audition.

Besides, he may or may have not started his path to a new destination with his ex-girlfriend. It hadn't gone unnoticed that the good mood he greeted her with never lifted once today.

That was apparently what love could do. She frowned. Was he in love?

Stop it. This is your first warning. She scolded herself for the silly thought. She continued to chat with all her customers while Tom took Alex's place in the kitchen.

The face-off had been a huge success.

She only hoped that, even without Alex in the kitchen, customers would come in the rest of the week and next.

Hopefully, the chance to win a four-course meal would be enough.

"What's all this here?"

Sloan turned to see Mia standing next to her. "Hey, it's good to see you again." She paused, adding, "If you're looking for Alex, he just left for the inn."

"Oh, I saw him on the street. He said he left a takeout bag for me with Justine."

Takeout. So now they were doing takeout?

Stop it. You should be grateful for the sale. It was not a big deal that he made a to-go bag for Mia, and so what that he did? *Warning number two.*

Sloan smiled and handed Mia a purple marker. "Feel free to sign the board under Alex's name for our four-course dinner contest. Everyone who purchased APOPs today will be entered to have Alex make their meal."

Mia scribbled her name as Justine came over with a brown bag. "Three APOPs."

Mia laughed, taking the bag. "When I told my parents Alex was serving this today, my mom changed our lunch plans."

"Yeah, it seems to be wildly popular." Sloan took the marker back, placing it on top of the whiteboard. With three APOPs that had been cooked before lunch service conclud-ed, that put Alex ahead of her. He'd won the face-off.

And he knew it earlier. Which was more comical than upsetting. "Why this town has gone absolutely gaga for something that could clog their arteries and give them massive heartburn is beyond me."

"You haven't tried it yet?"

Sloan stiffened. Mia the ex could take her accusatory tone right on out of here. Her unwillingness to taste it was not a slight on Alex. *At least I didn't break his heart.*

"I haven't yet," she admitted. "I should probably get back in the kitchen. It was nice seeing you again. Thanks for supporting the face-off."

"You're welcome. Anything for Alex."

Uh-huh.

Warning number three.

"Sloan."

Apparently, Mia wasn't done talking. She turned back. "Yeah?"

"Do you think you could give these to Alex?" She reached into her oversized black purse and pulled out two of her books. "I'm headed to New York City for a couple of days for an event, but promised I'd give him a signed book." She handed them to Sloan. "One is for Dee Dee."

"I'd be happy to." She glanced down at the now familiar cover.

"Thank you so much." Mia waved the takeout bag in the air. "Thank you, Justine."

"You're welcome, love. Stop in before you leave town."

"I will. Bye, Sloan. Have a great afternoon."

"You too." Sloan made her way back behind the counter.

"Don't worry about her," Hayden said, now working on a piece of chocolate cake.

"Why would I be worried?" She set the books on the counter.

"Alex is definitely not interested in getting back together. That ship sailed years ago." She licked the frosting off her fork. "And sank."

"It's none of my business."

Hayden reached for a napkin and pressed it to her lips. "I saw your face when he left with Mia last night."

"That. That was nothing. I was just tired. It'd been a long day on my feet and . . ." She could continue to deny it, but Hayden was clearly onto her. "Do you really think he's over her?"

She nodded. "Definitely."

"Maybe she wants him back. I mean, she asked him to give her a lift home last night"—Sloan nodded to the books—"and now she's dropped off signed copies for him and his aunt." Never mind her actually *liking* his APOP.

Hayden raised an eyebrow. "What did she write in his book?"

"I don't know."

"Well, open it. How she signed it could signal if she wants to get back together or not."

Sloan shook her head because that was wrong. "I'm not going to do that. I'm not that girl."

"Well, I am." Hayden picked up the first book and

opened it.

Sloan's heart began to race, but she'd be lying if she wasn't a bit curious.

Okay, more than a bit.

"This one is for Dee Dee." Hayden set it aside and picked up the second.

Sloan glanced around, feeling a bit sheepish, which was stupid since Alex wasn't even here. She shouldn't look. It was wrong to look.

But if the book just happened to open . . . She placed a hand on her neck and lowered her gaze.

Alex, I'd like your wishbone wish to come true. Your Mia Always

Sloan frowned, closing the flap. She had her answer.

Chapter Ten

ALEX CLIMBED UP the stepladder and began removing the old light fixture his aunt hadn't had changed out in years. After spending a few hours at the inn, he'd made his way back to the diner and, in no time, had gotten to work.

It'd been a great day. He'd had a blast cooking with Sloan earlier, and then when he returned to the inn, the good news had kept coming.

The shiny wood floors in the library were beautiful. His kitchen remodel had passed full inspection, and then the coolest thing happened. The inspector said it was one of the best kitchen remodels he'd ever inspected, and if it was okay, he'd like to float his name to potential clients.

He couldn't lie that the offer kicked up a little anxiety from deep within, but he pushed through it. It seemed he may have finally gotten his lucky break to expand his contract work.

Maybe it was time to seriously consider opening up his own business. Hang up his Brooks Bend Handyman title that he'd been holding onto probably longer than he should have.

But not right now. He came down the ladder, grabbed the new fixture off the table, and climbed back up with his power tool to install it.

While his dog would be tasting meals, he wanted to get a couple of things knocked off of his aunt's to-do list. He also had some news to share with Sloan that involved her, and he hoped she would be excited about it.

Or at least be a good sport.

He'd run into the high school football coach this afternoon on his way to the inn and they shot the breeze for a few minutes about the big game this weekend. One thing led to another, and he offered up something for the team that he hoped wouldn't send Sloan into a frenzy.

Since they were planning on Facetiming his aunt sometime tonight, he'd hold off breaking that news until then.

She couldn't kill him with his aunt on the screen.

He finished power screwing in the light fixture, then admired his work.

"Dinner's ready." Sloan came out of the kitchen, wheeling his aunt's utility cart. On it were two plates holding bread bowls filled to the top with butternut squash soup, a bottle of red wine, and two glasses. Also on the cart were three plates of what looked like mushy meat that he was pretty sure was for Oliver.

At least, he hoped.

He reached for one of the dog plates. "Yum," he kidded. "Can't wait to dig into this."

She snatched it out of his hand. "That is not for you. *This* right here is for the human." She picked up one plate with the bread soup bowl and handed it to him. "One curried butternut squash soup. I know I'm not supposed to break out my spices for paying customers but thought you wouldn't mind."

He glanced down at the velvety-thick mixture that looked so amazing he couldn't wait to get it into his belly. "What's the garnish?" he asked, admiring the swirly white on top.

"A swirl of coconut milk with chili garlic paste."

"Wow." He set it down on a booth table. "And red wine," he said, taking the bottle, glasses, and opener off the cart. "Don't mind if I do."

"I found that bottle in the pantry. I hope your aunt wasn't saving it."

"Nah." He glanced at the label. "It's a local wine from Long Island. One of her customers probably gave it to her as a Christmas present one year. She's not much of a drinker."

"Go ahead and try the soup. It's my grandmother's special recipe. I'm dying to know what you think."

She didn't have to ask him twice. He dug his spoon into the soup. His eyes rolled back because what he was tasting deserved it. "This is amazing."

"Thank you. It took me years to replicate."

"Your grandmother taught you to cook?" he asked, tugging down the sleeves on his navy-blue crewneck sweater.

He didn't really know anything about how Sloan got started as a chef. He reached for the wine, uncorking it. But he was going to enjoy hearing that story.

Because he couldn't deny it much longer.

He wanted to get to know her.

"She taught me everything I know. Okay, Oliver . . ." She picked up a plate of the mush, oblivious to the big confession his heart had just made.

"Wait," he interrupted. "Wouldn't you like to have dinner first before the soup gets cold?"

It was a simple question—at least he thought it was—but she blinked a couple of times before answering for some reason. "That's okay. You go ahead," she finally said. "You look nice tonight," she added out of the blue.

"Oh, thank you." He pulled up a sweater sleeve self-consciously, feeling like a stupid teenager. He should have worn his flannel.

She picked up one of the dog plates. "Can you hold Oliver back for a second? I'm going to put the three meals down across the room and see which one he chooses to eat first."

He grinned, sliding into the booth and then patting his thigh a couple of times for his pup to join him. "He'll take his medium rare on a bed of rice with lots of gravy," he teased as he draped an arm over the dog to keep him from jumping out of the booth. "Or no tip."

She sent him a sideways mock glare and crossed the room with the three plates, setting them down on the floor.

"These are three different variations on a pooch turkey casserole with lots of turkey and vegetables all safe for dogs to eat."

"And the spices?" He had to ask because he knew they'd been sprinkled in there. Although he wasn't really worried about them being safe. He knew she'd done her homework.

"The first one is with turkey gizzards tossed in turmeric; the second, I used turmeric and anise seed; and the third has anise seed and ginger."

"Yum." He tried to mask his sarcasm, but it was inevitable with those combinations.

"Make fun all you want, but I've been doing some research. These seasonings are all safe for dogs and have a ton of health benefits." She stood. "Okay, let the guest of honor loose."

Alex did just that, Oliver's tail moving fast as he ran over to Sloan. "Good boy. You can have any turkey pooch casserole you'd like."

Oliver sniffed the first plate and looked up at Sloan. "Go for it, sweetie. Any one you want."

He wagged his tail and came over to Sloan, giving her knee a nudge with his nose. "We can play later. Here." She picked up the second plate and set it right in front of him. "Have some yummy turkey gizzards with turmeric and anise seed."

Alex bit back a smile and the sarcastic comment bubbling up behind it while his dog sat down on his hind legs, uninterested in taking a bite.

"Hey, Alex"—she glanced over her shoulder—"does Oliver take his time in eating his dinner?"

"No, normally he goes to town." Which was what Alex was doing at the moment, taking her up on the offer to begin eating this soup, breaking off a piece of bread and dipping it in.

"Go ahead, Oliver honey, have your dinner." She slid the first plate close to his pup, who sniffed it and gazed up at Sloan.

"It's your Thanksgiving dinner," she said. "The one you wait *all* year for. Dig those chops in." She shifted her body toward Alex. "Did you feed him before he came here? Maybe he's not hungry."

"No, he didn't have anything other than maybe a bone from Hayden." Oliver trotted back to Alex, no doubt understanding the word "bone," and laid down by his feet.

Alex dropped a hand to pet his dog. He didn't know how to break it to Sloan that Oliver had given his final answer on her pooch casseroles. "Maybe he's just not into turmeric."

"Hmph." She put her hands on her hips. "I really thought I'd created something he would love."

"He's finicky. He's more of a dry kibble pup."

"He snatched a pizza from my hands the other night! I'd say that makes him more of an adventurous canine." She sighed and picked up a plate, bringing it over and sliding into the booth. "It's awful, isn't it?"

Alex stared down at the thick brown mush with hints of orange carrots poking out. "I'm sure it's delicious." He could say an extra Hail Mary before he went to bed for that exaggeration.

"There's one way to find out." She reached for her soup spoon.

His hand flew up. "Stop, right there." Call him crazy, but he wasn't about to let this woman he was majorly attracted to eat dog food. Before she could protest, he dipped his own spoon in and tasted it.

"Well . . .?"

He grabbed a napkin and spit it out.

"It's that bad?"

He took a long swig of his wine and then, when swishing it around in his mouth didn't work, he tipped his glass up to his lips and drained it. "It's . . ."

He could tell her it was probably fine for pups, but that wouldn't get her the audition. He was confident he was speaking for all dogs. "It's pretty bad."

She slid out of the booth without a word, heading straight into the kitchen.

"You dodged a big one, buddy." He gave Oliver's back a pat. "You owe me for taking one for the team."

Sloan returned with a large butcher knife, maneuvering behind the counter.

Alarmed, he shot up. "What are you doing?"

"I've spent half the night cooking up those plates, and

your dog hated all of them. I need some luck." She brought the knife up with both hands and started to slice into the lucky pumpkin Aunt Dee Dee had left her.

"Stop!" He joined her at the counter.

"Why? If there is a time that I need some major luck, it's right now."

"You're actually wrong about that." He gently took the knife from her, setting it aside.

He wasn't one to believe in his aunt's silly superstition that the pumpkin brought its owner luck, because it hadn't, the onetime she'd bestowed a lucky pumpkin on him. But Sloan didn't need luck when she had talent. "Why don't we wait and see how your next round goes? After that, you can reevaluate if it's time for you to slice into it."

She blew out a breath that sent her long bangs flying, and man, it took everything for him not to take his thumb and sweep them out of her eyes.

Her beautiful browns.

He gulped and pointed to the duffel bag he'd brought with him. "Why don't we see if we can reach my aunt now? I brought my laptop."

"I would really love that."

"Then let's do it." He slid out of the booth and grabbed the bag, pulling out his laptop. "I thought we could Facetime her on a bigger screen than my phone."

"Good idea."

It took him a couple of minutes to log in to the diner's

Wi-Fi and connect, but soon, he saw his beautiful aunt on the other side.

"Alex, Sloan!" She looked adorable in her tall white chef's hat.

"Do you wear *that* in your kitchen?" he asked Sloan.

"Not that tall."

"It's so good to see you both." Aunt Dee Dee clapped her hands together. "Sloan, you look as lovely as your picture in your kitchen."

"It's so nice to meet you, Dee Dee. Truly an honor." Sloan grinned, leaning farther in. "The picture you're referring to of my grandmother and me is one of my favorites. It was taken our first Christmas running the restaurant together."

"You two look so happy."

Sloan continued, this time with a chuckle, "I nearly burned the restaurant down before that picture was taken flambéing my grandmother's Christmas pudding. She spent the rest of the evening trying to make me feel better by singing Christmas carols, and that's when we had the shot taken by one of our line cooks. That picture always takes me back."

Alex sat silently, watching Sloan's glowing face. Her grandmother had been important to her. She hadn't talked about her parents, though. He leaned back with his wine.

"How are you doing, Dee Dee?" Sloan asked. "Is my team treating you well?"

ROBYN NEELEY

"I'm having such a ball. I've always dreamed of working in a big five-star restaurant with an enormous kitchen and a passionate team, and your staff has not disappointed me. They've been so welcoming and helpful—that Connor is a hoot."

Sloan laughed. "I know. I know. Have you had a chance to see San Francisco?"

"Some of it, yes. It's such a wonderful city," Dee Dee said, then added, "I did want to ask if it would be okay if I came back next Saturday. I'd love to meet you in person and surprise my husband, Fred. It's his birthday."

"Of course," Sloan said. "I'd love to meet you in person too."

"Great, I'm going to rebook my ticket tomorrow. How are things going in Brooks Bend?"

Alex's gaze met Sloan's as a couple of seconds ticked by and then a third.

Dee Dee cocked her head, her tall chef's hat tilting like the Leaning Tower of Pisa. "That good, I take it."

"I had a bit of a rough start letting go of my heavily seasoned dishes, but your nephew set me on the right path. I worked with Liam yesterday."

"Did you get to ring the bell three times?" His aunt's eyes lit up as he knew they would.

"Yes, ma'am, and I've got the red lunch box to prove it."

"Splendid. Sloan, dear, don't you fret for a second about how this week started. It's only how it ends that matters."

Alex smiled. He'd grown up with his aunt's sage words of wisdom, but it never got old when he heard her deliver some to someone who might benefit from hearing them when they needed to the most.

He suspected Sloan would take Aunt Dee Dee's words to heart.

They took a few minutes to fill his aunt in on what they were doing this week, including how successful the face-off had been. Sloan's spirts seemed to lift from the retelling of their bumping into each other in the tiny kitchen, and he reminded his aunt that he was ready to knock out the wall whenever she said the word.

"And the best news . . ." He reached for the wine bottle and refilled Sloan's glass. "I haven't had a chance to tell Sloan, but after the big homecoming game this weekend, the entire team will be coming here for my APOP special."

Sloan's eyes widened. "The *entire* football team."

"And a few fans," he said, downplaying it. "Mostly parents. They won't eat much."

"Do we even have enough room to hold that many people?"

"I was thinking of seeing if we could borrow the empty space next door. Set some tables up in there. Could grab Hayden's karaoke machine so they could have some fun."

"Karaoke," Sloan repeated.

His aunt Dee Dee seemed to like the idea, reminding them there were three people in this conversation.

"Well, Aunt Dee Dee, we should let you get back to work," he said.

"Yes. Sloan, thank you so much for this opportunity. Your restaurant is a special place. You have made this old lady's greatest dream come true."

Sloan moved closer to the screen. "You are very welcome and thank you for trusting me to run your charming diner and for having such an awesome nephew. I'm not sure I would have survived this week without him."

They said their goodbyes and Alex powered down his laptop. "Awesome nephew, huh?"

She shrugged. "I was just being nice." She sipped her wine. "Was it really Dee Dee's dream to work in a big restaurant?"

He nodded. "There was a time a few years before she bought the diner that she'd been courted to be the executive chef for a big establishment in Manhattan. A real fancy one."

"Fancy one, eh?"

"You know what I mean."

"Why didn't she take it?"

He pointed up to a picture on the wall of his aunt with one of her favorite customers. "That's her with Spencer Carmichael. He spent all of his time in here as a kid working on his drawings after school and eventually grew up to be a bigwig fashion designer of Christmas jammies."

"Christmas jammies?"

"Yep. He's actually a cool guy. We grew up together, but

he's a few years older, and we didn't hang in the same circles. He's now engaged to Dee Dee's stepdaughter, Charlie."

"And this Spencer is why she didn't take the job?"

He nodded. "Spencer's just one example of many who would come into this diner and sit in these booths, spending hours here working on their dreams with Dee Dee's encouragement." He laughed, adding, "And probably a free piece of pie here and there. This is where she wanted to be, encouraging residents in the town she loved to follow their dreams. She turned the offer down, and a few years later, bought the diner and renamed it."

"Wow." Sloan sipped her wine. "What a special woman."

"She's the best," he agreed. "This exchange was her shot to live out her dream of running a big kitchen."

"I'm glad I could give it to her. She means a lot to you, doesn't she?"

"The world. My mom died when I was eleven. My dad was never really in the picture. They divorced when I was young. I moved in with Aunt Dee Dee when my mom went into hospice. Aunt Dee Dee's always been a second mother to me."

Sloan gave him a soft smile. "I feel the same way about my grandmother."

He remembered her fond words for her grandmother at last night's Wishbone Wishes event and didn't want to pry, but he was curious about her life. "What about your parents?"

"They both died in a car accident when I was a baby. It was just me and my grandmother. She raised me."

"I can tell by the way you credit her for your dishes that you loved her very much."

"I wouldn't be the chef I am without her support." She leaned back in the booth. "It was her dream to expand our restaurant to other cities."

"Starting with Paris?"

She shook her head. "No, but she was so fond of the city. She'd been there as a teenager and fell in love with the history, culture, the food, its people." She sat silently for a moment. "She had a stroke six years ago, and I didn't know what to do. I had doctors telling me she should move into a nursing home permanently." She lowered her chin. "And I listened. Her living above the restaurant was no longer a safe option with the steep stairs. I knew it crushed her that she'd never step foot in the restaurant again.

"Admitting her that day broke my heart." Sloan reached for a napkin out of the dispenser and twisted it. "I told her that I would come visit every single morning, and we'd work on our plans for Seasons of Paris, everything from the layout of the kitchen and dining room to the wonderful dishes we'd serve, and even what special dessert we'd create for the opening.

"She said she would like that, but she passed away some-time that night." Sloan picked up her soup spoon and swirled it into the soup. "And that's why it has to be Paris.

It's what I promised her. I know it all probably sounds stupid."

He shook his head. Nothing this woman sitting across from him thought or did or dreamed was stupid. "I think your grandmother will enjoy that opening one day."

She looked up and her pretty brown eyes locked with his. "I hope so." She slid out of the booth and piled up the dog food plates. "I should probably call it a night. Try again tomorrow."

"I can walk you to the inn if you'd like." He slid out of the booth to help clean up. It was late, and even though Brooks Bend was probably the safest town in America, he'd rather escort her back and know she got to the inn safe.

"That would be nice, thank you." She disappeared into the kitchen, her mood much more somber.

He put the cork in the wine and gathered their dinner plates and glasses. So, Paris wasn't exactly Sloan's dream. He reached over and scratched Oliver behind his ears. But it's what she wanted to carry out her promise to her grandmother and why she needed to win the competition.

If only there was a way he could help her nail it.

He sat up. Maybe he could. He'd helped her change direction once this week, and he could do it again. He might not know how to cook dog food, but he knew what they liked.

He reached into his back pocket and pulled out his cell phone. He'd need an accomplice if he was going to pull this off. In seconds, he had the one person who was crazy enough to help him at this late hour. "Hayden, can you meet me at the diner in an hour? I need to fire up the kitchen."

SLOAN TURNED OUT the kitchen lights and slipped on her coat. She pushed through the double doors back into the dining room, grabbing her bag from where she'd left it under the counter.

She stole a peek at Alex playing with Oliver. Even though the dinner guest of honor had balked at her pooch casserole, tonight hadn't been all that bad.

Her gaze rested on Alex, looking all kinds of handsome in his V-neck sweater and jeans. His date night outfit, according to Hayden.

She bit back a smile and gathered her things, happy that the night wasn't ending just yet because she was really enjoying his company. Maybe once they arrived at the inn, she could invite Alex in for a glass of wine in front of the fireplace.

She bent down to retrieve a tube of lip balm that had rolled out of her bag and her heart stopped at what was still underneath the counter.

Mia's books.

Strike that. Mia's books with her declaration to Alex inside one of them.

She took a deep breath. It would be wrong to not give them to him tonight. "Hey, Alex. I forgot that I have something for you."

"What's that?" He stopped playing with Oliver and turned to face her with the lopsided grin that she was growing more and more fond of with each passing day.

"Here." She walked around the counter and handed him the books. "Mia dropped these off earlier when she stopped in to pick up her APOPs. I completely forgot until just now. She signed them."

"Thank you." He took the books and started to put him in his backpack.

Was he seriously not going to open them? Sloan could hate herself later for what she was about to ask. "Aren't you going to read what she wrote?"

He flipped one open and then the second, his expression not giving anything away. "You ready?" he asked, shoving them into his backpack.

That was it?! No wide-eyed expression at Mia's declaration that she was interested in getting back together. No lopsided grin.

"I know what she wrote," she blurted out.

"What?" A line formed across his forehead.

"Uh . . . I mean . . ." There was no sense walking it back now. "I had them on the counter this afternoon and Hayden and I were looking at them." She dropped her head. "I'm sorry."

When she finally had the guts to meet his gaze, his eyes looked more amused than miffed.

"There's nothing to be sorry about." He slung his backpack over his shoulder. "It's not a big deal."

She cocked her head. She didn't have a ton of experience, but an ex declaring *in writing* that they wanted to get back together seemed like a very big deal.

Alex opened the door. "Shall we?"

"Yes," she said, stepping outside. If he was done with the subject, so was she. She zipped up her coat to block the chilly air and slipped on her hat and mittens. "I don't know how you people live here."

"What this?" He tugged on Oliver's leash for the dog to stop sniffing the curb. "This is nothing compared to the ten degrees, or lower, we'll drop down to in the next couple of months."

"Brrr . . ." She couldn't even imagine what that would feel like.

"So, tell me about when you knew you wanted to be a chef," Alex said.

She smiled at that memory. "I think I knew when I was six. My grandmother would let me hang out in the kitchen, but never cook. Child labor laws and all."

He chuckled. "Of course."

"She did make me her official taste tester." She laughed. "At least, I thought I was."

"An important role, for sure."

She nudged a playful shoulder into his for that tease. "I took it very seriously. No soup could leave the kitchen without my stamp of approval."

"I can picture it now. Did you sneak any seasoning into the soup?"

She chuckled because she probably did. "When I could legally work in the kitchen, I did nights and weekends in high school and all through college. It's all I ever wanted. Cooking is what fuels me and makes me feel alive."

"I admire that."

She stopped for a second. "You do?"

"Yeah, most people have no clue what they want to do with their lives when they graduate from high school."

"Did you?" She kind of knew the backstory from Hayden at the *Pie or Die* event, but she was curious to hear it from Alex.

"Nah, I went into the Army to forget a girl."

"Mia?"

"Yeah. I mean . . . don't get me wrong. I'm proud of the years I served, but it was a huge struggle coming back and finding something to make a living at that made me tick."

"And now?"

"I like remodeling things. The work I did for the inn, especially the kitchen, really lit a fire in me. There wasn't one day that I didn't come to work feeling . . ."

"Alive?"

He grinned. "Yeah. Alive."

She pressed her lips together. With any luck, she'd have a lead soon on a new remodel job to fuel his passion. "Well, I think that sounds like an excellent path to pursue. The culinary industry is huge. So many kitchens to update."

"Maybe." They continued walking down the street, passing a couple holding hands. "So, if you could only make one dessert for the rest of your life, what would it be?"

"That's impossible to choose."

"You have to," he insisted.

"One dessert . . . hmmm . . ." She glanced up at him. "Only one?"

"Yep. There is a massive worldwide shortage on ingredients for all desserts but one."

"Well . . ." She laughed. "In that likely scenario, I would choose my grandmother's maple-ginger apple pie."

"That sounds delicious."

"It is." She nodded.

"Is that your signature dessert back home?"

She shook her head. "That honor would go to my spiced caramel-pumpkin cheesecake."

"Then why not pick that one?"

She knew the reason, and she didn't mind sharing it with Alex. "The maple-ginger apple pie was my grandmother's gift to me. She created it the first Thanksgiving after my parents passed away. My mother loved everything with maple and, apparently, apple pie was my dad's favorite." She sighed. "She wanted to have something that represented them both on our Thanksgiving table."

"That's so awesome."

"And it's delicious. We even put it at the end of our cookbook that was published a few years ago as the perfect end to a fall meal."

"I'll have to get a copy," he said, as they approached the inn, teasing, "and skip to the end."

She breathed in the cold air as they reached the inn. He was probably being polite. A different type of book with the ending he might really want was stashed in his backpack. "This place is so beautiful. I don't think I've ever stayed anywhere so quaint."

"I'm glad you're enjoying it." He chuckled, adding, "Except for the four a.m. wake-up calls."

She nodded her head. "I could do without them, but I totally get now why some chefs prefer breakfast service. I had a great time today. Even if you did beat me."

Alex gave a mock fist pump.

"Care to enjoy a celebratory drink?" she asked, stretching her head to get a good look inside the first-floor window. "I see Hayden's still got the fireplace going."

"Oh, um . . ." He glanced in the other direction, shoving his hands in his jacket pockets. "Actually, there's somewhere I need to be."

Disappointment raced through her. "Right. Of course. Well, I guess I'll see you tomorrow?"

"See you tomorrow, Chef."

"And you." She bent down to pet Oliver. "I'm not giving up until you eat my pooch casserole."

They said a final goodbye, and Sloan watched as Alex made his way with Oliver down the street.

She bit her lip. Had Mia returned from her book signing in New York City?

Maybe his rush to leave had been because he wanted to see her. To get started on being happy together once again. She sighed, recalling Mia's written words.

Maybe Alex was ready to get back together too.

Her chest tightened, and she closed her eyes. *Third warning, Sloan.* Or maybe she was on her fourth attempt to stop her mind from going there.

She headed up the wooden stairs. She could give herself another three hundred and fifty-two warnings, but it wouldn't change the fact.

She was developing feelings for Alex.

Chapter Eleven

"YES, HIS NAME is Alex Edwards, and he's ready for his next job. You won't regret it, Grant, if you do end up hiring him. His work is amazing and his infusion of modern culinary design, while preserving a kitchen's history and traditions, is remarkable."

Sloan sat down in Dee Dee's office chair. She'd come in moments ago to take the call from Grant Watson, an executive chef at The Langley, a historic hotel in New York City.

She added spontaneously, "There's simply no one like him in the industry. The pictures I posted were of family wood ornaments handmade decades ago by the inn owner's father. Alex made sure they were a special part of the remodel, renaming each station after a member of the family. He encased the wooden ornaments right into the stations."

"He sounds like the right person for this job. I want to preserve some of the spirit of the hotel's historic kitchen in the remodel," Grant said. "I'll give him a call later today."

"You won't be disappointed." She stood. "If you could do me a favor and not mention my name when you speak with him, I'd appreciate it." She didn't want Alex to think she'd called in a connection. She said a final goodbye and fist-pumped the air.

Her post had worked. Grant replied that he needed someone who could start after Thanksgiving and finish the job to reopen by Valentine's Day, one of their busiest days of the year.

Beaming, she returned to the kitchen, grabbing a dishrag to begin sanitizing the prep table. It had been a busy morning and her green apple-sour cream pancakes had been as much of a hit as her sweet potato ones.

Although, they would have been a lot better with a healthy sprinkle of her spices. But she was a woman of her word. Her beloved tiny bottles would remain in her suitcase until she returned to San Francisco.

After the table had been wiped and sanitized, she moved over to the restaurant's range and peeked in, sliding on her oven mitts. The turkey she was cooking was done. After failing miserably last night with the gizzards, it was time to try again with different turkey parts. There was nothing in the audition rules that she couldn't include other ingredients as long as she also used what was provided.

Setting the turkey down to cool before she carved it, she looked out into the dining room. The new light fixtures Alex had hung up looked great.

She thought back to her conversation with Alex. She hadn't meant to go there with him, sharing how she'd lost her parents or the guilt she'd felt over putting her grand-mother in a nursing home, but he had asked, and, in the moment, she felt comfortable opening up to the man with his warm blue eyes and sweet smile.

And she'd loved talking to Dee Dee. She couldn't wait until they met face-to-face.

Well, she could wait another week . . .

Don't go there. Alex is nothing but a new friend. She searched for a knife to carve the turkey.

She'd come to the conclusion last night, while flipping on one side, then the other, and then onto her back, that these feelings for Alex were utterly ridiculous, given she'd only met the man on Sunday. There would be no reason whatsoever to act on them because next week, she'd be rolling her suitcases down the train station platform and boarding the train for her trek back to San Francisco.

Now all that mattered was thanking him for everything he'd done by helping him land a new gig that could lead to incredible things for his future. He was going to do an amazing job for Grant if he got the job—scratch that—when he got the job, because she had no doubt that he'd be hired.

And it wouldn't be because of her post. She smiled and put down the knife. Reaching for her purse underneath the counter, she pulled out her wishbone wish. If her wish came true, Alex would finally catch his lucky break.

Remodeling a luxury hotel kitchen in New York City would, no doubt, lead to more work. He could make a name for himself.

Suddenly, the bell rang over and over, causing her to jump out of her thoughts. She spun around to see Justine poised to ring it again. She set the wishbone wish aside. "Sorry. Just daydreaming. Whatcha need? Another green apple-sour cream pancake special?"

"Chef, you've got to come out here. Grab your coat."

Why did she need her coat? Maybe there was something going on outside the waitress wanted her to see. She went to retrieve it out of Dee Dee's office and made her way through the doors. "What's going on?" Her voice trailed as she greeted Alex, who wasn't alone. Hayden, Kimmie, and Earl were all with him. "Hi." She cocked her head, more than a bit curious as to why her friends had stopped by.

My friends. Her heart warmed.

"What are you all doing here?" she asked, pointing to the kitchen. "Do you want breakfast?" Breakfast service was about to be suspended as she needed to switch over and begin prepping for lunch, but she had enough pancake batter left, if that's what they wanted.

"As much as I would love that"—Alex came up to her—"we're kidnapping you for a couple of hours."

"Kidnapping me?" she asked, taken aback. "To where?"

"It's a surprise." Hayden came up behind her and untied her apron. "You won't be needing this." She tossed it to Justine.

"Where am I going?" Sloan looked from Kimmie to Earl,

who were both holding large brown paper bags and looking like they'd each swallowed a canary whole.

"You'll see. Slip this on." Alex took her coat from her and held it out.

"I can't leave," she protested, refusing to put it on because this was absurd. "Lunch service is about to start, and it's too much to leave Tom by himself. We're still running the four-course meal contest."

When those reasons didn't seem to work on Alex, she pulled out the big guns. "Your aunt would be very disappointed to hear her nephew made me abandon her hardworking staff during the lunch rush."

"Tom and Justine won't be alone." Alex pointed to the old guy sitting at the counter, whom she'd totally missed when she came through the kitchen doors. When he turned around on cue, her eyes widened.

"Liam!" He slid off the stool and joined them. She gave him a big hug. "What are you doing here?"

"Enjoying some breakfast before my shift. Those pancakes had just the right amount of sour cream. Not too overwhelming with the green apples. Good job." He patted her shoulder and lifted an eyebrow at Alex. "Dee Dee still using that relic of an oven?"

Alex laughed. "Do you even have to ask?"

"Then I better get back there." He started to leave, but Sloan grabbed his sleeve.

"By shift, you mean you're working here?"

"Can I learn now where we're going?" she asked, reaching into her coat pocket and pulling out her hat and mittens.

"Good idea." Alex pulled out a blue knit cap of his own, putting it on and pulling it over his ears. "We're going to be outside for this adventure."

"You're going to love it, Sloan," Kimmie called out from a few feet ahead.

"Really?" She shot Alex some side-eye. "Before this ambush, I was carving a turkey to try again on my pooch casserole."

"Then I saved my dog from a bellyache."

Cute as he was in that blue knit hat that matched the color of his eyes, it did not save him from a punch to his shoulder. "I'm not giving up. I will make a meal so good, Oliver will be wagging his tail and asking for seconds."

"I don't doubt it. Got any new spice combinations?"

She let out a cool breath. "Not really."

"Maybe you need a nice fall day to clear your head."

"Is that what this is? Are we walking around the block?" If so, maybe they could stop in the Belle & Beau because she'd like to buy a hat and mittens set for Erika for Christmas.

They rounded a corner and started to walk up a dirt road away from town. "How far are we going?" she asked a few minutes into the walk, taking in all the pretty sunflowers and cornstalks on each side.

"About a mile or so," Alex said, picking up his pace.

"Okay, then." Her shoes crunched on all the fall leaves that had fallen onto the road. Alex had been right the other day. The leaves had begun their descent.

"You know what would make this walk even better?" he asked.

"If you told me where we're going?" she shot back.

"Apple-cider donuts. Earl, hit us up back here."

Earl reached into his brown bag and tossed one to Alex.

Alex snatched it and handed it to Sloan. "For you."

Despite being mildly annoyed that she was the only one in the group who apparently wasn't going to be clued in on their final destination, she slipped off her mitten and bit into the donut. Her taste buds exploded from the fluffy, sugary goodness. "Oh, my God, *this* is delicious."

"Bet you don't get donuts like that in San Francisco." Alex caught a second that Earl sent soaring over.

"No." She took another huge bite. "Not at all."

"You men are Neanderthals, throwing food like that. Here, Sloan. Us girls need to stick together." Hayden dropped back, handing Sloan a napkin. "Those donuts are from Hot Apple Cider Guy." She grinned. "We're going on a date tomorrow night."

Alex, who was easily listening, smirked. "To the home-coming game."

"Whatever. It's a date," she shot back, sticking her tongue out at him before rejoining Kimmie ahead.

Sloan laughed as she continued to eat her donut, still in

step with Alex. "So what fall Brooks Bend activities do I need to make sure I do next week? I'm guessing it's too late in the season for apple picking, and I'm all set in the pumpkin department."

He thought for a second. "The inn is hosting its annual Mulled Wine and S'mores event Tuesday night. It's usually a good time."

"I saw a flyer on it in the living room." She laughed. "Spiced wine, chocolate, and a fire. That sounds like a fall event that I would love."

"Then we'll have to make it happen."

"I'd like that," she said softly, finishing her sugary donut, while a vision of spending a relaxing evening sitting next to Alex, toasting their marshmallow sticks over a blazing fire, Alex blowing on her marshmallows to cool them as she got lost in his big blue eyes—

"We're here," he said, interrupting the daydream that he had no idea he was starring in.

Sloan pressed her lips together and glanced around. They'd stopped in front of a two-story white house with red trim. Off to the side was a huge red barn.

The group greeted a middle-aged woman wearing a heavy orange jacket. "It's so good to see you all." She turned to Sloan. "You must be Sloan. I'm Molly."

Sloan nodded. So, the stranger knew she'd be coming? "It's nice to meet you, Molly."

"I was in the diner yesterday. Those sweet potato pancakes were amazing. I put my name down for you to win the face-off."

"I'm sorry to disappoint you, Molly." Alex pumped up his chest. "But the better special won."

Sloan jabbed Alex in the ribs. "Thank you so much for supporting us, Molly. You still have a chance to win the four-course meal made by one of us."

"I'll keep my fingers crossed." Molly crossed them for good measure. "Are you all ready to get to work?"

Work? Sloan raised an eyebrow. What kind of work were they doing? She moved over to Hayden because it was useless to get Alex to tell her anything. Hayden would spill the beans. Girls needing to stick together and all.

"What are we doing here?"

"We're raking leaves." Hayden went over to the row of rakes propped up against the red barn and handed one to Sloan.

"Seriously?" She watched as the others picked out their rakes and started following Molly out back where there was, in fact, a yard full of fallen leaves.

"C'mon, Chef." Alex ran past her, waving for her to follow.

Sloan watched as the others went to town, raking the leaves. She'd left the warm diner during a busy lunch service to rake dead leaves in the cold.

Forget calling these people friends. They were certifiable.

"Chef, c'mon," he called out again.

She could either join them or she could walk down the hill back into town by herself, so she began to rake underneath a huge tree. She watched as Kimmie and Hayden took selfies, doing more jumping around than actual raking, but having a ball, nonetheless.

Earl, on the other hand, decided after a few minutes that the paperback in his back pocket needed reading. He found his way to a rocking chair on the house's wraparound back porch to do just that.

"Chef."

Alex nodded to an area of scattered leaves that needed raking. "Okay, okay." She began to rake, glancing down at the crispy leaves.

"You're not quite doing it right," he said, coming up beside her.

"Well, excuse me, Master Raker. When you grow up living in the second-floor city apartment above your grandmother's restaurant, you don't get this experience."

He chuckled and moved next to her. "You need to keep the rake close to your body like this and rake into the wind."

Feeling stupid, she attempted to mimic what he was doing. "Why doesn't Molly just get a leaf blower?"

He smiled. "Rake."

She rolled her eyes. "Like this?" She attempted again, pushing the leaves, but getting more stuck in her rake than in the pile.

"It's more like this." He dropped his rake into his ridiculously large pile for the short time they'd been there and came up behind her, both arms going around her.

Her mouth made an "O" as she inhaled his spicy cologne. Maybe being an inexperienced raker had its advantages.

"Bend your knees and keep the rake close to you, moving it like this." He placed his hands over hers and brought her rake back and forward. "Back and forward."

"Back and forward," she repeated, getting lost in his strong arms around her, his knit cap touching hers.

If anyone would have told her when she stepped off the plane at JFK that she'd end her week getting raking lessons in the arms of a really cute man, she'd thought they were delirious.

But in the strangest plot twist to her culinary exchange adventures yet, that was exactly what was happening.

"I think I got it," she said shyly as Alex released his arms and moved away to continue working on his pile.

She raked for a good thirty minutes or so, finally taking a break to bend down and pick up a burgundy one. "You really are beautiful," she said, twisting it around.

And wherever they were was quite nice too. She glanced over at the big red barn with a tractor in front of it. They must be at a farm. Maybe Molly owned it.

She turned to see Alex now picking up leaves and putting them in a brown bag he must have borrowed from Kimmie or Earl. "I didn't see you as a leaf collector," she teased as she came up beside him.

"I'm not, but some moments are worth collecting for when you need them most."

She rested her rake. "Thank you."

"For what?" he asked, slipping a leaf into the bag and folding the flap.

"For this. You know. Getting me out in the fresh New England air, taking in all of the Brooks Bend fall foliage before it disappears. I really appreciate it."

"Oh, that's why you thought you were here?"

"Isn't it?" she asked, as he dropped down his rake and set the bag next to it.

He grinned as Molly appeared on the back porch. "We're ready, Molly. Release your residents."

"You got it, Alex." Molly opened the back door and dozens and dozens of dogs of different breeds, shapes and sizes came flying out the door in their direction.

Her heart plummeted to her stomach. *What is happening?*

"This is what we're doing," Alex said, and before she knew it, he'd swept her up and dropped her in his huge pile of leaves, diving in next to her, as the dogs jumped in.

"Alex," she called out, trying to sit up and was promptly shut up by a golden retriever licking her mouth while several other four-legged creatures stormed the pile, demanding attention. "Okay, okay."

"Just give in and play." Alex tossed a few leaves at her and reached for a ball in the cutest little Jack Russell terrier's mouth, throwing it.

While she had fun in the leaves with the happy dogs all around her, Hayden and Kimmie chased a beagle and dachshund around with Frisbees. Even Earl got into the action, tugging a rope with a German Shepard.

Sloan could barely feel her stomach from laughing so hard.

"Need some help getting up?" Alex offered her a hand.

She took it, shaking leaves off her jacket. "I'm guessing we're at an animal shelter."

He nodded. "Molly's a family friend. She often opens up the shelter for kids to come up here and play in the leaves with the dogs during their playtime this time of year." He reached down and removed the brightest red leaf she'd ever seen from her hair. "I was hoping a couple hours with your future customers would inspire you."

She grinned. Oh, she was inspired, her heart pounding against her rib cage from his touch. A few other emotions were soaring through her too.

"And this is why Oliver couldn't join us." She bent down to pet the Jack Russell terrier who'd been playing with Alex. "Okay, okay, little one," she said as the dog leaped into her arms and licked her face.

"He would have been overwhelmed. Too many choices for girlfriends."

She laughed. "Thank you. I can imagine that was a big deal to leave him behind."

"You know, it wasn't that bad." He reached out and petted the Jack Russell, letting it lick his hand.

She nuzzled her face with the terrier's. "I'm not sure I'm closer to knowing what they want, other than hugs and kisses."

"And treats. They want snacks." He climbed up on the porch and picked up the brown bag next to where Earl had been sitting.

"Oh, I don't think they should have all that sugar, Alex." She kissed the top of the terrier's head and set it down. No. Apple-cider donuts were probably a no-no.

"Good thing Hayden and I made these pumpkin-peanut butter bones last night." He pulled one out, handing one to her.

"Last night . . ." She glanced down at the brown bone. "When did you make these?"

"After I left you. I met Hayden back at the diner, and she helped me."

He hadn't gone to see his ex.

No, instead he'd done something that was so incredibly thoughtful to help her with her career.

She took the bone and inspected it before giving it to the Jack Russell, who went to town, downing it in a few small bites. "Hmmm, I didn't realize that dogs liked peanut butter." She shoved her hands in her pockets. "I mean, I never grew up having one, so I wouldn't know."

"They *love* peanut butter, and pumpkin, too, and . . ."

He paused, pulling another bone out and handing it to a German Shepherd who had trotted on over. "You just happen to have a pumpkin waiting for you at the diner. It might be time for you to slice into it."

Her lips turned up. She was about to tell him that she couldn't agree with him more when his phone rang from inside his flannel jacket's pocket.

"Hold on one sec. Hmmm . . . 212 area code. I should take this." He handed her the bag. "Why don't you give your customers their snacks?"

She took the bag and gave a bone to a bulldog who'd made his way over, dropping his tiny, yellow ball at her feet. In no time, all the other dogs had swarmed around her.

Smiling, she looked over her shoulder at Alex, who was now leaning against a tree trunk while taking the call.

This amazing man had done something really incredible, once again, for her.

Her heart began to bloom. With any luck, that call was her thank-you.

"YES, CHEF GRANT. It was nice speaking with you too. Thank you for the invitation to interview. I look forward to meeting you next week."

Alex ended the unexpected call with the executive chef of The Langley Hotel, staring down at his phone. Had he really mere minutes ago been offered an interview for a kitchen remodel job for one of the most historic hotels in New York City?

Had he really just *accepted* the invitation?

His heart began to pound against his ribcage. *Holy cow.*

Who had recommended him to the executive chef? Was it normal to go from remodeling a small-town inn's kitchen to one in an enormous luxury hotel? Was he ready for this? What if he got the job and failed?

The questions kept slicing into his confidence, and he immediately reached down for Oliver, his fingers grasping air.

His throat began to constrict. *Oh, God.* Maybe another one of the dogs could fill in this one time. He glanced over at Sloan and the rest of the gang saying goodbye to Molly on the back porch steps. All the dogs had been taken back inside.

He inched to the other side of the tree trunk, whipping off his hat and throwing it to the ground before unzipping his coat. It couldn't have been more than forty degrees, yet he felt as if he were baking in an oven. He leaned against the tree and began his rhythmic breathing.

Breathing in through his nose for four seconds. *It's okay.*

Holding for seven seconds. *You're okay.*

Exhaling out of his mouth for eight seconds. *Everything's okay.*

Closing his eyes, he repeated his focused breathing again

and then a third time.

"Alex."

His eyelids flew open at the sound of Sloan's voice.

"There you are." She came up beside him.

"Hey," he said, pulling himself off the tree trunk.

"We're about to head back." She bent down and picked up his wool hat, handing it to him. "Everything okay?"

"Yeah." With the help of his rhythmic breathing, his heart rate and body temperature were returning to normal. He took the hat and placed it on his head, never so grateful for cold ears. "Sorry, I was taking a call."

"Didn't go well?"

"To be determined." He watched as Hayden and Kimmie came up to Sloan, each linking an arm with Sloan's to begin their trek back into town. The women talked a mile a minute about the fun time they'd all had, while he silently listened a few steps behind.

He'd thought he was ready to leave Oliver behind, but if he couldn't handle a couple of hours without him, did he have any business pursuing a job that probably wouldn't welcome a lead contractor with an emotional support animal attached to his hip?

Chapter Twelve

"WHAT'S THE SCORE?" Sloan asked, carving yet another turkey while Alex dipped a large spoon into a tub of mayonnaise for his macaroni salad. He was getting a head start on the APOP mix while she tried to make something that met Oliver's approval.

"Seventeen to ten in the third quarter. That gives us probably another hour or so for me to teach you how to make these."

"Oh joy." Sloan cut out the wishbone and handed it to him. "I wish I'd never agreed to this and was now in my cozy bed at the inn."

"I'm pretty sure that's not how that works." He took the wishbone, nevertheless, and tucked it in his apron pocket.

"Okay, fine." She continued to carve. When she agreed to do this, she'd assumed Tom and Justine would be helping out, but neither was particularly interested in overtime to serve a bunch of rowdy teenagers. Their friends couldn't be recruited, either, as Hayden was on her date with Hot Apple Cider Guy, and Kimmie was busy driving people to and from the game.

"Why do you keep fighting it?" Alex brought a fork over to her with a golden tater tot slathered in the macaroni salad and baked beans, and she pushed it away.

"Because it's disgusting. I don't get you East Coasters at all."

She moved into the pantry, returning with a couple of jars of peanut butter. Alex hadn't been around much the last two days, other than in and out here and there as he worked his way down his aunt's to-do list. She suspected he might also be getting ready for his interview with The Langley, but, because she wasn't supposed to know about it and he hadn't said a word, she wasn't quite sure.

She grabbed a spoon, twisted off the peanut butter top, and dipped it in. The visit to the animal shelter had inspired a pumpkin-peanut butter pooch lasagna with layers of turkey, peanut butter, and pumpkin. She coated a rectangular glass baking dish with thin slices of turkey, and then added in a generous amount of peanut butter, smoothing it out.

"I think I'm ready to puree my pumpkin." She pointed her knife at her lucky pumpkin, now on the prep counter from when she'd brought it in earlier. "Do I need to say any lucky chant?"

Alex laughed, placing an industrial-sized jar of baked beans underneath a can opener. "It's not a spell."

"Okay, then." She cut off the top and set it aside, digging her hands into the pumpkin, pulling out the mushy insides entwined with pumpkin seeds. It took her no time to puree the insides from scratch, setting the pumpkin seeds aside because Alex said the seeds toasted was his favorite snack.

She grabbed a spatula, then spread the puree over the peanut butter and seasoned it with her fall seasoning—the only bottle allowed out of her spice rack. After warming the dish up in the microwave for a few seconds, she was ready. "Okay, Oliver."

She placed it on the floor and backed up. That the dog dropped his pizza toy and came right over was a good sign—a really good one.

"Is he eating it?" Alex asked over his shoulder.

She put a finger to her lips. "Shhh . . ."

Alex stopped what he was doing, and they watched for a second as the dog sniffed at it. A few seconds later, he came over to Alex and lied down.

"Oh my God. So much for being a lucky pumpkin." Sloan threw up her hands. "I was positive he'd like this one. Sure of it."

"What spice did you use?" Alex picked it up and dipped in a finger, tasting it. "I taste cinnamon."

"And pumpkin. It's a fall spice that I make each year."

"I like it."

"Unfortunately, you don't count." She shook her head, taking the baking dish and staring down at it. "It's hopeless. I'm going to lose the audition."

"One dog's preference shouldn't deter you. Why don't

you put that batch in the refrigerator and test it out at the animal shelter tomorrow? I'll give you Molly's number."

She thought about it for a minute, pressing into the mixture with her fork. "I guess I could do that." She set the utensil aside and covered the dish, putting it in the refrigerator. "I'm going to take a walk."

"Good idea. Go reset with some fresh air so you can get right back in the game."

She gave "Coach Edwards" some serious side-eye as she pushed through the double doors.

Once outside, she took in the brightly lit street while inhaling deeply. *How do I turn this around?* She had two days to come up with not only an entrée, but two sides and a dessert too.

"I can do this," she gave herself a pep talk. Alex's idea to take the pooch lasagna to the animal shelter was a good one. If three dozen or so dogs turned their noses up at it, she'd have her answer.

She made her way into the space next door to call her agent. They'd set the space up earlier and now the room looked ready for business with long rectangle tables and checkered cloths.

Alex thought it would be a good idea to have board games on the tables in case the kids lost the football game. There would be something fun for students to focus on. He'd called Kimmie and Earl to help him out this afternoon, and they hadn't disappointed. Now each table included popular games like Codenames and Throw Throw Burrito.

Alex had even rolled in the whiteboard to run a game competition, with the winner of each game going on the board for diner gift certificates and leftover desserts from the week.

Just more of Alex being the wonderful, thoughtful guy he was.

She pulled out a plastic chair and sat down, reaching into her apron for her phone. In seconds, Erika was on the other side.

"Sloan."

Sloan cocked her head, barely able to make out her agent. *Was she outside?* They were three hours behind, but since it was evening there, too, it was pitch dark. "Where are you?"

"I'm in a corn maze," she whispered.

That wasn't a place she'd ever picture Erika. "You're where?"

"I'm in a corn maze." She raised her voice an octave higher. "Somewhere north of the city. That guy I had coffee with the last time we talked—we're on a date, and I got lost. Do you know how bloody scary it is being lost in a corn maze?" she asked as a corn stalk smacked her in the face.

Sloan suppressed a laugh. "Take a deep breath. I'm sure you'll run into a twelve-year-old who can escort you out."

"You think so?" That question came with a mixture of fear and hope.

"You'll be fine. Do you want me to let you go?"

"No, keep talking. How are your Puppy Palate meals going?"

"Well . . ." She could lie or at least exaggerate the truth, but that wasn't her style, and never with her agent. "It hasn't been as easy as I thought it would be, but I've got some ideas."

"Do you think you'll be ready to rock and roll by Tuesday?"

"Yeah." She stood and made her way outside. "I'm going to work all day tomorrow on them since the diner is closed. There's this animal shelter nearby where I'm going to recruit some doggy testers."

"Good, because I've booked your train ticket to go up to Boston on Monday afternoon and returning late Tuesday night, in case your audition runs a little longer. You'll be staying at the Omni Parker House."

Late Tuesday. *Oh shoot.* Disappointment shot through her. Of course, she'd love to stay at the legendary hotel and stroll Faneuil Hall, but it also meant she wouldn't be able to attend the Mulled Wine and S'mores event with Alex. She gazed inside the diner. Alex was tossing Oliver his pizza toy in the dining room.

"I'll be ready," she said. "I'm going to let you go. Watch out for Freddy," she joked, adding, "unless that's your date's name."

"Very funny. I'll call you on Tuesday."

"Talk to you then." She slid her phone back into her apron and continued to watch Alex play with Oliver for another second.

If only he lived in San Francisco.

Her heart squeezed. After next week, there would be more than three thousand miles between them.

But that wasn't now. At this very moment, there was no reason for there to be no more than three feet between them. She strolled inside and rolled up her sleeves.

"Hey," he greeted her. "Do you feel better?"

"Much." She breezed past him. "Let's go."

"Where?" he asked, giving Oliver back his pizza toy.

She flashed him a smile over her shoulder. "In the kitchen, so you can teach me how to make an APOP."

"ALEX, THE BOARD games were such a good idea." Hayden came up to him, digging her fork into her APOP. "The kids are having such a great time. So much better than moping around. I wish we did this after all the football games."

Tonight, the kids had lost by only a touchdown. When the bus had pulled up, they piled out with their heads down. He was glad that they could turn the collective mood of the team around—a lot of talk and laughter filled the room.

Hayden's comment was definitely intriguing. If his aunt had the right help, she just might go for it. There'd always been great energy after a football game. He wished they'd had a hangout place when he was on the team.

He'd talk to his aunt when she got back and maybe Colin, too, to see if there could be some sort of partnership with the Pizza & Pop Shop.

He glanced around at all the kids having fun and horsing around—the cheerleaders loving all over Oliver. Many of their parents were next door in the diner's dining room. "Hey, I meant to ask you." He touched Hayden's arm to get her attention. "Did you recommend me for a job in the city?"

"In the city?" she repeated, in between bites.

"New York City. A kitchen remodel job for a hotel."

"No." She shook her head, but then widened her eyes. "Did someone call you?"

"Yeah, this executive chef at The Langley said he'd heard about my work and invited me for an interview on Tuesday."

"The Langley." She whistled. "That's fantastic." She thought for a second. "I bet it was my dad. He's been squeezing in weekend golf games any chance he gets before the snow flies. He probably showed off some of his pictures of your work to his buddies. You know how guys talk on the links."

He actually didn't, never having acquired a taste for the sport. "Yeah. The guy said he saw some pictures."

"Sounds like my dad." She chuckled. "As long as my

When he didn't answer, she looked to Alex, who clearly was the ringleader of whatever it was that was going on.

"You got a full pantry in the back?" Liam asked, taking off his jacket, revealing his red chef's coat and black apron.

"She does," Alex said.

"Good. Good. C'mon, fella." Liam whistled for Oliver. "We've got some cooking to do. You kids enjoy yourselves. Oliver, Tom, Justine, and I will keep your customers happy."

Sloan narrowed her eyes as Alex made a nod to her to put on her coat that he was still holding. "Are you really going to leave Oliver?"

"I'm trying something new."

She smiled. Yes, she'd said that about leaving her seasoning suitcase behind at the *Pie or Die* event, but this wasn't a bottle of seasoning that she could live without. This was his emotional support companion. "Alex . . ." she started softly.

"It's really okay. He's in good hands. And I know I am too. I'll be fine, and so will you."

She studied him for a beat. He had to have something big planned to willingly leave his dog, even if it was for a short time. She owed it to him to see it through—whatever it was he had up his sleeves. "Okay fine." She slid her hands into the coat.

The group filed out of the diner, the cool fall wind hitting her cheeks as she stepped out onto the sidewalk. They headed down Main Street, everyone in exceptionally good moods.

mom doesn't see them before her Christmas surprise, I won't have to wring his neck. Are you excited?" She popped a loaded tater tot in her mouth.

"Yeah," he said, with as much excitement as taking Route 95 out of Manhattan during rush hour.

Hayden apparently took his apprehension as a case of the jitters. "Don't be nervous. They'll love you. You better remember me when you get your own show on HGTV."

"That's not going to happen."

"Why not?" she asked. Finishing her APOP, she took it to the bin and tossed it. "This could be your big break to starting your business," she said, licking a finger.

He paused, taking a deep breath. "Between you and me?"

"Of course," her voice softened as a line of concern formed across her forehead. "Alex, what's wrong?"

"Things didn't go well after the animal shelter."

"What do you mean? Did you have a fight with Sloan?"

"No. No." He shook his head, then dropped his chin to his shoes. Hayden was his best friend. He knew she'd understand, and there was nothing to be ashamed about. "I had a panic attack. I didn't realize it, but not having Oliver around, even for a couple of hours, really hit me later on. I couldn't let him leave my side all night."

"Oh, Alex." She rested her hand on his arm. "I'm so sorry."

"Thank you. I'll be fine. I saw my therapist yesterday. She thought it was a good sign that I tried."

"If you'd like, I could come with you to your interview and watch Oliver."

"Yeah, maybe." He looked away. Although he was pretty sure it was illegal for a prospective employer not to hire him for having an emotional support animal, he suspected they'd just find another excuse to say he wasn't the right fit. Did he really want to go through with the interview, only to be disappointed? "I'll think about it."

He gave his friend a hug. He didn't want to put a damper on the night because he was really feeling fine today and didn't want her to be concerned. He made his way back into the diner with Oliver. Sloan was single-handedly serving APOPs, and she looked adorable doing it.

"Hi." He came up beside her.

"I thought you ditched me now that I know your secret recipe."

"Never."

"How does this look?" She showed off her APOP.

"It's more of an AOP. May I?" he asked as they returned to the kitchen.

"By all means." She gave him the paper container.

"See . . ." He dipped a ladle into the honey baked beans, piling it on, adding more burger and macaroni. Once he had that pile to his liking, he added some cheddar cheese and finished it off with some gravy. "You need to pile it up."

"I was trying to save any of our customers from going into cardiac arrest."

He laughed, handing it over. "There. That is the perfect ratio for 'Alex's Pile-on Plate.'"

She shot him a smirk. "So that's what APOP stands for?"

"Uh-huh. You were missing the important step that differentiates my dish from others."

"I'm so sorry," she sent over a mock apology.

He shrugged. "You're a rookie. You'll get the hang of it."

She reached for a new carton and filled it with a macaroni base. He usually started with hamburger, but she could do what she wanted.

"So, what inspired you to create this, anyway?" she asked, getting into piling her plate.

"One of my high school football buddies went to college in Rochester, New York, where Garbage Plates are the rage, especially after a night in the clubs. I came back and experimented with the general idea, deciding my spin would be how much I piled up. The APOP was born."

She laughed as he picked up her finished carton to take it out to anyone wanting seconds.

"Wait."

He turned back. "Everything okay?"

"That's mine."

He shot up an eyebrow. "You're going to taste it?"

She grabbed it back. "It's the least I can do for the guy who tried my dog food—twice."

True, but he wasn't one to ever force his meals on anyone. "If you don't want to, you don't have to."

She flashed him a smile. "I want to." She reached for a fork and dug in, taking a rather impressive bite.

"Hmmm."

"Hmmm?" He grinned. "That's all you got?"

"It's okay."

"Oh, c'mon. It's amazing." He laughed, coming up beside her. "You're just threatened by my talent."

"So threatened," she deadpanned, and took another big bite.

They continued to joke and tease each other as they moved around the kitchen. The hour went by and then another as APOPs continued to fly off the counter. Sloan, stating that she felt a little bit guilty for being his piled-on plate sous chef, cut some fresh fruit and placed platters on each table, along with pitchers of water.

Two hours later, Alex finally said good night to the last of the team, making sure that the storefront next door was locked up as well as the diner.

Exhausted, he glanced at his watch. It was two a.m. They hadn't meant to stay open so late, but everyone was having such a good time.

He shlepped into the kitchen. With Sloan not in sight, he leaned against the wall, his legs giving in as he slid down. Sloan appeared from his aunt's office and picked up a small bowl, sliding down beside him.

"I am so beat," he said, as Oliver settled in on his other side. "You too, buddy." He draped a hand over his dog.

"I don't think I can feel my legs." She offered him the bowl.

"Toasted pumpkin seeds." It took some extra energy to lift up his lips, but he did it for her. She'd remembered that he'd said they were his favorite part of the pumpkin. He reached over and grabbed a few, popping them into his mouth. "Wow. Those have a kick."

She smiled and rested her head on his shoulder. "I broke into my spice rack when you weren't looking for some Kashmiri chili spice."

"I guess I can't take the spice out of the girl," he kidded, quite liking the feel of her head on his shoulder.

"Nope, you can't."

"Tonight was fun, wasn't it?"

"So much fun," she agreed.

"We should probably get going." He didn't make any effort to move and neither did she.

"Yes. We probably should." She sighed, barely lifting her lashes. "And I want to skip merrily down Main Street while eating your APOP out of a takeout tray," she murmured, sliding her arm over his chest and closing her eyes.

"We could do that." He grinned and rested his hand over hers.

Staying right here seemed fine too.

Chapter Thirteen

S LOAN MOVED HER arm, her eyelids flickering to see that
the inn's quilt comforter that she'd gotten quite used to
being cocooned in wasn't around her. Nevertheless, her arm
was wrapped in something warm and soft . . .

With solid abs.

Her eyelids flew open. Solid abs!?

She raised her eyes to see she was still in the diner's
kitchen. Her arm had slid between Alex's flannel and his
white T-shirt, his arms around her. She lifted off of him and
sat up.

Oliver came up by her side, wagging his tail. "How could
you let this happen?" she whispered, because when you were
caught having fallen asleep on a kitchen floor . . .

In the arms of the guy you had a major crush on . . .

But you haven't told him, and have zero clue how he
feels about you . . .

You, of course, blame his dog.

Her gaze rested on Alex's handsome face, still tan from
the summer, with just the right amount of chin stubble.
How could they have fallen asleep here?

Oliver nudged her arm with his wet nose. The poor pup probably needed to go out. She poked Alex in his side. "Alex. Wake up."

"Hey." His eyes opened slowly, looking adorably groggy.

She glanced away. *For Pete's sake. Stop looking at him.*

"Did we fall asleep here?" he asked, sitting up.

"It seems so." She brought her knees into her chest.

"Wow." He stretched his back, letting out a grunt. "I can't believe I passed out like that."

She stood, feeling all sorts of awkward, because this was not normal Sloan Leary behavior. This was . . . this was . . . She had no idea what it was or how to process it. "I'm going to get a pot of coffee started."

"Good idea. I'll take Oliver out back and then make us some breakfast. Eggs good with you?"

"Uh, yeah. Sure." How could he act so casually? They'd just spent the night together. Okay, it was innocent, but still. *I was in his arms.* She beelined for the double doors, needing some distance, but she paused before pushing through.

Stop overreacting. So they slept in the kitchen together. It wasn't a big deal unless they made it a bit deal, and he didn't seem to care. "I mean, breakfast would be nice, thank you."

Sloan made her way into the dining room, flipped on the lights, and got to work on their coffee. She shook her head as she waited for it to brew. Since it took forever, she could rewind and dissect everything that led to her falling asleep in Alex's arms.

It was simply two people utterly exhausted from not only a long night but an equally busy week. Her arm around him was merely her nightly ritual of getting comfortable.

An innocent unconscious move of her limb.

If it had been Tom or Liam instead, she would have done the same thing.

Yep. She gazed into the kitchen at Alex, who'd returned from his walk with Oliver and had set to work on their breakfast.

She gulped. Same exact thing . . .

"Hey, Chef, how do you like your eggs?"

"Scrambled please. How do like your coffee?"

"Cream and sugar, thanks."

She made his coffee and stirred in some cream and sugar, bringing the spoon eye level to catch a glimpse of her reflection.

She smoothed her hair with both of her palms. Hopefully, she didn't have major bed head. Then she did a quick breath test, breathing on the back of her hand and bringing it up for a sniff.

She wrinkled her nose. *Oh God.* She should have never eaten that APOP. She could still taste the onions he'd used in the macaroni salad.

She searched behind the counter for something that would kill her morning breath, or at least mask it, finally settling on a bottle of honey. "You'll do." She brought the bottle to her mouth, tilted her head back, and gave the bottle a generous squirt.

At that moment, she felt Oliver nudge her leg.

"What?" She looked down at the dog.

"You want some honey too?" From her research this week, she knew it wasn't harmful for dogs in small quantities, so she squirted some on her fingers and let him go at it.

"Ouch." She pulled her hand back. "Preserve the hand, please."

"Two scrambled eggs, hash and buttered toast." Alex dropped two plates on the counter and pulled out the stool next to her sitting down.

In seconds, he was full-on attacking his breakfast with not a word to be had.

She gave him a sideways glance. *How can this man eat so casually?* Wasn't he as weirded out as she was about this whole thing? She glanced down at the plate. "No macaroni salad this morning," she teased, rather grateful that there wasn't.

"I thought we'd go with a classic. It was a long night."

"Good idea." She dug into her eggs, still tasting the sweet, sticky honey on her lips. Maybe she needed to take a page out of his book and, at the very least, act cool, engage in some small talk. "So, what do you have on tap for today?" she asked, reaching for her toast and taking a bite.

"I thought I might get some errands done. I'm assuming you'll be working here?"

"Yeah, I'm going to go to the inn and freshen up, but

I've really got to buckle down and focus. I leave for Boston tomorrow afternoon."

"Boston, eh?"

"Yeah, that's where my audition is. My agent booked me a train ticket and a room at the Omni Parker House."

"Nice hotel." He smirked. "You're finally going to Bean-town."

"Yeah, but I'll be back late Tuesday night. I'm bummed that I'll miss the Mulled Wine and S'mores event."

"I'll save you some wine," he said, in between bites. "Feel free to text me if you want Oliver to try anything today. We can swing by."

"I will." She glanced around the dining room that needed a good sweeping. She picked up a pom-pom from a set a cheerleader must have accidentally left on the counter, shaking one in the air. "Give me an A."

He chuckled.

"What a night," she said.

"Yeah, it was better than I expected. I had a really good time." His gaze met hers.

Heat crept up the back of her neck. Better than expected, because they'd had such a large crowd or because she fell asleep in his arms?

"I didn't think all the parents would come, and it was nice to see some of my old team stop in too. That was fun."

Disappointment washed over her. And just like that, she had her answer. She set down the pom-pom.

"It was a lot of fun," she agreed. "Until we fell asleep."

"About that . . . um." He set his napkin down and turned to her, looking all serious.

Oh, God. He was going to apologize. He'd been so casual this morning, and now he probably wanted to clear the air that his arms around her were merely to keep her warm or something.

"You know, there is something we still need to do," she blurted out to save herself from any humiliation.

"What's that?" he asked.

"We need to pick our two winners for the four-course meal contest."

"That's right. How much did we raise?"

"We raised two thousand dollars, and I'm going to match it. I e-mailed the Walter Reed Medical Center yesterday to let them know a check would be coming."

"Thank you." His gaze met hers. "That's very kind of you."

"You're welcome. I'm happy to do it. Justine told me before she headed out yesterday that she left two bowls behind the counter with the entries of those customers entered to have you cook their meal and those that are hoping to win a meal from"—she wiggled her fingers—"these award-winning hands."

He groaned. "I can't believe I agreed to this."

"Let's see." She hopped off the stool and made her way around the counter. "Justine said we had a great week, recouping everything I lost on Monday, even after taking out the donation," she said, feeling a slight stabbing in her heart, reliving that royal mess-up.

"Hey, sometimes it's how you end the week that matters, not how you begin it. Remember."

She smiled. "I could use more of your aunt's wisdom in my life."

"She'll offer it to you anytime."

"I'd like that." She bent down. Though she was in no rush for the week to end, she was looking forward to meeting her. She found the two bowls, one with an Alex yellow Post-it taped to it and another blue Post-it with Sloan's name scribbled across it and set them down on the counter.

Alex peeked in and whistled. "You left me in your dust."

That she had, with a bowl filled to the brim with entries. Alex had a respectable number, given he'd cooked only one day of the four-day contest that ended with yesterday's lunch service; otherwise, he would have had more, given last night's success.

He finished his eggs and pushed his plate aside. "This feels a little anti-climatic, selecting names on a Sunday when the diner isn't even open."

She waggled her eyebrows. "Do you think we should call the mayor in? Make a formal announcement in the town's square?"

"No one wants that. Mayor Hertzberg is fine where he is at home in his bathrobe and slippers."

She giggled at that image. "We could each call our winner today and share the good news." She grinned because she couldn't help herself. "I'm going to make sure I send a bottle of antacid to whoever you get."

"And I'll send them a book on spices so they know what they're ingesting," he teased.

"Ha, ha, ha." She reached for the coffeepot and gave him a generous refill. "Okay, shall we do this?"

"I'm ready."

"On the count of three." She counted them down. "One, two . . ." They both put a hand in their respective bowl. "Three."

She pulled out her entry, seeing that Alex had done the same.

She glanced down at hers. "I got Hayden! How fun. I'm sure she'll want to have Hot Apple Cider Guy join her."

"Good." He snickered. "They can have a proper date that doesn't involve the varsity football team."

"It'll be so romantic. I have a ton of ideas of what I could cook for them. Who'd you get?" she asked. She probably wouldn't know who it was or recognize the name, given she only knew a handful of people in this town.

"Just an old friend."

"C'mon. Who'd you get? I promise I can give you some tips with your menu and even help cook the meal if you'd like. We can go grocery shopping together." An image of them joking around as they shopped for fruits and vegetables at a quaint farmer's market made her heart soar.

Maybe she was acting cool in front of him, but last night has meant something to her. They still had one week left to perhaps explore whatever was going on between them.

He set down the entry between them and she glanced down.

Mia Graves.

Her heart ended its flight abruptly, spinning in an uncontrollable nosedive. "Oh, wow." She'd forgotten about Mia and her takeout that had given her three entries. Sloan held her smile, trying her best not to show her disappointment.

Of course, of the thirty or so tickets in his bowl, he'd select his ex—the ex who was eager for their second chance. "I'm sure she'll enjoy whatever you cook. Could be a great start to rekindling your relationship?"

"Oh." His eyebrows furrowed.

"I'm sorry. I just mean what Mia wrote in your book." *Oh, Sloan. Shut up.*

"Right." He fiddled with his napkin. "She might enjoy my making something more than cheeseburger with macaroni salad."

Her stomach began to turn, and it was a tough call whether it was the mention of the APOP star ingredients or the fact that Alex could soon be planning a romantic dinner date for Mia that caused it.

Who was she kidding? She knew exactly what caused her

stomach to flip.

She pushed away her disappointment, attempting to be cool about it. "I am happy to help put together your menu. My grandmother had a fabulous autumn harvest brisket in one of her old recipe books that I picked to be my fall dish on my restaurant's menu this year. It's easy to make and delicious. I can text you the recipe."

"Thanks. That would be great." He pulled his phone out of his flannel pocket, and she gave him her number to send her a text. Shoving off the counter, he reached for his plate and Sloan's. "I should get going. Take Oliver for a long walk."

"Yeah. I've got so much to do." She spun around and fiddled with the coffeemaker. Alex's impending date shouldn't matter in the grand scheme of things—not with the Puppy Palate contract on the line.

She pressed the OFF button on the ache in her heart.

But the date did matter. A stray tear slid down her cheek.

"You'll text if you need us?" he asked.

"Of course," she said, not turning around. The last thing she wanted was for him to see her cry. She waved up a hand, not making eye contact. "See you. Bye, Oliver."

As she heard the back door close shut, she swiped her cheek and picked up the entry with his ex's name on it.

"Good going, Sloan." Figures a contest that she came up with to save her butt might also be the catalyst to bring Alex and Mia back together.

ALEX RUMMAGED THROUGH his closet, pulling out his old dark-blue suit that he wore on the rare special occasion. His aunt had lent him the money to purchase it when he was honored with a key to the town by the mayor's office when he returned from overseas.

He tugged at the wrinkled slacks that he'd have to smooth out later, after he picked up an iron at the nearby Target or borrowed Hayden's. He slid his arms into the suit jacket, making sure it still fit, and headed into his bathroom.

"So, Alex. Tell us about yourself?" he asked in the mirror, his mind immediately going blank.

"Um . . ." He lifted his gaze up to the ceiling to see if that would help shake out a good answer. "I served in combat for five years, and when I returned, I began doing handyman work around my town. That eventually led to my being hired to renovate The Bend's historic kitchen." He glanced out the doorway at Oliver, who was lying head up on the full-sized bed. "How was that?"

His pup laid his head down and closed his eyes.

"That riveting, huh?" He turned back to the mirror, adjusting the awkward suit that hung a little long. "It's a pleasure to meet you. I believe that with my experience, I am the right man to build you a new kitchen that helps bring in more customers based on . . . um . . ."

Seriously, dude.

He yanked off the jacket. This was hopeless. He'd never get the job with an answer like that. He left the bathroom and moved down the narrow hall into his kitchen, reaching for his flannel off the kitchen chair where he'd left it along with Oliver's leash. "C'mon, bud." He let out a loud whistle. "Let's get out of here and take a walk."

Minutes later, Alex sat down on the park bench while Oliver watered the grass. He inhaled the cool crisp air. The last thing he wanted to do was bomb the interview, but maybe he was in over his head.

His gaze moved across the way in the direction of the diner.

Was Sloan still inside, working on her audition recipes?

He'd left her earlier, inspired to nail his interview for The Langley job. She was putting everything on the line to achieve her dream and was willing to do something completely out of her comfort zone.

He found that inspiring. Yes, he'd lived through dark times, and some nights, he still did, but this Langley Hotel interview was his shot to step forward into new possibilities.

"Hey, Alex."

He glanced up to see Mia attempting to pet an uninterested Oliver, who came running over to Alex and lay down by his feet. "Hey. How was your book signing?" When they'd bumped into each other the other day outside the diner, she'd mentioned she'd had one in Manhattan.

"It was great." The scent of her strong floral perfume

made his nostrils twitch. He didn't remember her wearing particularly pungent scents while they were dating. Maybe that's what successful city women wore.

He couldn't help but steal another glance in the diner's direction. He'd rather enjoyed the fresh apple scent of Sloan's hair as her head rested against him.

Yeah, last night had been great, and if anyone would have told him passing out on his aunt's hard kitchen floor would be the highlight, he would have laughed in their face.

But despite a stiff back, the chef's arms around him had felt pretty awesome.

He turned his head to see Mia trying to engage Oliver, who got up and moved to Alex's other side.

Maybe he and Mia were both bad at misreading vibes. Sloan had made it pretty clear this morning she wasn't interested by her encouraging him to cook a romantic dinner for his ex.

Then when he got home, he found a text from her with the recipe for her famous fall brisket that looked amazeballs. She said she'd gotten his number from Hayden.

Perhaps this thing he was feeling for Sloan was just some stupid crush because he hadn't dated in a while, and it was time to focus on someone who—all signs indicated—was interested in him.

He glanced over at his ex, not quite sure how to begin. "Thank you for my book," he finally said.

"You're welcome."

He hunched his shoulders, threading his fingers. Should he address the 800-pound elephant sitting in the space between them, holding the book open to the first page with her note? He chickened out, saying, "I'm glad you're back."

She smiled. "Me too."

"And I have some exciting news for you."

"What's that?" She turned her torso toward him, causing Oliver to stand.

Alex dropped his hand to his dog. He doubted Mia would like brown fur on her purple wool coat, but for whatever reason, Oliver seemed ready to rumble. "You won my four-course meal."

"No way!"

"I don't know if I should congratulate you or offer my condolences."

She laughed. "Well, I'm sure I'll love it."

"Um . . . would you like to have the dinner on Saturday?" Flashbacks of his fifteen-year-old self, sweating profusely while asking Mia to the movies in front of their lockers, filled his mind.

His heart had been pounding so hard that day that he'd nearly thrown up his pizza lunch along with that invitation.

This ask came without debilitating nervousness. He dismissed that revelation. He could ask any woman out now without the urge to throw up. "That is, if you're not busy."

"I'm free," she blurted out, adding, "and I'd love to have dinner with you."

"Great." He leaned back. Maybe the lack of an endorphin rush was because they were adults. Not silly hormonal teenagers. Just two grown-ups wanting to spend a little more time with each other. "So, what are your plans this week?"

"Writing. I'm working on my sequel to *Pie or Die*."

"Wow. There's a sequel? The main character must have chosen pie, eh?"

She laughed at that. "You'll just have to read the book to find out."

He reached for Oliver's leash and moved off the bench. "Well, I should probably get going. I've got this interview in Manhattan and need to prep."

"Interview?" She stood, tugging on her leather gloves. "That's great. What's it for?"

"A hotel kitchen remodel job." He took a few minutes to fill Mia in, ending with, "I've never formally interviewed in all my life."

She inched up an eyebrow. "Seriously?"

He shook his head. "I worked for my aunt after high school and then went into the Army. I mean, I had an interview with a military recruiter, but it was pretty casual. Since then, I've gotten jobs by word of mouth with people I know. Bill Merry offered me the inn's remodel job over a beer while fixing the front porch steps."

"Tell you what." Mia linked her arm through his. "Why don't you come over to my parents' house for dinner tonight? I'm sure my dad would be willing to give you a few pointers, and we can do some interview role play."

"That doesn't sound painful at all," he kidded, adding, "I mean the role play, not dinner with your parents."

She laughed. "They will be so excited to see you."

"You know I see them around town all the time."

"Right." She removed her arm. "The offer still stands."

He thought about what Mia was suggesting and, given her father was his old high school guidance counselor, it was actually a great idea. "Are you sure your dad won't mind?"

"Of course not. We usually have dinner at six. Come on over."

"Sounds good. I really appreciate it."

"Great, it's a date," she quipped, her smile radiating as they left the park and crossed the street.

It's a date. He gazed down the street and caught Sloan on the other side, walking in the direction of the inn. His heavy heart cemented him in place for the moment.

In one more week, she would be leaving Brooks Bend to return to San Francisco and there'd be no reason to ever see her again.

Maybe it was time to explore a new beginning with a woman he had history with and not one who would be exiting his life as fast as she'd dropped into it.

He returned Mia's smile. "It's a date."

Chapter Fourteen

S LOAN SAT IN front of the inn's roaring fire, sipping her coffee. After a good nap and a long hot shower, she felt revitalized and ready to start again on her audition meals.

She'd decided before going to the kitchen, she'd take another hour or so to do more internet research to make sure anything she made wasn't harmful or toxic for dogs.

"Hey, Sloan."

Sloan looked up to see Hayden holding the pooch casserole she'd made last night. "Hey."

"I saw this in the refrigerator and thought I'd check with you first before I start serving it to our guests," she joked.

Sloan laughed, taking the casserole. She set it on a nearby table. "I'm so sorry. I brought it back from the diner. I'd hoped to serve it to some of the pups at the animal shelter this afternoon, but they're closed on Sundays."

"Is that your audition meal?" Hayden asked, adding, "You must be so excited."

"I was, and yes, it was to be the main course until Oliver snubbed his nose at it. That's why I need some different testers. Oliver is a bit finicky, and Alex has the wrong number of legs."

"You have to admit"—Hayden giggled—"they're pretty cute, though."

"Yeah, Oliver's got a good sturdy set on him," she joked back.

She'd thought about last night a little more while she was showering, and their falling asleep wasn't a big deal. This silly crush she'd developed on Alex was obviously one-sided, given his indifference this morning. It would end next week when she boarded the plane.

There was no point crushing on a guy who was on the other side of the country.

Sloan powered down her laptop and slid it into its sleeve. "I have some good news for you."

"What's that?"

"You won my four-course meal in the contest."

"I did?" Hayden asked. "No way."

"I would be happy to cook it anytime this week before I leave. You let me know what you like, what you can't stand, and if you and your guest are allergic to or have a food sensitivity to anything."

"That's so fun." She clapped her hands. "I'll see what Kimmie's doing."

"Or Hot Apple Cider Guy," Sloan suggested, with a raised eyebrow. "I could make something romantic for the two of you. I've got a bunch of special dishes I serve on Valentine's Day, but I can easily turn them into fall ones."

"Would we have it at the diner?" Hayden asked.

Good question. Nothing spelled unromantic better than a four-course meal by candlelight in a vinyl booth in a small-town diner.

An image of Alex in a suit and her in a pretty dress doing exactly that popped into her head.

She looked around. "What about here? I wouldn't use the kitchen, of course, since you're waiting to break it in for your family's Christmas dinner. It'd be easy for me to bring the meal over."

"I love it. We could set up a table in the new library." Hayden grinned. "I like how you think, Sloan Leary. I'm really going to miss you."

Sloan's throat thickened. "I'm going to miss you, too, and Kimmie, Earl, Liam, Justine, Tom. Everyone's been so wonderful to me."

"And Alex?" Hayden asked.

"I'm going to miss him and Oliver too." She paused for a second and then another, before finally blurting out, "I fell asleep in his arms last night." It was pointless to hide her feelings when Hayden already knew the truth.

"What?" Hayden slammed her hand on the arm of the chair. "You're just telling me now? Details, please."

Sloan looked over at her pooch casserole. "There's nothing to tell. It was well after two a.m. before the last person left. We were so tired and literally propped up against the kitchen wall. Honestly, we were both delirious with exhaustion and didn't know where we were."

"Oh, Alex knew." She grinned. "He was exactly where he wanted to be."

"You know, I got the sense this morning he didn't really care one way or another." She gazed for a second into the fire's dancing flames. "And here's an ironic memory for the flames. He pulled out Mia's name as the recipient of his four-course dinner."

"You're joking."

Sloan shook her head. "Nope. It's like I pushed them together, coming up with the contest, and all of this is silly and shouldn't matter at all, because I leave next Sunday."

"But it does matter."

Sloan held back the tears building up in her eyes from spilling onto her cheeks, lowering her chin. "It can't. I don't even live here."

"What if you did?"

Sloan looked up. That was a big hypothetical. "My restaurant is in San Francisco."

"Would you consider opening a Seasons of Boston or, better yet, a Seasons of Manhattan? That's an easy commute."

"It has to be Paris," she said softly. "That's what I told my grandmother I would do for her right before I put her into a nursing home she didn't want to go to. I can't let her down again. Please don't tell Alex about my crush. It's better if he doesn't know."

"I won't say anything, but I'm not sure I agree with you." Hayden seemed to have more to add on that subject, being the spokesperson she was for Alex's heart and who should have it, but the front door opened, and a young couple stepped in. "We'll talk more about this later." She got up and went to greet the couple.

Sloan let out a sigh as she gathered her things. It was time to head to the diner. If anything, getting back on the horse with her Puppy Palate meals would at least distract her because, like it or not, Alex and Mia had history going for them.

She reached for her bag, opening it. She and Alex, they had . . . they had . . .

Pizza.

She glanced down at Oliver's pizza toy next to her wallet. The dog must have dropped it in there at some point when he was playing last night.

She pulled it out, unable to stop her thoughts from re-winding all the way back to the moment the Labradoodle had snatched her pizza slice. He'd scared her out of her mind, while Alex ran across the street to her rescue, looking all cute in his baseball cap turned backward.

She gave the toy a squeak. If only she could come up with something as scrumptious to Oliver's liking as that pizza.

Or honey. She glanced down at her fingers Oliver had licked clean this morning. The dog would probably go bonkers if Alex squeezed some honey on the pizza toy.

Honey pizza . . .

Her thoughts drifted back to the sweetness she tasted on that Pizza & Pop slice. Almost baked into the crust . . .

Her hand flew to her lips as she shot up. "Oh my God. That's it!" How could she have not realized it? Honey was the last ingredient in the Pizza & Pop Shop's seasoning. Dried honey, to be specific. She'd bet all of her seasonings in her season rack on it. She gathered her things and threw on her jacket and hat, grabbing the pooch lasagna while her idea continued to form.

This could work. This could really work.

"Sloan, where are you going?" Hayden asked as she raced out of the living room and through the foyer, nearly taking out a huge coatrack.

She spun around. "Hayden, could you text Alex and have him meet me at the Pizza & Pop Shop right away?"

She raced out the door, flying down the porch stairs. When she got to the pizza place, she'd ask Colin if dried honey was the secret seasoning along with the basil and oregano.

And if that answer was yes—and she was one hundred percent sure it was going to be—she planned to ask if she could pay him a substantial amount to use the seasoning and additional royalties to come, should she win the audition.

This was going to work. She knew it.

She speed walked down the street, holding the pooch

lasagna tight. If dogs liked it, the sky would be the limit on what she could create. She could sprinkle the seasoning in and on top of other healthy sides.

Reaching the Pizza & Pop Shop, she took a deep breath and opened the glass door. Colin was alone behind the counter. "I think the last seasoning is dried honey. Dried honey, basil, and oregano. That's my final answer."

He grinned. "I knew you'd get it eventually, Sloan. Can I get you a slice?" He motioned behind him. "On the house, for the only person to figure it out in fifty years."

"Actually, there's something else I need."

She took a few minutes to fill him in. His expression was a mixture of flattered and stunned as she walked him through what she was doing and how she was confident that dogs all over America would go nuts for the seasoning. "I will make sure my agent works with Palate and their lawyers to include you as the creator of the original spice if I get the contract, and we'll pay you," she added. "There will be a lot of zeros on the check."

"Could I retire early to Florida?" He chuckled.

"Yes! Wherever you want. Florida, Costa Rica, you name it."

The front doorbells chimed, and Alex held the door open for Oliver. "Hey," he greeted her, coming up to the counter. "Hey, Colin."

"Hi," she said, barely able to contain her excitement. "Thank you so much for coming. I'm so glad you're here."

"Are you taking a break?" He unzipped his leather jacket midway. "Did you want to grab dinner?"

"Yes! I mean, no. I want to give Oliver his dinner. The one thing he loves the most." She smiled, turning back to Colin. "What do you say?"

"Let's do it." The pizza owner handed her his bottle of seasoning.

"What's going on?" Alex asked.

Sloan took the pooch casserole to a table. "So, we know what Oliver doesn't like, but we also know what he does. Your pup not only snatched my pizza, he nearly ripped off my hand that night because I had remnants of the seasoning on my fingers. Remember that?"

Alex laughed. "I remember."

She continued, so excited by this discovery. "Then this morning, when I gave him some honey, he nearly tore my fingers off again."

"Wait." A line formed across his forehead. "Why were you feeding him honey?"

"Not important to the story." She dismissed her cure for her bad breath. "And it's fine for dogs."

"So, you're going to add honey into the seasoning?" Alex asked, and she could tell he was doing his best to follow along.

"It's already in there." She lowered her voice because a family of four had come in, and she didn't want to spill any secrets. "The good people of this town have been enjoying oregano, basil, and dried honey mixed together on their pizza all these years." She grinned over at Colin. "I might be so bold as to suggest that you also butter the crust with honey butter."

"I'm not admitting anything else until I see a check," the pizza owner teased, while nevertheless nodding his head.

She couldn't stop smiling. Colin was going to be paid a pretty penny if this panned out like she hoped it would. She pulled back the lid to her pooch casserole.

The moment was here. Her moment. Her big dream could be on its way to coming true with a few sprinkles.

She sprinkled the seasoning over the dish, giving it a generous coating. Satisfied, she set it down on the floor.

Oliver looked to Alex and barked.

"Okay, go ahead, bud," he said, letting go of the leash.

The pup ran over to Sloan and lowered his head into the casserole dish, his tail moving fast and furiously as he gobbled it up.

"Finally! He likes it! Oh my God!" Sloan clapped and jumped in the air in celebration. She turned around and threw her arms around Alex. Before she knew what was happening, he'd picked her up and spun her around, her arms wrapping around his neck.

"You did it, Chef." His blue eyes locked with hers as she slid down his arms.

She could overanalyze the sweet moment later. Right now, she rejoiced in all of it.

224

"I'd say on a tail-wag meter scale, it's a hit," Colin joked, handing her a couple of bottles of seasoning. "Let me know if you need any more for your audition."

"I will." Sloan hugged the bottles to her chest. "Thank you, Colin, so, so much."

He laughed, shaking his head. "I always knew my pop's seasoning was wasted on humans."

They all laughed and continued to watch Oliver finish the casserole. When he was finally done, Sloan picked up the plate, and gave the Labradoodle an enormous hug before following Alex outside.

"Congratulations again."

"Well, I haven't won yet, but I feel really good about this." She paused. "Oh, and I have something else for my number-one taste tester."

"I don't need a present," he teased.

"It's not for you." She fished into her purse and pulled out the pizza toy and gave it to a happy Oliver. She gazed up at Alex. "He must have put it in my purse last night."

"I was wondering where it went."

After a couple of awkward, silent seconds, she motioned toward the diner. "I'm headed to Dee Dee's. Do you want to join me? I could cook us some dinner." She dropped a hand to Oliver's back. "Maybe Oliver would like some of my apple-spiced pumpkin pup pie."

"Oh." Alex glanced down at his watch. "Actually, I've got somewhere to be."

"Right. No worries. I probably should focus on my audition, anyway." She paused, studying his outfit. In all the excitement, she'd failed to compute that he'd ditched his flannel and was wearing a sweater and jeans.

She bit her lip to keep it from turning down. Did he have a date?

"So, I guess I might not see you before the audition," he said.

"Yeah, I'm headed to Boston after the lunch service. Kimmie said she'd give me a ride to the train station."

"One step closer to Paris." He smiled.

She nodded and repeated, "One step closer to Paris."

"Well, I look forward to hearing about your audition when you get back."

They said a quick goodbye that involved an awkward hug, nothing like the celebratory one in the pizza shop. Alex jogged across the street with Oliver.

"Alex," she called out spontaneously, just as he was about to get in the driver's side of his Jeep. "Thank you and Oliver for everything." She probably sounded like a crazy person, yelling across the street, but she didn't care.

"You're welcome. It's time to rock this, Chef." He grinned and headed away from Main Street.

She looked down at the casserole dish now holding the two spice bottles. She was one giant step closer to getting everything she wanted. To fulfill her promise to her grandmother.

She made her way, alone, down to the diner.

She was also headed in the wrong direction to exploring something that could have been really great.

Chapter Fifteen

S LOAN MOVED THROUGH the lobby of the Prudential Tower, confident and ready to take on the dog world. She'd gotten up three hours early to prepare her remarks.

Yesterday's meal creation had been a huge success. After leaving Alex, she'd pushed through that sadness, creating two additional sides and one dessert dish. With those, along with her turkey-pumpkin-peanut butter lasagna, she was confident she was as ready as she'd ever be.

"Sloan Leary," a slender woman in a black pantsuit, with her blond hair pulled back in a sleek ponytail, greeted her, carrying a blue padfolio the same color as the Palate logo. "I'm Vicky Wallen, chief officer for New Product Lines." She extended her hand. "Welcome to Palate."

"It's so nice to meet you." Sloan shook her hand.

"How was your trip in from Brooks Bend?" Vicky asked.

"Very nice. Such a beautiful fall day." The train ride up was simply gorgeous, especially around Rhode Island. She'd failed to pry her eyes from the window.

"And you've been there all week, Erika tells me."

Vicky's question pulled Sloan out of her photographic

memory. "Yes. Have you ever been?"

"No. I'm more of a city girl," the Palate executive admitted with a slight smirk. "I hadn't even heard of it until we shipped you your meal kit to prep for your audition."

Sloan shoved her hands in her coat pockets as Vicky excused herself to give the list of all the chefs that would be auditioning this week to the security guard.

She'd thought the same way about being a city girl only a short time ago. Her hands felt her mittens stuffed into the pockets. The ones Alex had picked out for her.

But things had changed somewhere along the week.

"Okay, Sloan. We're ready for you." Vicky waved for her to follow.

"It's time to rock this," she repeated Alex's words under her breath.

They took the elevator up to the forty-second floor while chitchatting about the Omni Parker House and Sloan finally tasting her first-ever Boston cream pie.

"I'm glad you enjoyed it." Vicky stepped off the elevator. "Did you have a chance to look over the itinerary we sent to the hotel yesterday?"

Sloan nodded. She'd spent last night curled up on her bed with not only the pie but also a basket of the Omni Parker House's famous rolls and a hearty New England clam chowder, while reading through the schedule and instructions.

She'd spend the first two hours of her audition making

her meals. Once they were plated, the judging would begin.

As she stepped off the elevator, she took in the giant PALATE bright-blue logo sign. Her heart began to pound against her rib cage.

Vicky escorted her past a sea of cubicles and offices, making a few introductions as they passed. "Our cooking studio is all the way at the end of the hall. I think you'll really enjoy cooking in it."

They stepped in and Sloan grinned. Though she was getting used to the coziness of Dee Dee's, she'd missed working in a big kitchen, and this one was spectacular, with its long cooking and prep stations and every pot, pan, and utensil imaginable.

"So, here's what's going to happen, Sloan," Vicky began. "You'll find everything you need in the refrigerator and in one of those bags on the counter over there that has your name on it." She pointed to a long row of brown bags.

Sloan quickly counted her competition. Sixteen other chefs would be vying for the contract. "Thank you so much." She removed her coat and set her purse on the counter. "Everything looks great." She paused, adding, "You received my e-mail yesterday regarding my bringing some spice, correct?"

"Yes, and that's fine." She looked over her notes. "Oregano, basil, and dried honey."

Sloan grinned, still proud she'd figured out the secret seasoning. "That's right."

"Interesting combination. Okay, I'll set the timer and leave you alone to cook. If there is an ingredient missing from the list you provided yesterday, you can call me at this number." She ripped a piece of paper out of her portfolio and scribbled on it. "But, unfortunately, we can't provide you any additional ingredients not on your list."

"I'm sure I'll be fine. Thank you so much, Vicky, for this opportunity to audition. Cooking for Palate is a real honor."

"You're welcome. I'll see you in a couple of hours with the other judges. Would you like any music before I go?" she asked. "We've got quite the sound system." She laughed. "We like to keep our chefs happy."

"I'm good, thank you." Sloan tugged her chef coat over her hips. Hayden had been a doll and not only washed it for her last night, while she was busy preparing at Dee Dee's, but ironed it too.

And her friends even got her a card. Kimmie had given it to her while dropping her off at the train station, instructing her not to open it until she began her audition or it wouldn't bring her luck.

Lucky pumpkins, lucky cards—she'd take it. She reached into her purse and pulled out the card, tearing open the envelope.

Her lips parted. It wasn't a card from everyone. She stared down at the bright-red leaf now pressed with wax paper with a note attached.

Chef, a moment for when you need it the most. Rock on!

Love, Alex and Oliver

Her pulse raced as she picked up the leaf Alex had removed from her hair that day at the animal shelter.

Just then, Vicky popped her head in. "One last check to make sure you're all set. You good, Chef Sloan?"

"Actually . . ." She grinned, knowing exactly what she needed to rock this audition. "About the music. Do you have any Air Supply?"

ALEX THREADED HIS fingers in his lap and leaned forward like he'd been instructed to do. "I've done several paid renovation jobs since returning from Iraq, and with that experience and growing up in a restaurant my entire life, I understand commercial kitchens." He took a breath, finishing his pitch. "The remodel of The Bend Inn in Brooks Bend deepened my interest in bringing old, beloved hotel kitchens into this century while preserving their historic foundation."

He smiled because he was told to end on one—a closed-lips one.

As the conversation wrapped up, he gave Chef Grant a strong handshake that he'd practiced on Sunday night with Mia's dad, looked the executive chef straight in the eye, and told him he looked forward to hearing from him soon because he was confident he was the right man for the job.

At his Jeep in the hotel parking lot minutes later, Oliver barely lifted his head in greeting.

"What did you do to my dog?" He smirked over to the passenger seat, where Mia had her laptop up and was typing away.

"One second." She read what she'd been typing out loud. "Monica left the dark and dusty attic, her bare feet creaking on the old wood. Her life was gone, but she wasn't." She turned to him, flashing a smile. "I just wanted to finish this chapter." She shut her laptop and turned to him. "I don't think your dog likes me. I suggested a walk, and he rolled over and shut his eyes."

"Did you hold up his leash?"

"Oh. Well, no." She sat back and reached for her seat belt. "How did the interview go?"

"I think it went well. Thank you again for helping me prepare." He started up the Jeep and backed out.

"Did you remember to smile at the end?"

He blinked. "I forgot."

"Alex."

"I'm kidding." He exited the parking garage onto the busy street. "Thanks again for coming."

"You're welcome." She shot him a smile. "I'm just in it for the dinner I won."

He laughed. They'd had a good chuckle over that, since he was more of a one-course kind of guy.

His phone began to vibrate in his jacket pocket. He

touched his Jeep's media screen to accept it.

"Hey, Alex. It's Grant Watson."

"Hi," he said, a little taken aback. He hadn't expected to hear from the chef so soon.

"Listen, I forgot to ask for references. I have one from Sloan Leary, but could I get two more by the end of tomorrow?"

Sloan was my reference? He sat at the red light, trying to compute what Chef Grant had said. How? When? Why? A loud horn from behind him slammed all those questions to the corner of his mind. He put his foot on the accelerator. "Uh, yeah. I mean, of course, I'd be happy to send you those."

"Great. Really look forward to keeping the conversation going, Alex."

"Me too. Thank you."

"Everything okay?" Mia asked, as Alex ended the call.

"Yeah." How was it possible that Sloan was his reference? Had she been the one to learn about the job and referred him? He hadn't actually confirmed that it was Hayden's dad.

Had Sloan even seen his final work at the inn? His pulse began to race. She must have. "Sloan was one of my references."

"That's so nice."

Yeah, it was. Why had Sloan done it? He pondered that question while making his way out of the city.

Mia's hands clapping pulled him out of his thoughts.

"We should celebrate."

"Uh . . . yeah. Although . . . it might be a bit premature. I don't have the job yet."

"You will. If they're ready to check references, it's yours."

He continued down the street. He didn't have experience in the job offer department, but this felt good.

Really good.

"What do you have in mind?" he asked.

"Hmmm . . ." She snapped her fingers. "The Mulled Wine and S'mores event is tonight."

He sat, silent. Sloan had wanted to go to that event, but wouldn't be getting back until later tonight. He couldn't help but wonder how her audition was going. Yesterday he'd pressed one of the leaves like his aunt had taught him and dropped it off to Kimmie with a card.

When Sloan had invited him to dinner Sunday night outside the Pizza & Pop Shop, he'd nearly said yes, but knew that he seriously needed the help prepping for his interview.

He'd made the card to show that he was rooting for her.

"Unless you don't want to go," Mia said, probably sensing his hesitation.

"Uh . . . yeah. I'm sorry." He stopped at a red light and turned his head toward Mia. She'd been so supportive, helping last night, not to mention offering to watch Oliver while he went into his interview. "Sounds like fun. Let's do it."

SLOAN SHOOK THE hands of the first three judges and then bent down to pet a cute little Boston terrier named Sox—the final judge with a big vote.

"Okay, Sloan." Vicky turned to her. "Please reveal your main meal, your two sides, and your dessert. You have five minutes and then we'll begin the taste test. Later on, there will be another round of taste testing with more dogs."

Sloan took a deep, slow breath. It's been an amazing two hours. She'd flown through the kitchen, putting her entire Puppy Palate meal together.

And now she was ready to begin.

"Thank you, everyone," she started, flashing her brightest smile. "It's such a privilege to come in and cook in your kitchen. When my agent came to my restaurant and told me the good news that I had been selected to audition for Palate, to say I was ecstatic was an understatement."

She grinned over at Sox. "When I learned that, ultimately, my meals would be going into furry bellies . . . well, let's just say, I wasn't sure if I had what it took."

She gazed down at the pressed leaf still on the table. "But I had the amazing opportunity to spend the week with my new friend, Oliver, a sweet Labradoodle who loves nothing more than snatching pizza right out of your hands.

"He and some other wonderful dogs that I had the chance to spend time with showed me that our fur babies aren't only lovable and cute. They work relentlessly each and every day of the year, never taking a break, wanting the very best for their humans, especially during this majestic season of the year.

"They are at the ready to fetch toys in the cool fall air; to snuggle up right beside you on cold autumn nights; and to jump in freshly fallen foliage, giving each leaf one last hurrah at life.

"Dogs work darned hard, dedicated to their owners. They deserve one day of the year enjoying a meal that is made for and celebrates them for all the love they bring into the lives and homes of their owners."

She waved her hands, displaying her plates. "It's my honor today to present to you Pupsgiving by Chef Sloan Leary, celebrating all of our dogs who love us so much."

It was time to rock this.

"First, I have a pumpkin-turkey lasagna with whipped peanut butter." She showed off the rectangular dish. "For the two sides"—she pointed to the dishes—"you'll find a sweet potato-stuffing-crust turkey pup pie and a cinnamon-butternut squash soup, finished off with a swirly tail of ginger and maple syrup." She moved along the counter to the final plate and picked up one of the barks. "And finally, for dessert, apple-spiced pumpkin bark."

She stepped back and watched as the plates were set down for Sox to taste. She tried to contain her excitement as the Boston terrier went straight for the butternut squash soup, slurping it up before attacking the turkey lasagna and then the turkey pup pie.

"I think it's safe to say Sox approves." Vicky clapped her hands and handed Sox a small piece of the dessert bark to finish his taste test. The other judges moved along the display, rating both Sloan's presentation display of the food as well as tasting it.

"That spice combination is really incredible," Vicky remarked, touching her lips. "Sweet and flavorful."

"I know," she said as Sox barked for more.

"I think our lead judge has spoken," Vicky said, and they all had a good laugh.

As the audition wrapped up, Vicky escorted Sloan to the elevators. "Thank you again for coming in. We will be in contact with all the chefs by the end of the week with our selection."

"Perfect. Thank you." Sloan extended her hand. "It's truly an honor to be considered."

"Enjoy your trip back to Brooks Bend."

"I will. If you ever get out there, stop into Dee Dee's Diner and order her chocolate pecan pie. You won't regret it." Sloan made her way to the elevator.

"Oh, Sloan. I forgot to ask. If you do get the contract, we'd need you in New England for a substantial amount of time for the product rollout and national promotion. We know your restaurant is in San Francisco. Is a temporary relocation something you'd consider?"

She blinked. *I'd get to come back for an extended period of time?* "Definitely."

She said a final goodbye and, after a quick trip back to the hotel via a taxi to pick up her luggage, she made her way to South Station, where she quickly realized she had enough time to make an earlier train that would get her in just after five p.m.

That would mean she might not have to miss the Mulled Wine and S'mores event after all. She made her way to the counter to see if there were any available seats.

In minutes, she was nestled on the train, heading back to Brooks Bend. She stared out the window as the train made its way out of Boston.

Today had been a great day.

She was confident that she had a shot at being awarded the contract. She reached inside her purse for her phone to call Erika, her fingers touching the pressed leaf.

She smiled as she pulled it out and twirled it. It was wrong to feel this way because, at this very moment, Alex could be beginning a new relationship with Mia. Still, this leaf and all of his support meant something.

If there was a chance that he might feel anything for her, she had to . . .

She glanced down at the leaf, butterflies starting to kick up in her stomach. Well, she had to try, because there was simply no way a day that was going this well could possibly end badly.

Chapter Sixteen

ALEX ENTERED THE inn with Oliver, shutting the door behind him. He'd meant to be here at the start of the event but had gotten preoccupied at the diner finishing up the remaining tasks on his aunt's to-do list and had lost track of time.

"Hey. How did your interview go?" Hayden greeted him, her arms full of marshmallow bags, one dropping to the floor.

"Good, I think. I should hear back soon." He picked up the bag and held it up. "Big crowd, I take it?"

"Everyone and their mother is here. We ran out of marshmallows. Earl just dropped these off." She handed a bag to Alex. "Here. Take a bag. The graham crackers and chocolate bars are outside in containers by each fire pit. Help yourself to some mulled wine."

"Don't mind if I do." He crossed the room to the coffee bar that held a large Crock-Pot full of mulled wine. He reached for the ladle and filled a cup. "Hey, is Sloan back?"

"Not yet. At least I don't think she is. Unless she's upstairs." She paused. "Why do you ask?"

"No reason. Just wondering how her interview went." He'd considered calling her this afternoon when he thought she'd be on the train but didn't want to bother her in case it didn't go well. "Is Mia outside?"

Hayden nodded. "She's been here for more than an hour."

"Oh, man." They hadn't agreed on a set time, but he should have made it a point to be here at the start of the event. That was a bonehead move. "I was at the diner, finishing up some work for Aunt Dee Dee, and lost track of time."

"Are you two getting back together?" Hayden asked, handing off the marshmallow bags to one of the inn's staff who passed by.

He took a sip of his wine. That was a good question. To an outsider, it might look that way. The problem was, he wasn't quite sure he was feeling it. "I don't know. I had dinner with her and her parents at their house on Sunday and that was nice. We agreed to meet up tonight to celebrate my interview." He paused, adding, "I get the sense she wants to start over."

"And do you?" Hayden asked, inching up an eyebrow.

He dropped his gaze to Oliver. "Maybe . . ."

"That sounds promising."

He lifted his chin to her sarcasm. Pathetic was what it sounded like. "I mean . . . it's been great spending a little time together this week, and, well, you know, we have history. If she's interested in getting back together, don't I owe it to her to explore the possibility?"

Hayden placed a hand on his shoulder. "Who you owe is yourself. You deserve to be with a woman that can make you happy."

"I think I could be happy with Mia again," he said, biting his bottom lip. It being a total toss-up if he was trying to convince Hayden or himself.

She gave him a smug look.

"What?" he asked.

"Nothing. Maybe give some thought to who you asked about first tonight."

"Who, Sloan?" He shrugged, taking another sip of the wine. There was no way he'd admit to Hayden his crush on a woman that would be on the other side of the country in a few days. "The spices in the wine made me think of her. That's all. I was just curious to how her audition went."

"Uh-huh." Before Hayden could say another word, a high-pitched scream from outside came through the inn. "Honestly, I didn't know that this event needed to come with 'Marshmallow Roasting 101' lessons. How hard is it to not put your stick all the way into the fire?"

Alex chuckled and followed his friend out back to see one of the half a dozen bonfires set up across the yard, the first a bit out of control with orange flames rising high.

He caught sight of Mia sitting alone by a smaller bonfire off to the side.

Guilt crept up the back of his neck. He really should have been here much earlier or sent her a text. He made his way over.

"Hi," he said, taking a seat next to her on a long log, instructing Oliver to lie by his side away from the fire.

"Hey, you." She turned, flashing a wide grin. "I was wondering if you'd stood me up."

"Never." He reached for a stick on the ground next to the chocolate and graham crackers container and opened the marshmallow bag. "I'm sorry I'm late," he added. "You look really nice."

"Thank you." She tugged on her heavy beige sweater and then took a marshmallow he offered, spearing it with her stick. "I found it in my parents' attic. Do you remember it?"

He glanced over. "Should I?"

"Your aunt made it for me for my seventeenth birthday. You were going to take me skiing, and she wanted me to have something warm to wear."

He laughed, now remembering. It'd been a fun afternoon at a ski resort not too far from here, teaching his frightened girlfriend how to go down the bunny slope. "I remember you falling quite a bit."

"I fell really hard that day." Her gaze met his and stayed there. "It was the first time I told you I loved you."

Oh, wow. She really was soaring down memory lane. He touched her sleeve, joking, "My aunt may have missed her calling as a warm wool sweater designer."

Mia grinned and began to roast her marshmallow, and he did the same, suddenly at a loss for words.

He moved his gaze over to Mia, the orange flames casting a glow over her pretty face as she desperately tried to blow out the fire on her marshmallow, but with little luck.

"Here. Let me help you with that." He reached for her stick. Tonight wasn't about giving her a ride home from the Wishbone Wishes event or her helping him ace an interview. It was about their spending time together. A night to enjoy each other's company while remembering happier moments between them.

She was all in. He should be too.

"THANK YOU SO much, Kimmie." Sloan got out of the passenger side and waved goodbye, carrying her suitcase up the inn's steps. The front door flew open, and a couple stepped out, talking and laughing.

She rushed inside and set her suitcase behind the check-in counter, hoping she hadn't missed the event. She'd changed into a sweater and jeans on the train so as to not waste time getting ready.

Approaching the coffee bar, she stopped to pour herself some mulled wine and took a sip.

Fennel seed. "I would have gone with star anise." No matter. It was still delicious.

"Hey, you. How was your audition?" Hayden came over to greet her, looking all cute with her blond ponytail pulled back by a pumpkin-orange wool headband.

"Great." Sloan smoothed her hair that she'd decided to leave down for tonight. "The judges seemed to like everything I presented." She laughed, adding, "Including the four-legged one. I really think I have a chance."

"That's fantastic. Congratulations. We're all rooting for you."

"Thank you." Sloan took another sip of her wine. Today had been fantastic, and she really hoped tonight would end just as well.

Speaking of which . . . The butterflies that had hitched a ride in her stomach on the train ride back to Brooks Bend began to take flight again.

"Is Alex here?" she asked, following Hayden out the back door.

"Sloan, about that . . ."

She glanced past Hayden at the backyard, set up with twinkling white lights and scattered fire pits, with everyone talking merrily and appearing to be having a blast.

Her gaze landed on Mia and Alex sitting close together on a log, laughing while they roasted their marshmallows.

Hayden touched her arm. "It's not what you think."

The butterflies fell to the bottom of her stomach and turned upside down. "That Alex and Mia are on the road to getting back together."

"It's not happening." Hayden shook her head. "He's gotten swept up in old feelings. When the tide settles, she'll go her way and he'll go his."

Sloan pressed her lips together. Try as she might, she couldn't look away. How could she have been ready mere minutes ago to confess to Alex that she'd developed feelings for him? "I think I'm going to call it a night," she finally said, turning to go back inside.

"No." Hayden reached for her arm. "Come sit with Earl and me."

"I'm good, but thank you." She waved over to Earl, not wanting to be rude. "I really should get to bed. I want to go into the diner early tomorrow."

"C'mon," Hayden pleaded. "Have one s'more with us."

"Maybe some other time." Sadness washed over her. There would be no "other time," because this wasn't her home.

Her gaze fell on Alex. She didn't belong here, and there was no reason to ever come back.

What she'd romanticized in her head had been silly, and the clear proof that her feelings were one-sided was less than twenty feet away. "I'll see you tomorrow, Hayden."

She turned but didn't get more than five feet when sudden paws to her back caused her to be thrust forward. She fell on all fours on the grass, her cup of mulled wine spilling all over her jeans in the process.

She closed her eyes for a beat. So much for a graceful ex-it. She flipped over and greeted Oliver, giving him a hug.

"Looks like someone doesn't want you to leave," Hayden quipped, nodding ever so slightly at Alex, who was now walking toward them.

"Hey, I'm sorry." He offered his hand.

Sloan slipped her hand in his, his touch sending tingles up her arm as he hoisted her up. "Thank you. He probably just smells food from my audition. My hands probably smell like the pizza seasoning. I should have taken a shower. I'm going to do that right now. Um . . . get the dog food scent off me before other dogs in the neighborhood chase me down." She spun around and squeezed her eyes tight.

Way to sound like a babbling fool.

"How'd everything go with Puppy Palate?"

She turned back around. He wanted to know about her audition. Given his dog had been a big part of it, she at least owed him an update. "Good. I mean . . . I won't hear until the end of the week, but the judges seemed to like what I prepared."

"That's awesome. I bet you'll get it."

She smiled. "I think I have a good shot." They stood in silence for a beat and then another, but Alex wasn't making any move to return to his log. "I see you took my advice," she finally said, nodding to Mia.

"Yeah." He shoved his hands in his pockets. "It's kind of weird. I mean, it's nice. I guess it's just strange after all these years."

Right. The reminder that the two had history. "Um . . . I should let you get back to your date. I mean . . . I should go." She turned and headed for the back door.

"Chef?"

She glanced over her shoulder. "Yeah."

Alex closed the distance she'd created between them. "I'm going to be making my four-course meal for Mia on Saturday. I was kind of hoping you might help me? I'd really like to try my hand at something that isn't served with ketchup on the side."

She couldn't help but smile at that request. She'd probably regret what she was about to offer. "I'm happy to help. We could . . . I don't know . . . go grocery shopping together. Kick around some recipes."

"Thank you. I'd like that . . . the help, I mean. I've got some things to do for Bill as we finish up the library tomorrow and Thursday, but maybe we could go to the farmer's market in the square Friday morning."

"Uh . . ." She froze, processing his words. He wouldn't be around the diner for two whole days. She forced herself to respond. "Friday morning would be terrific. I have to stop at the Belle & Beau to pick up a gift for my agent. Want to meet there, say, at nine thirty?"

"Great." He clapped his leg for Oliver to rise. "Well, I should probably get back."

"Right. Of course." She shoved her hands in her coat pockets. "Have a good night, Alex."

"You too."

Her chest tightened as Alex made his way back to Mia with Oliver. How could she have let herself fall in love with that wonderful man and his adorable Labradoodle?

Love.

She let that sink in. She could deny it all she wanted, but that is exactly what had happened.

She watched as Alex dropped down next to Mia, handing her a marshmallow. What awful timing for her heart to make that declaration.

Chapter Seventeen

S LOAN SET THE pretty cranberry-red hat and mittens on the counter and reached inside her purse for her wallet, pulling out her credit card. "My agent's going to love these."

"It's the last set I have in that color. I'm glad you grabbed them." Gwen wrapped the items in tissue and handed the bag to Sloan. "Thanks for coming in. I hope to see you again before you leave."

"I'm afraid this is the last time. I go home on Sunday," Sloan said, just as Alex walked by the boutique while talking on his phone, a dark-blue backpack slung over his shoulder. He caught her eye and motioned with his finger that he'd be a minute.

"This town grew on you, didn't it?" Gwen gave her a knowing wink.

"It did," she admitted.

It'd been a long two days since the Mulled Wine and S'mores event, where she agreed to meet up with Alex to visit the farmer's market for the ingredients he needed for his special date with Mia.

True to his word, he hadn't come around the diner. If he

had, she may have tried to get out of it.

However, last night, she'd realized if she didn't go, she may never see him again. He'd been so wonderful, helping her in the diner and with the Puppy Palate audition, thanking him and saying a proper goodbye was the right thing to do.

Even if it would break her heart.

She said a final farewell to Gwen, promising a meal on her if Gwen ever made it out to San Francisco, then stepped outside. "Hey," she greeted Alex once he ended his call, the fall breeze whipping through her hair.

"Hey, there."

"And hello, Oliver. I have something for you for being my Pupsgiving by Sloan Leary inspiration." She reached into her purse and pulled out some of the pumpkin bark. "I know it's not pizza, but I think you'll like it."

"Pupsgiving, huh?" Alex waggled his eyebrows.

"It just came to me in the moment." She looked down at Oliver. "I think your dog would have liked my presentation."

"I know he would have. I'm sorry we didn't get to really talk the other night. I'd love to hear about it."

She smiled. She'd had some time to process the evening and what she'd seen with her own two eyes, which was Alex on his way to getting back together with Mia.

She filled Alex in as they walked down the sidewalk toward the daily farmer's market in the square. "I even requested Air Supply be played on their sound system while I was cooking."

He laughed. "I knew you'd come around."

"So, how can I help with your menu?" she asked as they made their way into the park and toward the various fruit and vegetable stands.

"I've got most everything I need, but realized I only had three courses—the salad, entrée, and dessert. I forgot about the starter course and have no idea what to make." He picked up a tomato and tossed it. "Can I just go right to the salad?"

"No!" She shook her head. It didn't matter who he was cooking it for, she wasn't going to let him skip the most important part, as far as she was concerned. "The starter course sets the stage for the entire meal."

"Seriously? Isn't it an appetizer to tide you over before the entrée?"

"That's what most people think." She picked up a red onion. "But it's so much more. It's like the pre-game show or the opening act at a concert—it's a burst of culinary flavors for your taste buds. A promise that they'll get more."

"A promise for more." His gaze rested on hers.

"Yes." She pressed her lips together. "Mia's going to love it."

He broke their gaze, shoving his hands in his leather coat pockets. "So, I guess my infamous pigs in a blanket wouldn't work?"

"Yuck." She gave his arm a swat. "Your date will not be

eating processed meat in store-bought crescent rolls." She made her way over to the vegetable stand, picking up a yellow butternut squash. "I've got a simple starter dish that's perfect for a fall four-course menu—a butternut squash roasted ravioli with a dripped honey-sage browned butter. It's my favorite."

"That sounds complicated. I think I'll go with the pigs in a blanket." He grinned down at Oliver. "Sound good, buddy?"

Oliver barked.

"As much as I love your dog, I don't think he should be your dinner consultant. No offense, Oliver." She petted his head. "It's not hard to make. You aunt has some ravioli in her pantry, and I could hook you up with some of my ground sage."

"Thank you," he said, taking the butternut squash. "Are you excited to cook *your* dinner tonight, because Hayden can't stop talking about it."

She nodded. "It's all prepped. The dessert has been baked, and I'll be working after the lunch service on the rest. Although I could use a few more tomatoes." She inspected the ones a few feet away.

She was determined for this dinner to be a lot of fun for Hayden.

"You can use one of my bags if you'd like." Alex unzipped his backpack, pulling out a reusable bag from the small stack he'd brought with him. He handed it over to her.

"Be the person your dog thinks you are," she read out loud the words on the bag that also had a loveable picture of Oliver on it.

"Aunt Dee Dee had a bunch of them made up for me last year for Christmas. I think it's her way of keeping me in line."

She laughed. "Probably. I'm really looking forward to meeting Dee Dee in person."

"Not long now. I'm picking her up at the train station and bringing her right to the diner."

They made their way through the farmer's market, Sloan stopping to admire a stand with the most beautiful bouquets. She settled on the only one left made up of mostly bright-yellow and orange sunflowers. It would be a perfect center-piece for the dinner table.

"Sunflowers are my favorite," Sloan said. "My grand-mother once told me they represent unconditional love." She tapped it to Oliver's nose. "Like a dog," she teased. "They are at the ready to bring you happiness when you need it the most."

She glanced up to see Alex with a strange expression on his face, so she added quickly, "You should get these for Mia," she said, hurling the bouquet into his chest.

"Oh, I don't think . . ."

"It's fine. I bet she'll love them. I'll pick out something else." She reached for a beautiful assortment. "These lilies will be perfect for Hayden."

"Let me get those too." As Alex paid the woman behind the table, Sloan pretended to be fascinated by all the different varieties of apples available.

Maybe everything was happening for the best. Alex deserved to be happy, and Mia deserved flowers that represented unconditional love. She watched as he attempted to put the sunflowers in one of his bags, having all sorts of trouble.

"Here. Let me help." She pulled open the bag.

"Thank you." They proceeded out of the park in the direction of the diner. "So, when do you hear from Palate?" he finally asked.

Good question. She'd been checking her phone constantly. "They told me they'd be in touch by the end of the week, but so far, nothing. I'm assuming they'll call my agent first and share the news with her."

"Oliver and I are rooting for you."

"Thank you." She grinned down at Oliver, who took that as a sign to jump on her, paws to her chest. "And thank you too." She gave the pup what she suspected was one last hug.

"I've got some news too," he said as they exited the farmer's market, crossing the street.

She glanced up. "What's that?"

"Last week, I got the strangest call about a commercial remodel job in Manhattan. You wouldn't happen to know anything about it?"

Oh, shoot. She stopped in her tracks. He did get a call. Why hadn't he mentioned it? "Um . . ."

He cocked his head. "Apparently, a big-time chef in San Francisco recommended me."

Okay, she was busted. "I don't know if I'm big-time." She rested her gaze on him. He didn't look upset. That was a good sign. "I'm sorry, Alex. I should have told you I recommended you. When you didn't say anything, I wasn't sure if Grant even called you. I mean, he said he was going to, but you never know."

"Why did you recommend me?" he asked, his voice dropping.

He was upset. "I didn't mean to overstep. Hayden showed me the inn's kitchen. It's some of the best work I've ever seen." She paused, adding, "I sent a couple of pictures around to this executive chef's social media group I belong to. We're all alumni of the Culinary Exchange program. Grant reached out right away with his opportunity. I'm sorry."

"No, it's fine, and thank you. It was just a surprise to get the call out of the blue like that."

She parted her lips, afraid to ask the question. "Did you get the job?"

He smiled. "I got it. I got the call last night. I start after Thanksgiving."

"Oh, Alex, that's wonderful." She touched his shoulder. "I'm so happy for you."

"It's a big step, but I think I'm ready."

"I know you are." Just then, a group of men headed into the diner, one of them hanging back to catch up with Alex for a second.

She stood off to the side, waiting to say her own good-bye. How about that? Alex had gotten the job.

Her heart couldn't help but tick up. Maybe she hadn't gotten *everything* she wanted, but this outcome was high up there. Alex was on a new path to doing incredible things and deserved every bit of the success coming to him.

She had no doubt The Langley gig would lead to others, especially in a city as large and connected as New York City.

That she had something to do with it made her smile. Sometimes people came into your life for a short time for a reason and maybe they'd reached their conclusion—an end that would send them both on exciting new paths.

"Well, I guess I should go back in and help Tom and Justine with lunch service," she finally said, when Alex turned back to her. Her throat thickened, causing her voice to crack. "Goodbye, Alex."

"I'll see you tomorrow."

She lifted her chin, her gaze meeting his, causing her pulse to quicken. "You will?"

"When I drop off my aunt."

"Oh, yes, right. I'll see you tomorrow then." Before she could talk herself out of it, she threw her arms around him. "Thank you so much for everything. I truly can't thank you enough." She stepped back, her cheeks, no doubt, red, but she didn't care. "I didn't want to do that in front of your aunt."

She seemed to have rendered him speechless. Just then, Tom came out with a question for Alex.

She bent down, petting Oliver behind his ears. "You take good care of him." She nuzzled his fluffy ear, whispering, "Please, make sure his heart doesn't get broken."

The dog licked her cheek.

She patted his head. "I knew I could count on you."

Alex finished his conversation, and she stood. "Bye, Alex." She turned to leave.

"Wait. You forgot Hayden's flowers."

She spun around. "Thank you." Taking them, her gaze rested on the sunflowers still in his bag. Her favorite flower that would be given to Mia.

"I'll see you tomorrow, Sloan."

"See you." Her heart split in two as she made her way through the dining room and pulled out a stool, plopping down. That was the first time Alex had called her by her first name and not Chef.

"You okay?" Justine asked. Reaching for the coffeepot, she poured Sloan a cup.

Tears began to run down her cheeks. She brushed a few away and lowered her head. "I just really liked that dog."

Justine came around the counter, resting her hand on Sloan's back. "Why don't we go into the kitchen and whip

of humor. Hayden and Todd talked, joked, and took pictures with Sloan in between the four courses. It'd been a nice night.

Sloan smiled at the empty champagne flute glasses still on the table.

And speaking of champagne, there were still two bottles in the refrigerator. True to her word, all the cooking had been done at the diner, but Hayden had said Sloan could use the refrigerator.

It'd be fun to toast Dee Dee when she arrived, so Sloan made her way into the kitchen to grab the bottles.

Her heart slammed into her chest while her feet froze in the doorway at the sight on the counter. Four familiar grocery bags, each with a picture of Oliver on the front.

Why are Alex's grocery bags here?

Had he dropped these off late last night?

"Oh my, God." *Her hand flew to her mouth.* Was he cooking his dinner for Mia *here*?

No. The kitchen wasn't to be used until Christmas. "For a really special occasion," she whispered Hayden's words from last week when she'd given Sloan a tour.

Hayden had seemed to be "#TeamSloan," but Alex *was* her best friend. Had she given him permission to make his meal here?

That horrible thought spurred her into action. She opened the refrigerator and grabbed the bottles before turning on her heels.

She crept back up the stairs into her room, where she picked up her suitcase and threw it on the bed, flinging it open. Yanking open the top dresser drawer, she grabbed all her clothes in one sweep, bringing them over to the bed and throwing them in.

There was no way she was staying here tonight with the very likely possibility that Alex would be downstairs cooking his four-course meal, let alone enjoying it with his date.

Minutes later, she threw on her coat and headed down the staircase with her packed suitcase and the smaller one with her spices. Hayden hadn't returned, so Sloan didn't need to make up some stupid excuse as to why she was checking out early.

She'd work her shift and then head to the train station. She could spend the night at a hotel in the city.

Maybe get a last-minute ticket for a Broadway show or something.

She took a deep breath, determined to put as much distance between her and the inn as possible. She crossed the street and made her way down the sidewalk, reaching the diner, when her phone buzzed.

Erika. Sloan unlocked the front door and maneuvered her two suitcases in, flipping on the lights while accepting the video call.

"Oh, good. You're up."

"I'm at work. The better question is, why are you awake?" She cocked her head. It was two a.m. in San Francisco.

"Lucas and I were ice-skating last night with his son and daughter, and I was trying to bring back my old school Nancy Kerrigan spin to impress the kids—you know, the one where I extend my leg."

"Wait. Rewind that. Who is Lucas?"

"The coffee guy. The one who took me to the cornfield."

Despite her own broken heart, Sloan grinned, glad to see the coffee guy was still around. "You didn't tell me he has kids."

"Six and eight. I wanted to impress them and ended up in the hospital."

Sloan's eyes went wide. "Are you okay? Is there anything I can do?" The answer was probably "no," her being so far away and all, but she had to ask.

"No, I'm fine. The doctor said I got a mild concussion when my head hit the ice. My point is, Palate called while I was at the ice rink, but my phone was off."

Sloan's heart began to race. "They did. What did they say?"

"You won! Sloan, they loved you. You are the signature chef for their Puppy Palate line!"

"Oh my gosh!" Sloan touched her cheek.

"You smoked the competition. They want to get started right away. I'm going to work on the contract next week, and yes, before you ask, I got your e-mail about the seasoning, and we will work in payment to the pizza shop owner."

"This is amazing." Sloan basked in this moment, doing a twirl and then another. So what if it was barely dawn? It was a moment and a feeling she'd remember for the rest of her life. "Thank you so much for all of your encouragement, Erika. I couldn't have done any of this without you."

"You're welcome. Paris, baby!"

She stopped mid-twirl. *Paris.* The enormity of what just happened hit her, and the tears came down fast.

"Sloan, you've worked so hard. Your grandmother would be so proud."

"I know." She reached for a napkin out of a booth dispenser, dabbing her eyes.

"The Palate team will be in touch with you after we finalize the contract. They'd like you to be in Boston shortly after the new year for six months. I can work on getting you some temporary housing. We'll find you a cute place in Back Bay."

Six months. Vicky had said they'd want their chef to be in Boston for a temporary relocation, but she hadn't realized it would be half a year.

"Okay, I'm going to go back to bed. Have a safe flight tomorrow. I'll see you when you get back."

"Talk to you later, and please take care of yourself." Sloan ended the call fist-pumping the air. She rolled her suitcases into the kitchen and set them off to the side as she flipped on the lights.

Her gaze moved to the wall where she'd fallen asleep in

Alex's arms. Could things have been different if Alex knew she was coming back to New England for a much longer stay?

ALEX GLANCED AT himself in the Belle & Beau Boutique's long mirror and grimaced.

"You look so handsome." Gwen came up beside him, patting his shoulders.

Thirty minutes ago, she had squealed when he'd come into her shop, asking if she could help him pick out a suit jacket and tie. He wanted to look nice for tonight's dinner date. He also didn't want to wear his ill-fitting suit jacket that he'd worn for his interview earlier in the week.

Gwen had flown behind the counter, not stopping until she'd selected a handful of jackets and ties.

He glanced again in the mirror and tugged on the skinny red tie that made him look like a preppy nerd going to a Christmas party. "I'm not sure about this one. It's so bright." He glanced down at Oliver. "Should I go with it?"

Oliver made a sound and brought his paws over his eyes.

Alex laughed. "Yep. I thought the same thing."

"I've got a couple more colors in the back. Hold on a second." Gwen disappeared into her storage room.

He hadn't realized how difficult it would be to select a jacket and tie. He undid the red one and laid it back on the table with the others.

His gaze landed on the next table filled with hats and mittens.

He smiled, picking up a pair of burgundy mittens, the same color as the ones he'd chosen for Sloan.

He set them down while his thoughts raced back to yesterday outside the diner. That hug of hers had knocked all the words out of him for a split second. He chalked it up to being a little sad that she was leaving.

That's all it was. She was a cool woman that he'd enjoyed getting to know. He'd see her later today for a final goodbye when he dropped off his aunt.

"Okay, Alex. What do you think of either of these?" Gwen came up beside him, holding up a mustard-yellow tie and a burgundy one. He immediately went for the burgundy.

But first, he needed a second opinion. "What do you think, buddy? Do you like this one?"

Oliver sat up and barked, causing both Gwen and him to laugh.

"I think we have a winner." Alex slid the tie around his neck and tied it like his aunt had taught him. "It's perfect."

Chapter Nineteen

S LOAN PICKED UP a dishrag, wiping down the prep table. With the last burger sent out of the kitchen ten minutes ago, she'd called it a wrap. Her time at the diner had reached its end.

"Sloan, can you come here a minute?" Justine asked from the service station. "We've got a customer out here that says his burger tastes funny."

"Tastes funny?" Sloan scrunched her face.

"Did you spice it up for your grand hurrah?" Justine raised an accusatory eyebrow.

"If I did, it would taste much better." Curious as to who was complaining, she tossed the dishrag and followed Justine out the double doors.

Her eyes went wide at the sight of the diner full of customers on their feet. All of them started clapping.

For me? She glanced at Justine. "What's going on?"

"We wanted to give you a proper send-off. We know it wasn't easy when you first arrived, but you quickly won us all over."

Aw shucks. Sloan stood, feeling a little awkward, but this was way better than chasing truckers out the diner's door for not eating her saffron chicken.

Justine continued, "And so you don't forget us, we wanted to give you this." The waitress handed her a picture frame.

Sloan smiled down at the picture of Justine, Tom, Alex, and her from the face-off, Alex and her with their backs to each other, both of their arms crossed. "I will cherish this always."

Justine wasn't done. "We also have this for you."

Sloan laughed out loud at the bottle of ketchup with a giant blue bow around it. "I will put this in my kitchen and . . ."

"Never use it," Tom finished her sentence. "We know." He gave her a hug. "It was an honor to cook with you, Chef."

Her eyes began to water. "The honor was all mine. I will miss all of you, but I know starting next week, every belly will be much happier eating the meals made by Dee Dee's hands."

Sloan spent the next thirty minutes in the dining room, saying goodbye to all the customers who continued to mill about and taking some fun selfies with several of them.

She finally sauntered into the kitchen and fist-pumped the air.

I did it. She'd won the Palate contract, and she survived a culinary exchange that had thrown her for a loop.

Her gaze rested on the bowl she'd put Alex's pumpkin seeds in, a few seeds remaining. She slid them into her purse.

They'd eventually get thrown away, but not today.

The bell ringing caused her to jump. "I'm sorry. The kitchen is closed."

"Even for the owner?"

"Dee Dee!" She dashed out of the kitchen. "I can't believe you're here."

The old woman came over, giving Sloan a huge hug. The kind of embrace that, on contact, reminded her of her grandmother's.

"It's so nice to finally meet you in person. How was your trip home?" Sloan gazed around the dining room for Alex, who'd said he'd be dropping his aunt off, but he was nowhere to be seen.

"It was good. It's great to be home."

"I've got a surprise." Sloan moved back into the kitchen as Dee Dee caught up with Justine and Tom.

She cut the cheesecake she'd prepared into four slices, warmed up the caramel sauce, and finished each slice off with her special seasoning. With Justine's help, they brought the dessert into the dining room with four full flutes of champagne.

Dee Dee's eyes lit up. "What's all this, dear?"

"I wanted to celebrate," Sloan said, as she and Justine passed around the beverages and plates.

"You didn't have to do this," Dee Dee said, admiring the

cheesecake and then winking at Sloan. "But I'm so glad you did."

Sloan held up her flute. "So, when I first stepped off the train and saw the BROOKS BEND sign, I thought for a second about turning around and getting on the next plane back to San Francisco. Then when I tried to get the town to embrace my spice cooking . . ." Her gaze moved to Tom and Justine. "Well, let's just say your amazing staff had been given the gift of enough time to sharpen their crossword puzzle skills to win any tournament."

They all got a chuckle out of that.

She continued, "With everyone's help, and especially your nephew's, I quickly realized how much this diner is the heartbeat of this town, and everything you cook sustains it. Wherever the future takes me, I only hope that I mean as much to my customers and my community as you mean to Brooks Bend." She turned to Dee Dee, the old woman's gaze glossing over.

"You told me it was not how I started, but how I finished that mattered. As I wrap up today, I truly hope I lived up to your hope for me and thank you for giving me these two weeks. I'll cherish my time here always." She raised her glass. "To Dee Dee and this amazing diner."

Dee Dee held up her glass, tears streaming down her face. "To Sloan for making this old woman's dream come true."

They cheered and dug into their cheesecake, while chatting and reliving their time in each other's restaurants. Sloan thoroughly enjoyed hearing how Connor had shown Dee Dee how to salsa dance in between shifts.

"You know . . ." Sloan took another bite. "Your nephew also likes to have a good time in the kitchen. He rocked out to Air Supply while making his APOPs." She showed Dee Dee the framed picture Justine and Tom had given her.

Dee Dee could only laugh. "He told me all about his having the opportunity to bring out his legendary meal."

Sloan raised an eyebrow. "Do you like it?"

"Not so much." She rested her hand on Sloan's. "Don't tell him, though. It would break his heart."

"I promise the secret will go with me back to San Francisco."

"Speaking of San Francisco, I brought back some of your city's amazing coffee. Let me brew some up. I'll get the fancy cups out from the storage room."

While Dee Dee did just that, Sloan got up and began to gather her things. She couldn't help but pause in front of the booth that she had sat in with Alex the night she'd shared why opening up a restaurant in Paris was so important to her.

"Are you taking off now?" Dee Dee came over to her with two mugs.

"I thought I'd take the train into Manhattan tonight and see some of Times Square before I leave, but I have time for coffee." She sat down in the booth and Dee Dee did the same.

"Do you need a ride to the station?" Dee Dee asked. "I can call Alex."

"No. I'll just send Kimmie a text. I'm actually going to stop by the Pizza & Pop Shop and grab a slice for the road." The last thing she wanted was for Alex to take her to the train station. Besides, he was probably cooking his dinner for Mia right about now.

Her throat thickened, and she tried to fight through the feeling so that she could enjoy her final moments with Dee Dee. "I'm going to be in Boston in the new year. Perhaps I can come down for the day."

"I'd like that." Dee Dee sipped her coffee. "Does that mean you got the Palate contract?"

She blinked. "Yes. I did."

"Congratulations! That's so wonderful."

"Did Erika tell you about my audition?" Sloan asked reaching for her coat. She'd left her hat and mittens at the inn, but there was no way she was going back for them.

Dee Dee nodded. "She did when she first called me about the culinary exchange. She asked me if coming here would give you time to work on your audition meals. I told her we could suspend dinner service for you."

Sloan's hand flew to her heart. "You suspended your service for me? A stranger?"

Dee Dee rested her hand on Sloan's shoulder. "I did it for a fellow chef chasing her dream. I'm glad I could help you in a small way."

Sloan had done a good job holding back the tears this afternoon, but that did it. Alex had told her that his aunt spent a lifetime helping others achieve their dreams. "I'm sorry." She caught the tears with her knuckles. "I don't know why I'm crying. Opening a restaurant in Paris to honor my grandmother is all I've ever wanted."

"But is it what you need?"

Sloan blinked. "It's been my driving purpose, but now that I might be able to financially pull it off, I just feel . . ." She lowered her head. "Empty."

"Maybe it's not what you needed after all." Dee Dee smiled, slid her hand into her sweater's pocket, and handed her a slip of paper.

Sloan glanced down at the familiar paper and the words she'd scribbled at the Wishbone Wishes event.

I wish Alex would catch his lucky break.

She'd forgotten she'd left it in the kitchen.

Dee Dee reached for Sloan's hands, folding her own over Sloan's. "I hope you'll come back to Brooks Bend soon."

"I'd like that." Sloan slid out of the booth. It was time to go and stop burdening this kind woman, who probably wanted to go home and celebrate her husband's birthday. "I should go. Thank you for everything. I hope we can cook together the next time I'm here."

"I'll make sure of it."

Sloan said a final round of goodbyes and made her way

out to the sidewalk with her suitcases. She glanced down the street in the direction of the inn before letting out a deep sigh and turning around for her last walk to the Pizza & Pop Shop.

It was time to start her trek home.

ALEX PULLED OUT the ginger-maple apple pie from the oven, placing it on the cooling rack next to the fall salad he'd made earlier with roasted pumpkin seeds.

He'd been grateful that Hayden had changed her mind about waiting until next month to break in the kitchen. He promised to not only leave her generous leftovers, but he would help her make that special Christmas meal for her family.

"What do you think?" he asked his partner in crime, who'd come over today after his lunch shift to help out.

Liam looked up from the prep counter where he was putting the final touches on the butternut squash roasted ravioli with a dripped honey-sage browned butter. "Looks magnificent."

"I really tried to follow the recipe. I hope Sloan likes it."

"Is Sloan joining you for dinner too?" Liam asked, taking the bottle he'd filled earlier with browned butter and dripping it over the ravioli.

Alex blinked. "Um . . . no." He thought for a second,

realizing his mistake. "Oh, I'm sorry. I meant Mia. I hope Mia likes it."

His gaze moved over to the cookbook that was flipped open to Sloan's grandmother's ginger-maple apple pie recipe.

He'd have to save Sloan a slice. Since his dinner was taking place at the inn's library, like hers had been for Hayden's, it was entirely possible that he'd see her at some point this evening.

Liking that idea, he reached for a small plate from the counter and set it to the side so he wouldn't forget. It'd be nice to have a reason to see her and say a final goodbye.

He'd meant to go inside the diner and see her earlier when he dropped off Aunt Dee Dee, but his aunt showing off the *A Dish for Every Season* cookbook that Sloan's agent had given her as a welcome from Sloan had given him the idea. He'd taken his aunt's luggage out of his Jeep, asked if he could borrow the cookbook, and then headed straight to the grocery store to buy the ingredients he'd need to make Sloan's grandmother's special pie.

"Hey, your date's here." Hayden breezed into the kitchen, all smiles. She'd been in an exceptionally good mood all day, no doubt, still living her high from her date last night.

He glanced down at his watch. "I hadn't realized how late it was getting."

Hayden walked over and reached for the bowl of leftover pumpkin seeds, popping some into her mouth. "She's in the library. I offered some of the apple cider champagne you made, but apparently, she doesn't like apple cider. I'll open a bottle of red wine."

"Thank you." He whipped off the blue apron he put on earlier over his shirt and tie and slipped on his jacket before grabbing the ravioli plates from Liam. "This looks amazing."

He left the kitchen, moving down the hallway to the library to see Mia dressed in a fire engine-red sleeveless dress that showed off her long legs and California tan.

He glanced down at his tie. Maybe he should have gone with the bright-red one.

She had made herself at home, sitting on a long couch in front of the bay window, chatting on her phone.

He set down the ravioli plates and took a seat, playing with Oliver while he waited for Mia to finish her call. He glanced up at the oak bookcase that looked spectacular in the room. Maybe Dee Dee would be willing to let them put Sloan's cookbook in the library for guests to enjoy.

Perhaps Hayden could have an event one night, where they cooked one of the cookbook's recipes and video conferenced Sloan in from San Francisco . . . or Paris.

He smiled. It'd be fun to see the chef in her dream restaurant, even if it was only on screen, knowing that he and his dog had played a small part in getting her there.

"I'm so sorry," Mia finally said and joined him. "That was my editor, checking in. She's really anxious to read my manuscript."

Alex stood and pulled out her chair. "No problem. I

hope you like the starter. It's a roasted butternut squash ravioli with a dripped honey-sage browned butter."

Mia's hand flew to her mouth. "Oh, Alex. I'm so sorry. I should have told you. I'm allergic to butternut squash."

"You are?" That was news to him. Although, to be fair, their dinner dates growing up mainly included burgers and shakes.

"Yeah. Any squash, really. I break out like crazy." She scratched her bare arms.

He reached for her plate, setting it far away from her. "We can't let that happen." She wouldn't be able to eat the fall salad he'd made either.

"You go ahead." She picked up a piece of bread from a bread bowl that Hayden had brought in earlier and pulled it apart, reaching for a butter knife. "This is fine."

"I'm so sorry."

"It's not a big deal." Her phone buzzed. "Do you mind if I take that? It's one of my friends back home. We're planning a girls' trip to Palm Springs, and she's booking our accommodations this weekend."

"Sure."

"And please eat."

He picked up his flute. First, the apple cider champagne that she didn't care for and now the butternut squash ravioli that could send her to the hospital. He was really batting a thousand. He glanced down at his burgundy tie that majorly clashed with her red dress.

He flipped the tie with a finger and let out a sigh. Or maybe this was a clear sign.

Mia returned to her seat, setting her phone in her purse.

He squared his shoulders. It was time to be a man and admit what he wasn't feeling. "Mia, can I be honest?"

"Sure."

He collected his thoughts for a minute. There was no turning back. Still, he wanted to be polite and show her respect. "I was extremely flattered by what you wrote in your book, but I don't think this is the direction we should be taking." He glanced down at Oliver, feeling like a total heel.

Afraid to look over, he finally did, and her nod that kept going was not what he'd expected. "I feel the same way." She laughed. "Or not the same way."

Relief washed over him. "You do?"

"Yeah. I guess I got caught up in how great we were in high school. It was fun to get swept up in our past, but I really can't be with a man whose dog doesn't like me."

"He likes you," Alex insisted, as Oliver got up and left the room.

"No, he doesn't," they both said in unison.

"Alex, I think our next chapter is going to be one of friendship," Mia said.

"I'd like that. It'll be a good one." He glanced down at his plate. "I'm really sorry about dinner. I've got a fall brisket in the oven if you'd like to move on to the entrée."

"If it's okay with you, I think I'm going to go." She rose

from the table and grabbed her coat from the sofa where she'd left it. "I have a lot of writing to do." She hugged him goodbye. "I promise to let you know the next time I'm in Brooks Bend."

"You better." As she left, he picked up his flute, taking a sip. *Well, how about that?*

He stared at the bubbly apple cider, and an image of Sloan—smiling while sitting across from him, sipping the drink that reminded her of her grandmother—popped into his head.

He swiped his hand down his burgundy tie. A tie he picked because it was Sloan's favorite color.

His pulse quickened. This entire meal had been about Sloan, from the starter course she'd said was her favorite all the way to the dessert out of her cookbook.

His heart pounded a loud wake-up call against his rib cage. Sloan should have been his date, not Mia.

He sprung up and beelined it for the kitchen. How could he have not seen it?

"How's the starter course going?" Hayden asked, while Liam examined the beef brisket still in the oven. "Are you ready for your salads?"

He grinned down at the goat cheese salad. Yep, his sub-conscious had been way ahead of him. Even the salad had roasted pumpkin seeds, reminding him of his special night cooking APOPs with Sloan that had led to her falling asleep in his arms.

"Change of plans." He reached into his pants pocket for his phone. He had an important call to make. "C'mon. C'mon."

"Dee Dee's Diner."

He recognized the older voice on the other end.

"Hey, Aunt Dee Dee. I'm looking for Sloan. Is she there?"

"No, dear. She left a while ago for the train station."

His racing heart slammed against his chest. "Wait. Say that again." He couldn't have heard that correctly. She must mean that Sloan left for the inn. He snapped his fingers for Hayden and Liam to be quiet for a second.

"She said she was going to spend her final night in New York City."

He turned to Hayden. "Did Sloan already check out?"

"No, why?" Hayden came up to him.

"Aunt Dee Dee says Sloan's headed to the train station. She's leaving tonight."

"I know how to confirm this." Hayden raced out of the kitchen with Alex right behind her.

"Did Sloan say why she was leaving early?"

"No, dear. But she promised to come back when she moves to Boston."

Alex stared at the phone in disbelief. "She's moving to Boston?"

"For a few months. She didn't tell you that she got the Puppy Palate contract?"

His stomach tightened. "No. She didn't." Why wouldn't she have shared that news with him? Why was she leaving tonight?

"She'll be back soon enough. Maybe when she gets back, Fred and I can have you both over for dinner."

"Yeah. I'd like that." Stunned, he ended the call with his aunt and waited in the foyer for Hayden to come down from Sloan's room.

In minutes, Hayden climbed back down the stairs, holding Sloan's hat and mittens.

"Her luggage is gone, but she left these." She handed him the hat and mittens. "They were on the dresser."

Alex glanced down at the soft burgundy mittens. "Did you know she's coming back?"

"She's coming back here tonight."

He shook his head. "No. In the New Year. She won the Puppy Palate contract."

Hayden clapped her hands. "That's amazing."

"Why would she rush out without telling us or saying goodbye?"

Hayden looked away.

He studied his friend. "What aren't you telling me?"

"Your feelings for Sloan aren't one-sided. I'm sorry. She begged me not to say anything. She probably didn't want to stay here tonight, knowing you'd be with Mia."

His lips parted. "Sloan has feelings for me?"

Hayden smiled, touching his shoulder. "And Oliver."

She gave a playful shrug. "Probably more for your dog."

He grinned and flew down the hallway to the kitchen. If Hayden was right, there was no time to waste because he wasn't going to wait until after the first of January to see Sloan again.

"What are you going to do?" Hayden asked, right on his heels.

"Throw a Hail Mary pass and pray she doesn't get on that train." He slid his hand into his apron and pulled out the wishbone he'd put in there days ago, sliding it into his pants pocket.

He leaped into action, grabbing a sunflower out of the vase.

Minutes later, he met Hayden and Liam beside his Jeep, briefing them on the plan that included his friends taking a detour to pick up some important passengers before they met up with him. "I'll see you both soon."

"And you . . ." He bent down and placed Sloan's hat over Oliver's head, then opened the passenger door. "You have the most important job. Okay, buddy, let's go get our girl."

Chapter Twenty

S LOAN LET OUT a breath as she took a seat on the platform's cold cement bench. She crossed her legs at the
ankles, looking out onto the dark train tracks.

Her decision to leave tonight had been a good one. She
knew that, regardless of how much it hurt. It would have
been far worse to stay at the inn, risking seeing Alex on his
date with Mia.

She brushed away a stray tear.

This is all for the best, she said to herself for the ump-
teenth time as she opened her to-go pizza-shaped container
and took a bite of the slice.

If she said it a few thousand more times, her broken
heart would catch up eventually.

She glanced down at the cheesy pie with a hefty coating
of the seasoning.

How could a slice of pizza literally have changed her life
in so many ways, from her meeting the man and his dog who
would both inevitably steal her heart her first night in Brooks
Bend to discovering the seasoning would be the secret
ingredient to her winning the Puppy Palate competition,

setting her off in a new direction?

It was all surreal.

One loud bark, followed by several more, caused her to jolt. Racing down the platform toward her was Oliver, wearing her black knit hat, the burgundy ball bopping. "What are you doing here?" She stood and snatched it off his furry head. "How did you get this?"

Oliver answered by lunging for the half-eaten slice in her other hand, scoring a perfect 10 in his pizza snatch.

"You can have it. Don't take off my fingers." She laughed as he devoured it at her feet.

"I knew he'd find his dinner here," said a deep voice, and she glanced up.

Alex. "What are you both doing here?" she asked, her breath catching as she took in his black suit jacket and burgundy tie. Why would he have left his date to come to the train station?

"You didn't say goodbye, Chef." He closed the distance between them handing over her mittens. "And I kind of thought you'd be doing that tomorrow."

"I'm sorry." Her head dropped to the mittens. Hayden must have found them in her empty room and given them to Alex. "It just seems like a better time to leave now, given your aunt's back and all." She paused and lifted her head to ask the question she didn't really want to know the answer to. "Aren't you supposed to be on your date right now?"

"I was." He smiled.

"Oh." For some reason, he didn't seem all that put out. "You didn't need to leave on my account. I don't want your date angry with me."

He bent down and attached the dog's leash to his collar, flashing a smile. "Mia's just fine."

"Did you do the starter I recommended?" she couldn't help asking, always the consummate chef.

"I sure did—with Liam's help."

Wow. It was bad enough Hayden had given him full access to break in the inn's kitchen. He'd even gotten Liam involved for his special dinner.

"I also prepared the most awesome fall brisket."

"Wow. I'm impressed." She stood as bright lights from the inbound train lit up the platform.

As much as it was nice to see Alex one last time, it didn't change the fact that his looking *really* handsome was for another woman.

Who he would be going back to the minute she boarded the train.

"I guess this is goodbye." She grabbed onto the handles for each of her suitcases. "Bye, Al—"

"The thing is, I had it all wrong. The meal I was preparing had never been for Mia." He interrupted, reaching into his coat, and pulling out a sunflower, extending his arm. "I'm hoping I can give it to the woman that I should have invited to dinner. There's so much I want to thank you for, including the job opportunity."

Sloan stared at the bright-yellow sunflower that was part of the bouquet she'd picked out yesterday, while trying to comprehend what Alex had said.

It was another example of his just being thoughtful. Dinner celebrating his new job offer would have been fun.

But her time here was up.

The train made its stop, and the doors flew open. "Good luck with everything, Alex. If you find your way to San Francisco, stop by the restaurant." She grabbed her suitcases and maneuvered onto the train. Tears ran down her face as she rolled her suitcases down the aisle, while the conductor came on a loudspeaker, saying they'd be here for a five-minute schedule adjustment.

"Sloan, wait!"

She whipped around to see Alex had boarded the train with Oliver. "What are you doing?" she asked as Oliver came racing toward her.

"I'm horrible at this, clearly." He reached into his pants pocket and pulled out a wishbone. "But I really can't let you leave until you let me make my wish."

"Alex . . ." Her heart melted at the sight of the wishbone she'd given him last Saturday.

"May I?"

She smiled, petting Oliver. "It better be a good one."

He stepped closer, holding it up. "If I pull the bigger half, you and your spices will get off this train with me and stay here in Brooks Bend for one more night, and then when you come back, we spend every weekend together, because my dog really likes your cooking."

It *was* a good one. She laughed. "I see your aunt told you about my temporary relocation to Boston."

"She might have mentioned it." He held up the wishbone. "What do you say, Chef?"

She inched up an eyebrow. "You're going to put all your faith in a tug of a wishbone?"

He returned her suspicion with a wide grin. "I'm in if you are."

All of a sudden, a picture of them in the inn's kitchen, laughing and kissing while they cooked a Thanksgiving feast for all their friends, flashed in her mind. He'd be trying to sneak in his APOP for an appetizer, and she'd be dropping down to the kitchen floor a special seasoned plate for Oliver.

Dee Dee's question from earlier rang in her ears. She still wanted Paris and that wouldn't change, but she finally knew what she needed.

She wrapped a finger and thumb around her end as Alex did a countdown.

Maybe it was his strength or that she barely pulled on her end, but the smile now on his face told her everything as he brought her into his arms. "Thank you for my wish coming true," he said, stroking her cheek with the back of his knuckle. "And congratulations on the Puppy Palate contract."

"Thank you. I couldn't have done it without you." She

lifted her chin, her gaze meeting his. "Are you even curious what my wish was going to be?" she asked.

"A new shipment of seasoning?" he answered playfully.

"Oh, that would have been a good one." She wrapped her arms around his neck. "That the man with the adorable Labradoodle I met my first night in Brooks Bend would kiss me right now."

"I think I can make that come true." His lips landed softly on hers, and her legs went all wobbly. She'd probably make a thousand more wishes in her lifetime, but nothing would ever top this one.

"How much seasoning was on your pizza?" he joked when their lips finally broke apart.

She gave him a playful swat as he lifted her suitcases and they deboarded the train, Oliver right behind them.

"Oh, please be careful with the smaller one," she joked.

He laughed. "You won't need your seasonings tonight." But then his voice grew serious. "I know Brooks Bend isn't Paris. It may never be what you want."

"What I *need* is more moments in Brooks Bend with you and all of my friends." She bent down and gave Oliver a kiss. "And you too."

"Good." He reached for the door handle to the train station. "Because you're about to get it."

Sloan's jaw dropped at the sight of her new friends inside playing with several dogs. Hayden and Todd were finishing pouring apple cider into flutes on a round table. Liam and

Kimmie were uncovering chafing dishes. Earl was catching up with Dee Dee and an older man, whom Sloan suspected was her husband, Fred, off to the side.

"What is this?" she asked, eyeing the empty dog bowls on the floor as a Jack Russell, who she was pretty sure was the same one from the animal shelter, came up to her, nudging her leg until she picked it up. It immediately showered her face with wet kisses.

"It's your Pupsgiving!" Hayden and Kimmie said in unison to a round of applause.

"Is that my grandmother's maple-ginger apple pie?" She eyed the pie on the table.

Alex nodded, wiggling his fingers. "From scratch." He picked up a flute off the table. "I thought I was making a meal for Mia, but really, I was subconsciously making a dinner inspired by you." He handed her the drink. "And for you."

She smiled, her cheeks warming as she took a sip. "Apple cider champagne."

She grinned as Alex put his arm around her. "Do you think Mayor Hertzberg will declare Pupsgiving an official Brooks Bend holiday?"

Alex laughed. "Paw, yeah." He leaned over and kissed her a second time while Kimmie and Liam served the "four-legged" guests of honor, dropping down their bowls.

"Bone-apetit, everyone." Sloan raised her flute to the pups, basking in all the tail-wagging merriment. Dee Dee was right. It wasn't about how you started but how you finished, and this evening was the perfect way to end her culinary exchange and begin something brand-new with this amazing man, his adorable Labradoodle, and this wonderful town.

This autumn to remember was exactly what she needed.

Epilogue

SLOAN TUGGED DOWN her burgundy chef's jacket over her hips and reached for a bottle, turning it upside down and sprinkling some seasoning onto the dish she'd waited forever to make. She grinned down at her masterpiece. It wasn't her spiced caramel-pumpkin cheesecake, but she knew her special dinner guest would devour it all the same.

She took the plate and pushed through the double doors to the front of the house.

"*Bon soir*, Natalie," Sloan greeted her food and beverage director. "*J'espère que vous passez une merveilleuse nuit.*"

"Chef, your French is getting so much better," Natalie said in her thick French accent, eyeing the plate. "But *that* in your hand is letting your American side show through."

Sloan laughed. "It's for my dinner guest." She eyed the round table for three that had been set in front of the window, with candles and a beautiful arrangement of sunflowers in its center. "The table looks gorgeous. Merci."

The two walked outside, and Sloan said a final "*au revoir*" to Natalie and to have a nice day off with her boyfriend tomorrow. At least, that's what she hoped she'd said. She'd been taking morning classes to learn the language.

She breathed in the evening summer air, letting the scent of this vibrant city float through her lungs.

She couldn't help but grin, taking in the sight of the Eiffel Tower in the distance.

She was growing more and more fond of Paris with each passing day, and this view would never get old.

It'd been a year and a half since she'd won the Puppy Palate contract. She'd thrown her all into making meals that would get furry tails wagging. Last fall, the product line launched to huge commercial success.

The executives at Palate had immediately turned around and signed her for a five-year contract as their exclusive Puppy Palate chef.

And that wasn't the only contract she'd signed. She smiled up at the red Seasons of Paris awning. She'd found the perfect space for her new restaurant, and moved to Paris earlier this year to begin the process of registering it.

Seasons of Paris was scheduled to open next week, and she was more than ready. In addition to Natalie, she'd hired a team of front and back of the house staff. Erika had helped her connect with a local PR company who was in charge of publicizing her launch.

It'd been a busy time—consuming every waking moment. She couldn't wait for the grand opening.

But tonight, the only thing on her mind were the special guests who would be breaking in her restaurant, and she couldn't wait to feed them.

All of a sudden, a familiar bark came from behind. She spun around to see a Labradoodle sprinting down the sidewalk straight for her.

Her Labradoodle.

"Oliver!" Her heart sped up as she held her arms open, trying hard not to drop the plate holding a small pizza she'd made especially for him.

Her guys were finally here.

"We flew all the way across the Atlantic for pizza?" Alex asked, crooking up his lips.

She missed that lopsided grin. She missed that man.

She handed over her slice to an ecstatic Oliver, and then wrapped her arms around Alex, kissing her boyfriend. "I promise you you're going to love my dinner. How was your trip?"

"Good. I think Oliver got the phone number of two flight attendants."

She laughed.

"And I got the hotel interview. It's the day after tomorrow."

"Yes!" Sloan hugged him again. They'd been apart for months, while Alex finished up a private kitchen remodel job for an A-list celebrity in the Hamptons and set his sights on finding his next gig in Paris.

They had agreed Sloan should stay here for two years to establish not only her restaurant but also her presence in

Paris. The Palate team loved the idea of her here, wanting to tap into a larger global market for Puppy Palate.

"I hope you're hungry?" she asked, opening the front door and letting Oliver run in.

"Careful, buddy," Alex called out. "I'm going to guess that you didn't take my recommendation to add an American cheeseburger to the menu."

"Sorry. You'll have to wait two years for that."

He let out a groan and followed her into the kitchen.

"Man, this is some of the finest work I've ever seen," he said, running a hand across the seasonings rack that had been installed on the kitchen island, exactly like her grandmother's in the Seasons of San Francisco kitchen that Connor was now running as her executive chef. "Who did it?"

"Oh, just some guy whose dog knocked me to the ground for my dinner."

He grinned and brought her in for another kiss. "I missed you, Chef," he whispered into her hair.

She finally pried herself away from Alex's arms to finish cooking their entrée. In no time, she garnished the three *filets de saumon à la crème ciboulette* and handed him their two plates, then reached for the third—the one for her very special guest of honor who she'd suspected had been right by her side for every exciting step in opening this wonderful restaurant.

They returned to the dining room where Sloan had set the summer *salade verte* with a spiced honey vinaigrette and the peach melba she'd perfected weeks ago, adding to the raspberry sauce and vanilla ice cream a sweet cinnamon she'd found in an outdoor market. The ice cream she'd place inside small ice bowls, so it wouldn't melt.

"Are you ready for this?" he asked after they set down the plates. He wrapped his arms around her.

His supportive embrace rushed through her because this moment was finally here.

She smiled and placed her hands on his arms, her gaze resting on Oliver who had made himself comfortable next to the pulled-out chair by the window.

The one that she knew in her heart her grandmother was sitting in at this very moment, admiring the dish Sloan had made especially for her and enjoying every second.

She took the seat Alex offered and reached down to pet Oliver. "I'm ready to enjoy this night with everyone I love." She winked. "Let's make this a summer to remember."

The End

Brooks Bend series

Book 1: *Jingle Jammies*

Book 2: *An Autumn to Remember*

Available now at your favorite online retailer!

More books by Robyn Neeley

Honey Springs series

Book 1: *Bee My Valentine*

Book 2: *Love Pops Up*

The Sweet Texas Secrets series

Sweet Texas Charm

Available now at your favorite online retailer!

About the Author

Robyn Neeley is an east coast gal who loves to explore super cute small towns; watches way more reality TV than she cares to admit; can't live without Dunkin Donuts coffee; and has never met a Christmas cookie she didn't like. She writes contemporary romance with heart and humor.

Thank you for reading

An Autumn to Remember

If you enjoyed this book, you can find more from all our great authors at TulePublishing.com, or from your favorite online retailer.

TULE
PUBLISHING

Printed in the USA
CPSIA information can be obtained
at www.ICGtesting.com
LVHW041148081023
760500LV00030B/655